Alec's eyes met Julia's, his expression rueful, but he kept quiet

It was miracle enough that he was willing to do as much as he did. Even to completely uproot and move. When she'd asked Josh to choose between his family and his dangerous, high-adrenaline job, he'd chosen the job. It scared her to think Alec might hate it here in Angel Butte, so far from the high-adrenaline job *he'd* loved. From what he'd said, he was now stuck behind a desk, probably the last thing he'd ever wanted to do with his life.

I didn't ask him, she argued with herself. *He offered.*

But that didn't mean he wouldn't blame her if he began to chafe at a life shaped by his sense of duty.

He kept insisting they were his family, but they weren't really, were they?

The fact that she wished they were would remain her secret.

Julia's attraction to Alec might not remain secret for long...especially if her son can't keep out of trouble! Read on for an exciting, emotional tale in this latest book in Janice Kay Johnson's The Mysteries of Angel Butte series.

Dear Reader,

Forget *The Taming of the Shrew.* What I love writing about is the taming of a rebellious teenager! Truthfully, I've always had a soft spot for teenagers, maybe because I have way more vivid memories of the year when I was thirteen than I do the younger years. Emotions are all so extravagant. I hated my mother! My life would be ruined if that boy didn't notice me, or my mother refused to let me date an eighteen-year-old! How dare she? Ah, well. How your attitudes change when you become a parent instead.

In *All a Man Is,* thirteen-year-old Matt Raynor is positive he hates his mother, but in his case it isn't all teenage angst. My hero—and Matt's uncle—Alec Raynor thinks of his nephew as being tamped gun powder. This boy is hurting, but until he finally blows up, his mom and uncle won't know what's really wrong. Poor kid. I'm almost ashamed to tell you how much fun I had writing about him!

Best of all, *All a Man Is* includes one of my favorite themes— forbidden love. Sister- and brother-in-law, in this case. Not really taboo, but...touchy. This pair have banded together to raise Julia's two kids. Yes, her husband died a year and a half ago, but does that make these feelings they're having for each other okay? What if one of them makes a move and finds out the other one is still in the brother/sister mode? Do you dare risk a relationship that is essential for the kids' sakes in hopes of having something sublime? What if it all goes wrong?

I've had a great time writing these The Mysteries of Angel Butte books. Such a good time, in fact, that I've written another one. Jane Vahalik is a strong character in all three of the stories. The balance between being a woman and being a tough cop who has risen to the rank of lieutenant is a perilous one, and I found I kept thinking about her.

So look for her story coming in July 2014.

Thanks for visiting Angel Butte. Please come back!

Janice Kay Johnson

PS—I enjoy hearing from readers! Please contact me on Facebook, or through my publisher, at Harlequin, 225 Duncan Mill Road, Don Mills, ON M3B 3K9, Canada.

JANICE KAY JOHNSON

—

All a Man Is

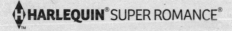
HARLEQUIN® SUPER ROMANCE®

Recycling programs for this product may not exist in your area.

ISBN-13: 978-0-373-60832-4

ALL A MAN IS

Copyright © 2014 by Janice Kay Johnson

Printed in U.S.A.

ABOUT THE AUTHOR

The author of more than eighty books for children and adults, Janice Kay Johnson is especially well-known for her Harlequin Superromance novels about love and family—about the way generations connect and the power our earliest experiences have on us throughout life. Her 2007 novel *Snowbound* won a RITA® Award from Romance Writers of America for Best Contemporary Series Romance. A former librarian, Janice raised two daughters in a small rural town north of Seattle, Washington. She loves to read and is an active volunteer and board member for Purrfect Pals, a no-kill cat shelter.

Books by Janice Kay Johnson

HARLEQUIN SUPERROMANCE

SIGNATURE SELECT SAGA

*The Russell Twins
**A Brother's Word
***The Mysteries of Angel Butte

Other titles by this author available in ebook format.

This one is for Pat,
a great friend when times get tough,
and an unbeatable plotting partner

PROLOGUE

HALF A DOZEN MEN and three women sat around the conference room table. Some had laptops open, others notebooks.

Lieutenant Alec Raynor found his attention kept wandering to the five red pins stabbing a map on a display board propped on an easel. Each pin represented a particularly brutal rape and murder, all similar enough for detectives to have linked them to a single perpetrator. One of those pins was within his jurisdiction, his responsibility, the Los Angeles Police Department. Two belonged to the county sheriff's department, one to Beverly Hills P.D. and the most recent to Santa Monica P.D.

This killer liked his victims to be upscale.

The task force had been formed after the third murder. Unfortunately for the detectives working the crime, the killer was smart and clearly well educated in the collection of trace evidence. Result: they had next to nothing to go on.

Alec's phone vibrated and he barely glanced at it, intending to let it go to voice mail. The name displayed, though, had him rising to his feet.

"Excuse me for a minute. I need to take this."

He answered as he left the room. "Julia?"

Unless it was prearranged, his sister-in-law never called him during normal working hours. Certainly not in the middle of the afternoon like this.

"I'm sorry to bother you, Alec." The stress in her usually melodic voice ratcheted up the worry that had gripped him the minute he saw her name on the call display. "I should have waited. If you're tied up—"

"I can take a minute. Something's wrong."

She laughed, a sharp sound. "As usual, it's Matt."

Both her kids had been named to honor Alec and his brother's mother and her Italian family. Matteo had recently turned thirteen. Alec kept hearing that girls were hell on wheels at thirteen, but boys had to mature for a couple more years before they were ready to rebel. Not Matt.

Thank God Matt's sister, Emiliana—Liana for short—was, at not quite eleven, still a little girl.

Alec's niece and nephew had both been slammed by their father's death a year and a half ago. Liana's grief and bewilderment seemed normal, while Matt's original shock had come to more closely resemble a bomb packed with gunpowder. It was dangerous to handle and had so many explosives tamped down inside, Alec expected the worst when it blew. Some days, he had trouble recognizing the boy he loved in the sneering, foulmouthed shit he'd become.

What bothered him most was that he had no idea what was going on in the kid's head.

Julia didn't call after every one of his escapades, and certainly not in the middle of the day.

"What happened?" Alec asked.

"He was caught stealing a bottle of whiskey from the Grove Street store. From Mr. Santana."

Mr. Santana had to be seventy-five if he was a day. He'd had cataract surgery recently on one eye but the other remained clouded. He'd continued running the store after his son was killed in an armed robbery and he was left to care for his daughter-in-law and her three children. The oldest boy, Javier, was an earnest seventeen-year-old who helped his grandfather every minute he wasn't in school. Sweet Mr. Santana was known throughout the neighborhood for his kindness to children.

Matt had very likely gone there to shoplift because he knew Mr. Santana's vision was poor.

"It gets worse," Julia warned, and now Alec could hear fear along with anger in her voice. "He was already drunk."

Son of a bitch. His thirteen-year-old nephew had gotten wasted? "Where is he?"

"Oh, his room." She sounded hopeless. "But you know how much good putting him on restriction does."

Alec knew.

"I've done some thinking today, Alec. I'd...like to talk to you if you can come over whenever you get off. Or—it can wait until tomorrow if you're tied up."

"No," he said roughly. "I'll be there after dinner sometime."

"Thank you." All the grief he'd begun to believe she was letting go of was there again, so heavy he could feel the weight. "Tonight," she said, and was gone.

ALEC STOOD IN Julia's kitchen, leaning one hip against the edge of the tiled counter, and tried to conceal his shock at Julia's announcement.

He couldn't help watching her as she busied herself pouring them both cups of coffee. Julia—his brother's widow—was a beautiful woman. Elegant, but not flashy. He remembered being surprised the first time he met her, because Josh usually went for buxom blondes, and the girl he was suddenly serious about was neither. Petite, no more than five foot three or four, she had the fine-boned build of a dancer. Alec learned later that she actually had taken dance classes for years, without being serious enough to consider it as a career. Her straight brown hair was a rich color with a warm cast, more like maple than mahogany, he had decided. And then there were eyes of a witchy green-gold she had passed on to her daughter but not her son.

When he'd first arrived this evening, he'd spent a few minutes with Liana. Skinny and small for her age, she had darker hair than her mom. He heard about her fascination with the algebra her fifth-grade advanced math group was currently studying.

"There's this boy who likes me," she had added shyly, pink tingeing her thin cheeks. "I mean, I guess he does. His name's Tyler. He told Jose, who told Brooke." Brooke, Alec knew, was Liana's best friend. "He wants me to be, like, his girlfriend or something."

Girlfriend! He'd had damn near as much trouble grappling with the concept of this little girl having some guy after her as he did with the idea of Matt boozing. They were turning into teenagers before his eyes.

They had been at just about the worst possible age to lose their father.

Alec hadn't trusted himself to talk to Matt yet. Instead, he'd left Liana instant messaging with friends and retreated to the kitchen.

"What happened to playing with Barbie dolls?" he asked plaintively.

Amusement lightened Julia's distress, if only for a moment. "What's she doing?" When he told her, she laughed. "Oh, she still has her Barbies and plays with them, too, but mostly by herself. She's not sure which friends will think it's totally uncool and childish."

"She's ten."

"Almost eleven. Sixth grade is in the middle school, you know. There'll be dances."

"Older boys," he said with the voice of doom.

He expected her to laugh again, but she didn't. "Alec, I think I need to take the kids away from L.A. You're so important to them." She bit her lip. "To me, too. That's why I've been so reluctant to do this. But you know my parents would like to have me close, and I have to believe Matt would do better in a small town."

The small town where she'd grown up was on a lake somewhere north of Minneapolis. Half the country away. More than half.

Alec felt sick. He had the impending awareness of devastation. In a distant part of his mind, he'd known he loved his niece and nephew, and, sure, Julia, too, as much as he dared let himself. When Josh had been killed in Afghanistan, Alec had naturally stepped in, assuming some of his brother's responsibilities. Julia and the kids were family. That was what a man did.

Until this moment, he hadn't understood that they were the three people he loved most in the world. He didn't know how he could survive without them.

"Your mother drives you crazy," he heard himself say hoarsely.

"I wouldn't move in with them. I'd get us our own place." Her face was pinched as she searched his face. "What would you suggest? That I close my eyes and stab a pin into a map, pick someplace to go at random?"

For a second he had double vision, those red pins floating before his eyes, and he thought with an astonishing burst of anguish, *Julia.* What if somehow, someway, that creep came across her? Los Feliz, the part of L.A. where she and Alec both lived, was upscale. She was pure class and beautiful. *He*—whoever *he* was—would like her. Want her. Hate her.

She and the kids would be better off, safer, away from overcrowded, smoggy, crime-ridden Southern California.

This was the moment when Alec realized he would do anything at all for her, Matt and Liana. Anything for them, and to keep them in his life even if he was painfully aware he was destined to remain on the outside looking in.

"*We'll* pick somewhere," he said. "I should be able to get a job running a police department in a peaceful small town somewhere. Don't go home to your parents. Let's stay together."

The shock in her green-gold eyes was such that, for a terrifying instant, he thought he'd blown it. And then those eyes filled with tears. "I can't ask you—"

"I'm offering." He couldn't let himself touch her, so he didn't move. "I'm ready for a change, Julia."

She pressed fingers to her lips, laughing and crying at the same time. "Oh, God. If you mean it…"

All the fear left him in a rush. "I mean it. I'll go online and start looking tonight. I'll let you know where I find possible job openings. You can research the towns. We'll find the perfect one. I promise."

There was a minute there when he thought she wanted to throw herself into his arms. But, as always, she turned away. Snatching up a dish towel, she began mopping her face.

"Do you think this is what Josh would want us to do?"

She always did that, produced his brother's name as if she were lighting a candle at his altar.

And I'm pathetic to feel jealous. Worse than pathetic, he thought in disgust. Why wasn't he glad she'd loved his brother so much?

"Yeah." He pulled a smile from the hat. "Josh would say go for it."

CHAPTER ONE

"Ew, GROSS! MO-OM! Mattie just spit on the floor," Liana whined.

"Tattletale," her brother snarled. "And don't call me Mattie again or I'll make you sorry!"

The dull throbbing in the left side of Julia Raynor's skull sharpened until she felt as if a drill bit was viciously driving through her forehead. She stole a glance in her rearview mirror to see her children glaring at each other.

She should have separated them by letting one ride in front, but she'd lost her temper this morning when they started fighting about whose turn it was.

"Both of you," she'd snapped, "backseat. No argument. We're not doing this."

She'd wonder why Matt wanted to ride up front, given how thoroughly he seemed to detest her, except she knew. Keeping his sister from getting what *she* wanted seemed to be one of his few pleasures.

Julia's only consolation was that she was pretty sure the sibling warfare was normal, no matter how aggravating it was from her point of view. So little about Matt seemed normal now, she'd take what solace she could.

The entire trip had been the closest thing to hell she could imagine. A step beyond purgatory. It should have been fun, an adventure. Not that long ago, it would have been.

Before Josh died. Before Matt became so angry.

Silence simmered behind her. It was like driving with a feral animal in a trap on the backseat right next to a fluffy, cheerful Maltese terrier now getting whiny and snappy out of fear, and Julia was beginning to wonder if the trap door was secure.

We could have flown. Been here in a few hours instead of the longest two days of my life.

Clenching the steering wheel, she wished she'd followed Alec's example and sold the damn car and bought a new one when they arrived. She'd been worrying about how much life her eight-year-old Volkswagen Passat still had in it anyway. Clinging to the familiar was one thing; clinging to a cantankerous car that would *not* like cold winters was something else again.

"We're almost there," she said, hoping to stir some tiny remnant of excitement. Not that Matt had ever felt any. He was bitterly resentful about the move.

So what else is new? she asked herself wearily. For the past year and more, her son had bitterly resented every word she spoke, every decision she made.

"You keep saying that," Liana said sulkily. Even Julia's good-natured daughter was wearing down.

"Because we *are* getting closer. The sign we just passed said eighteen miles."

"Oh."

This time, a glance in the mirror assured her that they were both at least looking out their respective windows, as if some curiosity had surfaced.

The landscape was intriguing and very different from the brown hills and canyons of their most recent home. No ocean beaches here in central Oregon, either, although Alec assured her there were countless clear, cold lakes. The highway had been following a beautiful, tumbling river for some miles now. This stretch of Highway 97 was wooded and… knobby. Those lumps couldn't all be volcanic cinder cones, could they? If so, they'd become overgrown with pine trees.

The fact that she was moving her children to a spot in the heart of volcano country made her a little nervous, especially now that they were here and she could see the evidence of it all around. Earlier they'd passed signs pointing to Crater Lake, which was the water-filled caldera of a truly monstrous volcano that had wrapped the entire world in black ash when it erupted 7,700 years before. She was already planning a trip back to the park in the next few weeks. Even Matt would be impressed, surely.

To the east was Newberry National Volcanic

Monument, which was described in the literature as "potentially active." The smaller cinder cones in the area—including Angel Butte—were like pimples scattered on the edges of Newberry Volcano, which didn't rear into the sky like Mount Rainier or Saint Helens. It was a shield volcano, she'd read, primarily made up of lava flows.

Julia had educated herself about volcanoes before agreeing to this move. In the end, she'd decided that her family was in more danger from earthquakes in Southern California than they would be from the unlikely event of a volcanic eruption.

Of course, Minnesota didn't have either. But it also didn't have Alec, which was the deciding factor.

The truth was, she would admit only to herself, she'd have gone anywhere he'd chosen.

Not because she needed him, although she did, but because Matt needed him, too.

"It's kind of pretty," Liana said timidly.

"There's nothing here." Matt sounded stunned. "It's, like, the middle of nowhere."

Short of moving to a village in Alaska accessible only by fishing boat or small plane—and, oh, how tempting that idea was—Angel Butte was the closest she and Alec had been able to find to the middle of nowhere. Or so they'd convinced themselves. Alec was discovering this town had considerably more crime and corruption than he'd imagined. She could only pray it didn't reach the middle school, where Matt would start eighth grade this fall.

The silence in the car had a different feel when they saw the sign for the turnoff to Angel Butte. They really were only minutes away from their new home. Julia was only sorry they'd have to wait a few days for their furniture and other possessions to catch up with them. Although Alec had bought the duplex where they were going to live, she and the kids would have to stay in a motel until their beds arrived.

The narrower two-lane highway swept through forestland that gradually became more open. To each side were Old West–style ranches with split-rail fences and a few horses drowsing in the midday heat. Horse-crazy Liana gazed in delight. More houses appeared, closer together, and finally a Shell gas station. With startling suddenness after that, Julia felt as if they could be back in Southern California. Alec had said a little drily that she'd be able to buy anything she needed when she got here, but he hadn't mentioned that their small town in the middle of nowhere had Target and Walmart stores, a Petco, Staples, Kentucky Fried Chicken, McDonald's and Red Robin.

"I'm hungry," her daughter whined, predictably. How could she be, after snacking all day long?

"You know Uncle Alec is eager to see us. He said he'd take us to dinner."

Matt didn't say anything. His respect for Alec

was the only hope keeping Julia going, but he'd even been sullen with Alec during the occasional weekend visits he'd managed these past few months. Julia wasn't sure whether Matt was afraid Alec was trying to ditch them or whether he was mad at Alec, too, because he'd conspired with Julia to move him away from his new and not-so-savory friends.

Maybe she should have stayed in San Diego after Josh died instead of uprooting the kids to Los Angeles almost right away so that she could lean on Alec.

As exhausted as she was, she wasn't going to let such a well-worn worry take root. It was too late. She and the kids had moved, and the truth was she hadn't wanted to stay in San Diego when all of her friends were the wives of navy SEALs. As a widow, her very presence would cast a shadow on them, and she hadn't liked thinking about what Josh had done for a living.

"There really is an angel up there," Liana said suddenly. "I can see her."

"Where?" her brother demanded.

Julia, too, lifted her gaze to the top of the small butte with steep sides made up of rusty red cinders partially masked by clusters of small pine trees. Yes, there it was. She, too, caught a glimpse of white, almost a gleam, although she couldn't make out details, not without taking her eyes from the road longer than she dared.

"Weird," Matt pronounced. Occasionally he forgot his angry persona and still sounded like the thirteen-year-old boy he was.

"Get Uncle Alec to tell you the story of how the angel came to be there," Julia suggested.

"You mean, she didn't fly down from on high?" her charming son sneered, having recollected himself.

Poor Liana, stuck back there with him.

Poor me, *stuck with him.*

Immediately Julia felt guilty for the unmaternal thought.

Julia spotted the sign for the hotel where Alec had made reservations. She found a parking spot, set the emergency brake and reached for her phone.

Alec answered on the first ring. "Julia?"

"We're here," she said simply, with vast relief complicated only a little by her apprehension and guilt.

ALEC USED THE EXCUSE of steering her through the restaurant door to lay a hand on Julia's back. Feeling the small flex of muscles beneath his fingertips filled him with exultation. He was embarrassed by the strength of it. He felt like an idiot teenager whose crush had finally agreed to go out with him. This was ridiculous. Nothing had changed between them.

He couldn't seem to squelch it, though, damn it. He all but had neon lights in his head flashing, *Julia is here, at last!*

Trouble was, he'd spent months living for this day.

Waiting for the kids to emerge from the restaurant behind them, the two of them paused. He reluctantly let his hand drop.

"Let's at least drive by the duplex," Julia suggested, and after a moment Alec nodded.

He wasn't looking forward to showing her, never mind the kids, their new home. Compared to the one they'd left, it wasn't very impressive.

Julia, of course, had seen photos online and knew it didn't match the charm of the Spanish-style stucco bungalow she had bought when she moved the kids to L.A. from San Diego after Josh's death. There were charming houses in Angel Butte, of course, but once Alec saw the duplex for sale, he'd been so struck by the advantages of them living side by side, he'd called her to see what she thought. The idea of sharing the cost had appealed to her, too, he suspected; being able to hold on to some of the money she'd made from selling her house eased the urgency of her job hunt. She could take her time and find something she really liked. Down the line, they had agreed, they might keep the duplex as a rental property.

Dinner had been at a chain restaurant where the kids already knew what they wanted to eat. Alec was less enthusiastic, but he'd seen how exhausted Julia was and knew a fancier meal would be wasted on her. Besides, this place shared a parking lot with the hotel where he'd booked a room for her and the kids. The hotel wasn't anything special, but it was clean and decent and had a swimming pool. He had known without asking that she wouldn't accept if he offered to put them up at one of the area's nicer, lakefront resorts. She had become increasingly prickly about money, probably because she worried about depending on him too much. Alec had enough pride himself to admire the same quality in others.

"I'll drive," he said, leading the way to his Chevy Tahoe. After flying here in February for the initial job interview and getting stuck for an extra day because of a snowstorm, he'd known his Camaro wouldn't do. It was time, even if he hadn't needed four-wheel drive. He'd wanted a vehicle suitable for a family. Now he felt satisfaction as the kids clambered into the back and Julia hoisted herself into the front seat.

If only they were *his* family rather than his brother's.

"Your Camaro was so cool," Matt said from the backseat. "But this is okay, I guess," he conceded grudgingly.

Alec grinned at him in the rearview mirror. "Thank you." He glanced at Julia. "We'll take a spin through downtown, which is a lot more attractive than this stretch." He explained that the commercial strip had grown up outside the city limits until a fairly recent annexation changed that. He didn't figure they needed to hear about the headaches that annexation had brought to an understaffed police department. Once he'd been on board long enough to see the big picture, he had begun an aggressive campaign to increase funding for the department. He didn't much like his boss, Mayor Noah Chandler, but had to concede Chandler was backing every budget demand he'd made to the city council.

He drove down the main street, once the traditional downtown when Angel Butte's population had been a third of its current size. The hardware store, dry cleaner's and newspaper office had retreated to side streets; the false-fronted buildings here now housed trendy bistros, boutiques, galleries and sporting-goods stores. The economy had become heavily dependent on tourism. From what he'd been told, the change had happened so quickly, old-timers were still in shock.

Thus, he figured sardonically, the reluctance to admit a small-town police department was no longer adequate.

He pointed out the redbrick public-safety building where he worked and the historic courthouse with a wing that housed city hall. They detoured by the middle school, bland as schools built in the 1970s usually were, and then the more modern elementary school where Liana would go.

Finally, he drove past the upscale part of Old Town where people with money lived, and then to the neighborhood of modest ramblers where the worker bees felt lucky to own homes. The duplex he'd bought was on a corner, which gave it a slightly larger-than-average lot, but he hadn't done anything yet that could be called landscaping. Right now, a lawn with sun-browned patches surrounded it. A few overgrown shrubs crowded front windows. The only thing he had done to the exterior was to have the place painted, going for a dark green with cream-colored trim.

He pulled into the driveway on his side of the duplex, set the emergency brake and turned off the engine. In silence, all four of them stared at the forty-year-old rambler clearly built as a rental. Each side had a single-car garage. Two concrete walkways led from the sidewalk to the identical front doors.

Matt broke the silence. "You're kidding."

"This is only temporary," Julia said uneasily. "You know that. Having Alec right next to us is ideal."

He cleared his throat. "It's a good neighborhood. Liana can walk to school. You can get almost anywhere in town on your bikes."

He'd actually considered a place outside of town so Matt *wouldn't* be able to get anywhere on his own, but that had other drawbacks.

"Can we see inside?" Julia asked, unhooking her seat belt.

"Sure," he said, sounding hearty and phony even to his own ears. They got out and approached the door on the side he'd decided would be theirs. He made a business of taking the key from his ring and giving it to Julia. "Uh…it's pretty bare-bones still," he warned.

He was glad they hadn't seen it before the work was done. He'd discovered that beneath the badly worn brown carpet were hardwood floors. Instead of replacing the carpet, he'd had the oak refinished to a glossy sheen. Bathrooms on both sides had new vinyl floors and shiny new fixtures. Julia knew he'd had the floors refinished, but not about the bathrooms, and he had no intention of telling her the duplex hadn't come this way.

The kitchens he hadn't touched yet, on his side because he hadn't been home enough to bother, and on Julia's side because he figured she would have her own ideas about what she wanted to do.

They moved over the threshold in a clump, even Matt sticking close to his mother. There was no entryway to speak of; the front door let straight into a cramped living room with white walls and a white-painted brick fireplace. The floors looked damn good, if he did say so, but Alec still winced at the comparison with the living room in the house Julia had just sold. It had had a bay window, glass-fronted built-ins, high ceilings and open, dark wood beams.

"There are three bedrooms," he said, "but only one bathroom."

"We're going to have to schedule morning showers," Julia said lightly.

They all peered into the bedrooms, two of them the standard ten-foot-by-twelve-foot boxes with inadequate closets. The master bedroom was only slightly larger.

He saw Julia breathe a sigh of relief when she saw the bathroom.

"Brace yourself," he said in a low voice just before they reached the kitchen with some extra floor space optimistically designated as dining area.

Dark brown Formica countertops went with the ugly dark cabinets, which were scarred in places. The flooring was a dated orange-and-yellow vinyl that at least was in good shape.

"You should have let me have this remodeled before you got here," Alec said, feeling inadequate as he watched them inspect their new home.

Despite her tiredness, Julia appeared undaunted now that she'd seen the worst. She smiled at him. "We'll eat with you while the kitchen is torn apart."

"Mine's no better," he admitted, looking around. "I bought new appliances, but that's as far as I've gotten."

"It'll be fun," she insisted.

The kids stared in disbelief. Even Liana seemed shell-shocked. Matt had an expression Alec didn't like. There was something a little smug about it, as if he'd hoped the new home sucked. Did he imagine his mother would turn tail and retreat to L.A.?

"Who wants which bedroom?" she asked gaily, as if the two rooms weren't virtually identical.

"I call first choice!" Liana declared, racing back toward the bedrooms.

"Like, who cares?" her brother said disagreeably, but he thundered after her anyway.

"Hey." Seeing Julia's expression, Alec violated his own rules and wrapped his hands around her upper arms. "You okay?"

Her laugh broke. "I'll recover. The drive was horrible. The only time they quit squabbling was when Matt was sulking. Liana was almost as bad. She sobbed when we drove away from our house. She was sure she'd never see her friends again."

"She may not," he said softly.

Her face crumpled. "I know. Oh, God, Alec. Did we do the right thing?"

He wanted to promise her they had, that Angel Butte was the idyllic town they'd hoped for, but he was beginning to wonder if there was any such thing. He'd grown up in Southern California, used to the tangle of overcrowded freeways and the yellow light of smoggy mornings. He wondered guiltily what her Minnesota hometown looked like.

"I think so," he said, unable to resist a gentle squeeze before he had to let her go. "It's not like Liana knew her friends that long. Maybe moving so soon after the last time is hard on them, but I have to think doing it quickly is better than waiting." He hesitated. "I'm sorry the house is so, uh, unprepossessing."

"What?" She lifted her face to his, surprise in

those extraordinary eyes. "Don't be silly. The duplex looks like it did in pictures, except better. You've had more work done than you admitted to, haven't you?"

He didn't say anything. Normally careful to keep his distance, he hadn't been this close to her since he'd held her after the funeral. Her skin, tanned to a pale gold, was as smooth as a child's, her lashes surprisingly long without any help from mascara. Her upper lip had an unusually deep dip in it that made him think of the pretty mouths painted on dolls.

If he bent his head just a little...

Her eyes widened at whatever she saw on his face.

Clenching his jaw, he released her.

"What if I keep Matt tonight?" he asked. "I've got one of the bedrooms set up as a spare."

"Really? You'd do that? Don't you have to work tomorrow?"

"Yes, but I could drop him at the hotel on my way. We could all have breakfast at the Denny's there."

"I would love that," she admitted. "I've got to tell you, I've been having distinctly unmaternal thoughts about him."

Having regained his self-control after a brief but significant battle, Alec was able to laugh. "How shocking. And this was the first time?"

She chuckled, a delicious ripple of sound. "Okay. You're right. There have been a few previous mo-

ments I'd have put him up on Craigslist if I thought
I'd get any offers."

"It's a phase. He'll get over it." Alec hoped.

Julia smiled. "They're fighting again."

"Then let's go separate them."

"Okay, but first—" She astonished him by stepping closer to kiss his cheek. She was blushing
when she sank back to her heels, but her eyes held
his. "Thank you. I can't tell you what this means to
me, so I won't even try. But I want you to know—"

He shook his head and took a chance, placing
his finger over her lips, feeling them quiver. "No.
I love those kids, too. If you'd taken them away, it
would have destroyed me."

For a moment they only looked at each other,
their defenses lower than usual. He hoped she
couldn't see the part he didn't say: losing her would
have destroyed him, too.

Especially losing her.

"How come *you* get the biggest room?" his
nephew said, startling Alec, who hadn't noticed
the kids coming back into the kitchen.

Alec leveled a stare at the kid. "Because she's
the adult and pays the bills."

Matt contented himself with rolling his eyes.

"Uncle Alec suggested you spend the night with
him," Julia said, her tone neutral.

The boy shrugged and ducked his head. "I guess
that's okay," he mumbled.

Not exactly enthusiastic, but close enough.

Alec studied Matt, sorry to see that he hadn't grown to speak of in recent months. He'd been a shrimp at this age, too, a curse he had especially resented because Josh, two years older and therefore taller at every stage anyway, had grown steadily all along. The height and physical-maturity issue might have something to do with Matt's behavior, if he'd been trying to convince his buddies that he was big and bad, too.

He was a good-looking kid, though, with the same dark hair and eyes as his dad and Alec. Alec could see Josh in his face, more square-jawed and less angular than Alec's face. The shape of his eyes came from Julia, though.

"Then let's take your mom and Liana to the hotel."

His eyes narrowed and that square jaw jutted out. "Wait. Then they can go swimming and I can't."

Julia looked at Alec, a hint of panic in her eyes.

"It's late," he said. "The swim can wait until tomorrow."

Matt grumbled during the entire drive back to the hotel. Alec contemplated how his own father would have dealt with that kind of back talk. Maybe there was something to be said for old-school parenting.

Saying good-night took only a few minutes. Julia had checked into her room earlier but their suitcases were still in the trunk of her car. Alec walked her and Liana into the lobby and watched them get onto an elevator. He couldn't make himself move until the elevator doors closed and cut off his last sight of her. Then he went back out into the warm night, where Matt waited by the Tahoe.

Alec unlocked the doors. "Long drive, huh?"

He was treated to more bitching. Why did they have to drive? Even if Mom wanted to, she could have let *them* fly. Or hired someone to drive the car here.

"Every time I played my iPod, she made me turn down the volume. What difference does it make to *her* how loud my music is?"

"Do you know what you sound like every time you talk about your mom?"

Matt gave a one-shoulder shrug that said louder than words, *Who cares?*

"My father would have taken his belt to my backside if I'd talked about my mother that way."

"You don't know what she's like."

"I know your mother pretty well," Alec said mildly.

"You just *think* you do," Mattie sneered.

Alec signaled to turn into his driveway. "You make life pretty unpleasant for everyone around you when you act this way."

Matt turned his head away. "So, who cares? You don't have to see me. I wish you'd just let us stay in L.A. Why'd we have to move, too?"

"Because it was the right thing for all of us as a

family." Alec turned off the engine. Laying his forearm across the steering wheel, he turned enough to look at his nephew. Into the silence, he said, "Your mom and I talked to you about it."

"I was happy there."

"No, you weren't." Alec let his voice harden. "A happy thirteen-year-old boy doesn't get drunk. He doesn't shoplift or get in fights at school. I can't remember the last time I saw you smile. Happy kids smile."

Matt flashed him a dark look. "I smile with my friends. When I had friends. Which I don't now, thanks to you. And *her*."

"You'll make new ones." Alec watched him, then shook his head. "Come on, let's grab your stuff."

Maybe he should have saved the lecture. He'd become the enemy now, too. But damn it, he wasn't willing to tolerate such disrespect for Julia, either.

They walked into Alec's side of the duplex. Matt looked around. "At least you have a TV."

He wanted to say, *So does the hotel room,* but he'd seen the relief on Julia's face when Matt had agreed to sleep here, and nothing would make him return her demon spawn to her tonight.

"How'd your grades end up?" he asked casually, although he already knew.

Matt had the sullen shrug down pat.

"I hope you plan to try here, Mattie."

The boy rounded on him like a cornered badger. His eyes glittered. "*Don't* call me that."

"I've called you that for years."

"I'm not some dumb little kid anymore."

Alec let his eyebrows climb. "Your dad called you Mattie."

"*You're* not my father!" the boy spat.

He needed a second to be sure he could respond calmly. "No. But I loved Josh, and I love you."

Matt stared down at his toes.

"Matt it is," Alec said after a moment. "Come on. You're the first person to sleep in the guest room."

Leading the way, he heard a muttered "Oh, wow."

Man, Alec hoped the kid wasn't as big a shit to everyone else as he was to his mother and now him. To the people who had authority over him, it occurred to Alec. Didn't bode well for teachers or coaches.

Grimacing, he had to wonder if Matt *would* make friends in Angel Butte. Even the way he dressed was going to stand out. Around here, boys his age didn't wear pants with the crotch hanging down around their knees and T-shirts three sizes too big. Alec hoped there wasn't already a tattoo hidden where his mother hadn't seen it, but where the other boys would in the locker room. Maybe not every kid at the middle school here in Angel Butte would be wholesome, but they tended to put up a better front.

Sooner or later, he and Matt would be having a serious talk about what was and wasn't acceptable. Alec could hardly wait.

"Why don't you come out to the kitchen once you're settled?" he suggested.

He was treated to the sight of the bedroom door shutting in his face.

CHAPTER TWO

AT HIS FIRST SIGHT of people clustered at the base of the Public Safety Building's front steps, Alec's mood darkened.

And he'd been feeling unusually good, too; how could he not, having started his day over the breakfast table with Julia and the kids?

He pocketed his car keys, mentally braced himself and strode forward. If he wasn't mistaken, that was a press conference, and no one had told him. He was even less pleased when he spotted, as the focus of the small crowd, Captain Colin McAllister, who worked immediately under him heading investigation and support services. McAllister had served as acting police chief until Alec's arrival and really should have been given the job permanently. His resentment had never been a secret, although he saved most of it for Mayor Noah Chandler, who had blocked his hiring.

Alec had really enjoyed watching Chandler fall for McAllister's sister. Neither of the men had been very happy about the prospect of becoming family.

Now McAllister stood on the top step, surrounded

by microphones. He wore a well-cut suit and was listening to a question with his head slightly bent.

But damn, Alec was going to be pissed if McAllister had some big news he'd chosen not to share with him before holding an attention-grabbing press conference.

Closer up, he saw that some of the crowd were police department employees and passersby, drawn by curiosity. His experienced eye identified a pair of reporters, one with the *Bend Bulletin* and the other with the *Angel Butte Reporter*. A third might be a stringer for the *Oregonian* out of Portland, and, more annoyingly, a huge TV camera from a local news channel was there and filming.

As he neared, he couldn't help noticing that McAllister's expression was not expansive.

"Mayor Chandler has endorsed me," he said with the tone of a man repeating himself. "Feel free to take your questions to him."

Jim Henning from the *Reporter* caught sight of Alec. He swung away from McAllister. "Chief Raynor!" They all turned to him, faces avid.

Feeling like fresh meat, Alec took the stairs until he was at his captain's side. "I wasn't aware of any excitement this morning."

"Word has been leaked that the mayor blacklisted Captain McAllister as a candidate for the position of police chief. Were you aware of his action?"

Alec flicked his captain a sidelong glance. Mc-

Allister spread the fingers of one hand in a subtle *what the hell?* gesture.

"I was aware," he said.

"And yet you and he both have endorsed Captain McAllister for county sheriff," Henning said.

"That's correct." He looked from face to face. "May I ask who leaked this information?"

The stringer from the *Oregonian* answered. "The tip came from Sheriff Brock's campaign manager." He sounded slightly sardonic. In not quite three months on the job, Alec had already heard plenty of stories about the incumbent sheriff, who was certainly incompetent and very probably corrupt.

"I see. As I believe Captain McAllister has already suggested, you might want to take your questions to the mayor."

"You must know Mayor Chandler's reasoning," Jim Henning shot back.

Damn it. He hesitated, debating whether to stonewall the question or not. "I do know," he said finally, "and I can tell you honestly that if I had been in the mayor's position, I would have hired Captain McAllister. I have only the highest respect for his expertise as a law-enforcement officer, his leadership ability and his integrity."

He smiled crookedly. "I'd have been the loser, of course, so I can't altogether regret the decision. That said, I'm aware of the frustration many sheriff's deputies feel with inadequate equipment and salaries, a substandard crime lab and a lack of support from the top. It's my belief Captain McAllister is exactly what this county needs to upgrade the department. As chief of the county's largest city, I look forward to working closely with him once he becomes sheriff."

He held up a hand. "Now, if you'll excuse us, the two of us *are* currently employed by the city." He eyed them. "Since I assume you're heading to city hall next, I wouldn't want you reporting to the mayor that we're doing nothing but hanging around chatting with all of you."

There was general laughter. Ignoring shouted questions that were more of the same, he and McAllister entered the building.

"Why don't you come on up to my office?" he suggested.

Without saying a word, the captain stepped onto the elevator with him, got off with him and accompanied him down the hall to the door that said Police Chief in shiny gold script.

His assistant greeted them and brought two cups of coffee before Alec had even sat down behind his desk. The moment the door closed behind her, McAllister growled, "That son of a bitch."

"Brock?"

"Who else?"

Alec felt a spark of humor. "You might have been talking about Chandler."

Colin sprawled into a chair. "That works, too." He brooded for a moment. "He's okay."

"Your sister seems to have mellowed him some."
He grunted.

"Do you think there's any chance Chandler's responsible for this leak?"

"No." A half smile lifted Colin's mouth. "I didn't ask for his endorsement, you know. He offered it."

"He could very easily give with one hand and then take back with the other," Alec pointed out.

Colin gave a bark of laughter. "Cait would geld him if she found he'd done something like that."

Alec had to grin.

"No," Colin repeated. "I didn't like his decision not to support me to take over the department here in Angel Butte, but I do understand it. He didn't try to hide what he'd done or why. No question he can be ruthless, but he's not underhanded."

Alec mulled that over for a minute. He didn't know Noah Chandler as well as McAllister did, but finally he nodded his agreement. "You're right. He's been honest with me. He didn't want to hire me, either, you know."

He wasn't quite sure why he was telling McAllister this, but the time felt right.

Colin's eyebrows rose. "No, I didn't. Why not?"

"Apparently he'd chosen a candidate who was already doing essentially this job and wanted to move up to a larger city. Chandler didn't believe I had the administrative or political experience required."

"Guess he was wrong."

Alec offered a smile that had been described by

his officers as feral. "He was wrong." Seeing McAllister's amusement, Alec added, "He was also less than thrilled because I'll be going back to L.A. a couple of times to testify. One trial in particular may pull me away for as much as a couple of weeks."

"Unusual for a lieutenant."

"I wasn't one when I made this bust." He quirked an eyebrow. "You ever read *Bleak House* by Dickens?"

Colin laughed. "The never-ending court case?"

"That's this one, but it looks like it's finally coming to a head." He hesitated. "The murder was related to drug trafficking. I arrested the head of a cartel."

"So you feel right at home here," McAllister said ironically.

He lifted a shoulder in acknowledgment. "Back to my hire. I didn't know it at the time, but I suspect a majority in the city council was seizing the chance to slap our mayor's hand. They went along with his decision not to hire you, but reveled in the chance to also refuse to give him what he wanted."

"Petty, but that's politics."

"Yeah, it is." Alec took a swallow of his coffee. "It'll be interesting to see what His Honor the mayor has to say to our press corps."

"Goddamn," Colin growled. "I was looking good in the polls."

"Better this came out now than later," Alec suggested. "If I'd been running Brock's campaign, I'd have waited to spring it on voters until the final weeks before the election. As it is, you have time to counteract any dip." Four months, to be exact. Julia had waited until school let out in L.A. to move the kids. Today was only—he glanced at the small calendar on his desk blotter—June 26.

McAllister rose to his feet. "Thank you for the support out there." He sounded a little stiff, no surprise for a man who disliked having to depend on anyone else.

"Early on, I told Chandler he had his head up his ass. He should have hired you."

"I'd have liked to be a fly on the wall."

"I phrased it a little more circumspectly at the time."

Colin was outright grinning now. "You mean, you have some political instincts after all?"

"Appears so."

They were both laughing when McAllister left Alec alone in his office.

"Do you mind if I turn on the local news before we go to dinner?" Alec gestured to the television in the hotel room.

He'd offered to spend the evening with her and the kids again. Julia was immensely grateful but was also unpleasantly conscious of being the object of his well-developed sense of obligation.

"Of course not," she said. She narrowed a look at

her daughter, who had already opened her mouth to whine.

Lately it seemed as if the kids could eat nonstop. Maybe they were both on the verge of a growth spurt. If so, she hoped they'd get it out of the way before she bought back-to-school wardrobes.

She sat next to Alec at the foot of one of the room's two queen-size beds. Liana sat cross-legged behind them, reading. On the other bed, Matt sprawled with his eyes closed, listening to music on his iPod. Great way to shut everyone else out.

Uncomfortably aware of Alec so close to her, Julia tried to concentrate on the news.

There had been a head-on accident on Highway 97, just south of Sunriver. The anchor told viewers solemnly that there had been one fatality and a second person who had been riding in the same car was clinging to life. The driver of the vehicle that had crossed the center line had walked away. Police were awaiting the results of tests for alcohol and drug use.

Julia's gaze slid to Alec's profile, clean-cut, sharp-edged. She drank in the sight of his jaw, darkened by the beginnings of stubble.

The second piece came on, and Alec used the remote to raise the volume. Watching intently, he leaned forward, forearms braced on his thighs. His interest made Julia pay attention, too.

"Scandal broke today in the race for Butte County sheriff," a young man told them. He was positioned in front of the historic courthouse in Angel Butte. "Staffers for incumbent sheriff Eugene Brock learned that police captain Colin McAllister, who has been leading in recent polls, was denied the job as police chief in Angel Butte when the mayor blacklisted him for reasons no official wants to discuss."

The camera focused on a tall man with a craggy face. "Mayor Chandler has endorsed me," he said tersely. "Feel free to take your questions to him."

The reporter said, "Angel Butte police chief Alec Raynor also commented."

Alec had joined the other man on the steps. A muffled voice could be heard. "You must know Mayor Chandler's reasoning."

Julia watched with intense interest.

"I do know," he said, maintaining what she thought of as his cop face, "and I can tell you honestly that if I had been in the mayor's position, I would have hired Captain McAllister. I have only the highest respect for his expertise as a law-enforcement officer, his leadership ability and his integrity." He smiled faintly. "I'd have been the loser, of course, so I can't altogether regret the decision."

The picture returned to the reporter at the courthouse. "Mayor Chandler has been persuaded to speak to us about the rumors," he said and held out the microphone. The image broadened to include a big, homely, tough-looking man who appeared distinctly annoyed.

"I gather Sheriff Brock is feeling challenged and felt it was time to start slinging mud." Muscles flexed in his jaw. "All right. I'll be blunt. Five months ago, when we first started the search for a new police chief in the wake of Gary Bystrom's resignation, I was disinclined to hire a candidate from within the department. We had some issues that I cannot discuss without interfering with ongoing investigations. I chose to go with an outsider. I have since apologized privately to Captain McAllister. I have become convinced he would have been a top-notch police chief. My original hesitation had nothing to do with Captain McAllister himself, not personally and not with his job performance. He has my full support in this campaign. That's all I have to say."

The camera cut back to Alec, who was saying, "I'm aware of the frustration many sheriff's deputies feel with inadequate equipment and salaries, a substandard crime lab and a lack of support from the top. It's my belief Captain McAllister is exactly what this county needs to upgrade the department. As chief of the county's largest city, I look forward to working closely with him once he becomes sheriff."

"There we have it, Peter," the reporter said, shaking his head in apparent bemusement. "The full support of Angel Butte's mayor and police chief—but no real answers."

The anchor thanked the reporter, and the channel went to a commercial. Alec turned off the television.

"That was you," Liana burst out. She draped herself over his shoulder. "Why were they asking you questions, Uncle Alec?"

Julia saw him look sideways toward Matt, who had taken the buds from his ears and was listening, too, even if he didn't want anyone to realize he was.

Alec hugged her. "Because I'm an important man around here, sweet pea." More seriously, he explained that he had two captains who worked directly under him at the police department. One of them was campaigning to become sheriff of the entire county. Reporters were asking some questions about him, and of course one of the people they'd want answers from was Captain McAllister's boss.

"That's you," Liana said in her often solemn way.

"Right."

Julia had been absorbing everything he said, wanting to know what he did every day and about the people with whom he dealt. He'd already told her a bit about Noah Chandler, the mayor, who didn't sound all that likable. She sensed undercurrents to this news story that she hoped he'd explain when he had a chance.

Alec smiled at Julia and Liana, then turned to include Matt. "Anybody hungry?"

"Yeah!" Liana bounced a few times on the bed, bobbing her mother and uncle up and down. Matt didn't say anything, but got up and shoved his feet into the sloppy athletic shoes that made his feet look enormous. As usual, he left them untied.

Alec suggested pizza tonight and took them to a place that was already a favorite of his. After their order was in, both kids snatched the money he offered and disappeared into the small video arcade, from which beeps and roars and yelps of triumph already emerged. Matt dropped back, undoubtedly to be sure no one watching would think he was with some little kid, and a girl at that. Julia hoped there was an appropriate game for Liana. She'd have followed to help her get started, but knew Matt would resent having his mommy trailing him. Also—she couldn't help it, but she wanted time alone with Alec, who was frowning as he took a drink of beer.

"So, was the television piece halfway fair? Or did they leave out the stuff you really wanted the public to see?" she asked.

"Huh?" He focused his dark chocolate eyes on her. "Oh, no. It was fine. In fact, I'm a little surprised they slipped my endorsement in at the end."

She thought about it. "Do you suppose the news team is secretly anti Sheriff Brock?"

"That's a possibility," he said. "The guy's scum." He glanced quickly around as if to be sure no one was close enough to hear, then smiled crookedly. "I didn't say that."

"Of course not."

"I confess, I didn't realize small-town and rural-county politics were as dirty as the big-city version." He shook his head. "Naive of me, I know."

"Oh, we had a hideous mayoral race when I was in high school." She laughed. "The challenger was a woman, which outraged the guy who had held the office for something like twenty years. According to my parents, half the time he'd run unopposed. He was heard to make some highly sexist remarks that may have appealed to the good old boys in town, but offended female voters. When she roared ahead in the newspaper poll, he dug up the fact that she'd had an abortion many years before. Unfortunately for him, he hadn't done his research. She did have an abortion, but only after she and her husband did some soul-searching and decided not to go to term with a fetus doctors knew was unlikely to live much past birth. No matter their politics, most people sympathized with her. Mayor Anderson was thereafter doomed."

"Deservedly so," Alec said, amusement curving his mouth.

"Indeed. Even my father, who is terribly conservative, voted against him. Or so he claimed, anyway."

"Your mother?"

Julia took a deep breath to combat a stab of pain. "Oh, Mom probably voted for him. I doubt she thought a woman should be in office, either."

Alec raised his eyebrows and watched her thoughtfully. When she clamped her mouth shut, he stirred. "Isn't it your mother you have the difficulties with?"

"Yes. Oh, both, to some extent. They're…" She tried to think how to explain her parents. "For one thing, they're older. I suspect I was an 'oops' baby. My brother and I are ten years apart, and Mom was forty-two when I was born. She's seventy-five now, Dad a year older. They were always stricter than my friends' parents, more rigid. Big on gender roles. To this day, I know nothing about cars or how to get a lawn mower started if it stalls." She shook her head in frustration. "They were shocked when I wanted to go to college. I had a high school boyfriend who planned to keep working with his father on the family dairy farm. He asked me to marry him, and they were stunned when I said no and not only left for college, but went all the way out to the West Coast."

"I didn't know any of that." A couple of lines had formed between his eyebrows that made him look perturbed. "You were only nineteen when you married Josh."

"Yes, and I blame my parents for that." She grimaced at his surprise. "Don't get me wrong, I loved Josh. But we didn't have to rush out and get married. I should have gotten my degree first. But in retrospect I realize that, once I did commit to a man, childhood conditioning kicked in. The little woman should step right into the support role. So much for the great escape from my past. Josh was already navy, and he wanted me with him when he was transferred. I could keep taking classes, he insisted, but, oh, gee, I got pregnant right away."

"With the demon spawn," Alec murmured, a smile forming.

She laughed. "You didn't say how the night went."

"Let's just say I have a new appreciation of the Craigslist option."

Oh, dear. Their number was being called, and the kids came bursting out of the arcade as if they'd been wandering in the desert for a hundred days and suddenly saw the vision of a feast laid out before them.

Julia shook her head, although the smile didn't want to leave her lips. "Have I mentioned that I love him, too, despite everything?"

"Yeah." Alec reached across the table and laid his hand over hers, one of the rare occasions when he voluntarily touched her. His voice was a little gravelly, but also…tender. "I know you do."

The kids appeared, Matt bearing one pizza and Liana another, the different options the only way Julia had seen to achieve peace when they ordered.

"Can one of you go back and grab plates?" she asked.

Liana trotted off. Alec moved over on his side of the booth and Matt slid in beside him. He grabbed a slice of pizza and lifted it, cheese stretching into a long string that kept his slice attached with an umbilical cord to the mother ship.

"You might want to cut that," Alec suggested, his tone mild but still firm.

Her son shot him a resentful look, but wound the string of cheese around his finger.

Of course, he contributed almost nothing to the conversation as they ate, although Liana chattered happily, having learned to ignore her brother's scathing glances.

Alec had finished and pushed his plate away when he shifted on the bench seat and produced a flyer from his back pocket. It was obviously a local effort, photocopied on green paper. Tilting her head, Julia saw a logo for Angel Butte Parks & Recreation at the bottom.

"These are summer classes and activities, mostly for kids," he said. "I spotted a few things like ballroom dance for adults. But I know you'll want to get the kids involved, and this seems like a good way."

Matt reared back in outrage. "No way you're signing me up for some kind of camp for little kids!"

Julia glanced at Alec, then said only, "We'll see."

She spread open the brochure, Liana pressing close to her so she could see, too.

"Can I take swim lessons?" she begged. "Ooh, look. A horse camp!"

Alec smiled at her. "I knew that's what you'd go for."

"There's a two-week soccer camp," Julia read aloud, "and orienteering." She moved her finger on the paper as she read the fine-print description. "You'd like this one, Matt."

"I don't need to be babysat."

"Learning to use a compass and make your way through the woods can be useful," Alec commented. "Your dad would have been an expert. Navy SEALs have to be able to navigate wherever they're dropped."

"This description mentions that the course is based on U.S. Army training," Julia chimed in, trying not to sound unacceptably bubbly. "Minimum age is...thirteen. Wow, you qualify."

"You mean, I could go somewhere without my little sister?" he asked sarcastically.

Liana couldn't hide the flash of hurt, but she had enough spirit to stick out her tongue at her brother.

Alec met Julia's gaze, his expression rueful, but he kept quiet. She'd seen him biting his tongue enough to know he wouldn't always handle Matt's snotty attitude the same way she did, but he was very careful not to act the part of a parent.

Depressed, she asked herself who could blame him. It was miracle enough that he was willing to do as much as he did. Even to completely uproot and move. When she'd asked Josh to choose between his family and his dangerous, high-adrenaline job, he'd chosen the job. It scared her to think Alec might hate it here in Angel Butte, so far from the high-adrenaline job *he'd* loved. From what he'd said, he was now stuck behind a desk, probably the last thing he'd ever wanted to do with his life.

I didn't ask him, she argued with herself. *He offered.*

But that didn't mean he wouldn't blame her if he began to chafe at this new life.

He kept insisting they were his family, but they weren't really, were they?

The fact that she wished they were would remain her secret.

HE NOW HAD a new challenge, Alec was disconcerted to realize: keeping his mind on the job now that he had the distraction of family. Alec was known for having a single-minded, intense focus. Back in L.A., Julia and the kids hadn't affected him so much, because he didn't see them daily. Apparently, things were going to be different now.

They hadn't even been in town forty-eight hours, and whether he was conducting meetings, talking on the phone or working on procedures, his attention was split. Worry about Matt was constantly on his mind; happiness tumbled with the bleak knowledge that Julia was going to be a big part of his life, but wasn't his.

This meeting was a good example. Alec rose to usher Naomi Wallace out of his office, hoping he'd actually taken in everything she'd told him. She was the community liaison working for the police department. This was their first meeting of any substance, although of course he'd met her and they had both attended the same meetings a few times. He shouldn't have put this off for so long.

He thanked her for letting him know how the police department was involved in both the Fourth of July parade and fireworks and the upcoming arts-and-crafts fair taking place later in the month. "I'll look forward to Frontier Days," he lied, but knew Julia would love an art fair that would take over eight city blocks for three days.

Yeah, throughout the discussion he'd been thinking, *I have to tell Julia about that* or *Good, that'll be great entertainment for the kids.*

The parade and fireworks slated for the Fourth would be a hit with Liana for sure. He was assured that this one included not only the traditional floats, honking fire trucks with firefighters throwing candy, the high school marching band and a lawn-mower drill team some local men with a sense of humor had dreamed up, but also horses. Lots of horses. The princess chosen by the Angel Butte Merchants Association didn't ride on a float; she was slated to ride a palomino horse. Liana would be in seventh heaven. He had hopes even Matt would come around, since Alec had been told a motorcycle-stunt and drill team also participating was enough to make the most hardened citizens gasp. The Fourth was always a headache for law enforcement, but he'd already made up his mind to take the evening off. He'd keep his phone with him if he was needed, but he wanted to watch the fireworks with Julia and the kids. The Fourth was a family holiday, and he now had family.

This meeting, he reflected, was a part of the job he'd been least prepared for. He actually had learned a great deal from Naomi Wallace about his department's role in special events—closing off roads, patrolling for maximum safety and ensuring activities met city codes.

Now, by God, he had to get back to his current focus, projecting manpower requirements and documenting his findings in a way he could sell to the city council.

He'd called up the folder on his laptop and was trying to remember whether he'd received the statistics on calls logged by patrol that he'd requested from Brian Cooper, the captain on the patrol side of the department, when his cell rang. Since he'd been struggling to focus anyway, he glanced at it with irritation.

The number was unfamiliar. Nonetheless, he picked it up. "Chief Raynor."

"We saw you on television." The voice was weirdly muffled. Not metallic, as if it was being electronically altered. More as if something was between the mouth and the phone receiver.

"Who is this?" he asked sharply.

"You will withdraw your support of Captain McAllister for the position of sheriff." Muffled or not, the speaker sounded deathly serious. "If you don't do as we ask, we can make you very sorry."

The click was audible. His caller was gone.

The phone number was local and clearly a landline. After a moment's hesitation, he called it. It rang half a dozen times with no answer. He redialed. Another half-dozen rings. Again.

This time he got an answer. "Jerry's Tavern and Pool Hall," a man said brusquely. "What can I do for you?"

"This is Police Chief Alec Raynor. Not two minutes ago, I received a call from this number."

"Customers use it sometimes. Maybe it was a wrong number."

"No," he said coolly, "it was a threat."

Silence. "I sure as hell didn't call you."

"I wasn't suggesting you did. I'm asking if you saw who used the phone last."

"I'm afraid not. Uh, I'm Jerry. This is my place. I was down in the basement grabbing a keg. There are a couple of locals in here. Let me ask."

Jerry covered the phone, but Alec could still hear him call, "Hey, Billy! Marvin, is that you? Yeah, either of you just use the phone?" Their answers were indistinguishable. "Uh-huh," Jerry said a couple of times. Then, "You see somebody making a call? Just a minute ago?"

He came back on. "They were playing a game of pool. Neither of 'em could see the hall from there. I had the back door open." He sounded apologetic.

"This isn't a real busy time of day. I was bringing in supplies from a Sam's Club run. Afraid pretty much anyone could've walked in and used the phone quick, if they were of a mind to."

Alec asked a few more questions, but knew it was hopeless. Out of curiosity, he thought he might drive by Jerry's and see how easily a passerby could have seen a way to slip in and use that phone, unseen.

He wanted to think it was a prank call, but well-developed instincts said no. One of Sheriff Brock's increasingly desperate staffers? More likely. If so, Alec doubted the threat was real.

He couldn't dismiss it altogether, though. Fanatics could be found anywhere. Frowning, he sat thinking about the call. He wasn't worried about himself. He'd been a cop too long to ever be anything but wary. What he didn't like was knowing that he now had an Achilles' heel.

Three of them, to be precise. And, although his home address was and would stay unlisted, it wouldn't be hard to follow him home. Or even just ask around. This small city more often felt like a small town to him. Everyone knew everyone. And anybody watching him would see quickly that the woman and children living on the other side of the duplex weren't just renters.

But the caller hadn't mentioned them, he reminded himself. Anyone in law enforcement got used to being threatened. This one hadn't been atypical. He couldn't deny that it had unsettled him, though.

Tell Julia?

No. All he'd do was upset her and make her over-protective, which wouldn't go over well with Matt right now.

He swore aloud, disconcerted when he heard his voice. Damn it, he was overreacting.

One thing he could do was check with Noah Chandler and find out whether he'd had a similar call. Chandler wouldn't be any more likely to give in to that kind of pressure than Alec was, but, like Alec, he had recently acquired an Achilles' heel of his own. In fact, if Alec wasn't mistaken, Chandler's wedding to Colin McAllister's sister was only a couple of weeks away. He had an invitation.

Alec wondered if any security had been planned for the wedding.

It was a good ten minutes before he could drag most of his attention back to his required-manpower projections for the city of Angel Butte.

CHAPTER THREE

Two DAYS LATER, they were moved into the duplex, a huge relief to Julia after the aeon she and the kids had spent trapped together, first in the car and then the hotel room. At least with three bedrooms, each of them had a refuge. She would have been ashamed to admit to anyone else how grateful she was for the hours Matt usually spent holed up in his bedroom.

The one drawback was that the kids' bikes arrived on the moving truck along with the furniture, and now that he had wheels, she couldn't think of a good reason to forbid Matt from disappearing to who knew where.

Thank heavens for the positives she was able to cling to as the first week in their new home went on. Number one, of course, was Alec. He was *there*. Eating with them every evening, quietly interceding with Matt, teasing Liana, giving Julia a sounding board. He was everything she'd wanted Josh to be, and while making a comparison like that disturbed her, she was too grateful for Alec's solid presence to let herself dwell on whether she was a dreadful person for contrasting him with Josh.

Second, Matt had yet to pull anything awful, like get drunk or be caught shoplifting, or even get into a fight. He wasn't exactly a delight, but she was letting herself hope, if only a tiny bit. Could having Alec so much more involved in their lives be making a difference?

And then there was the fact that, despite her shyness, within a day Liana had made tentative inroads with a neighbor girl.

Bothered that the girl seemed to be home alone all day, Julia kept an eye out the front window near the end of the third day. When she saw a car turn into that driveway, she strolled over to meet Sophie's mother, who introduced herself as Andrea Young. Obviously feeling a need to explain why her daughter was alone during the day, Andrea immediately started talking about her divorce and the fact that her ex had shortly thereafter moved to Texas. To her credit, she kept an eye on the girls to be sure her daughter wasn't overhearing her. The ex called occasionally, Andrea said with some bitterness, and that was about it.

"I count my blessings he's paying his child support so far." She cocked her head. "You on your own, too?"

"I'm a widow." Julia hated saying that, seeing the instant sympathy. "My husband was military. The blessing is that we do have death benefits, so I'm not as strapped financially as most single mothers. As soon as we're settled in, I'll be job hunting, though." She explained about her relationship to Alec and said that they'd decided to move to a smaller town for the sake of the kids, without being specific about her troubled son.

Both women continued to watch the girls, who were playing hopscotch on the sidewalk, having drawn the squares with colored chalk Julia had provided. Sophie was apparently artistic, as she'd gotten Liana to help her decorate the sidewalk for several additional squares in each direction with elaborate, intertwined curlicues. They'd probably had more fun doing that than they were having now playing such a childish game, even though they kept making mistakes—seemingly on purpose—and then giggling madly.

Julia mentioned Liana's upcoming birthday, when she'd turn eleven.

"Sophie's twelve," Andrea said, a slowness in her voice. "It's legal to leave her alone now, but I'd rather not. Full-time day care is so expensive, though, and she begged not to have to do it, anyway. This in-between age is hard. She'll be able to ride her bike to some of the Parks Department activities. I make her call me anytime she leaves the house."

She sounded helpless and maybe hopeless, too. Julia sympathized. Both emotions had become familiar to her.

"I plan to sign my kids up for some of those activities, too. If she's interested in any of the same things Liana is, I'll be glad to chauffeur Sophie, too."

When Andrea invited her in for a cup of coffee, Julia was happy to accept. The two mothers pored over the Parks & Recreation Department schedule. Then they called the girls in for a consultation.

The two-week horse day camp was a definite go, as were swim lessons. Sophie and Liana weren't quite at the same level, but the advanced class took place right after the intermediate, and Julia insisted that it wouldn't kill any of them to hang around the pool for an extra half hour one way or the other. Sophie wrinkled her freckled nose at the idea of ceramics class, but thought she might like tap dancing.

Studying the two girls, Julia was disconcerted to see that, only one year older, Sophie was developing a figure. She didn't wear a bra yet, but she probably would be before she started back to school. Which, in her case, would be middle school here in Angel Butte. In L.A., Liana would have been starting middle school, too. Thank goodness she wasn't here. The fact that the two girls would be separated for school in September would probably kill this budding friendship, but as far as Julia was concerned, if it lasted the summer, she'd be happy.

Now, if only there was a nice neighbor boy Matt's age.

But she didn't kid herself that Matt would want anything to do with a nice boy.

Which left her worrying about what he was doing when he rode away on his bike and didn't return home for two or three hours at a time.

When she asked, he only glared at her. "There's nothing *to* do around here. I'm just, like, riding my bike, okay?"

Her offer to help with Sophie was rewarded only a few days later, when Sophie shyly invited Liana to go to a movie with her on Friday night. The invitation included Matt, too, if he would like to see a blow-'em-up thriller that Andrea had noticed was also at the multiplex and running at close to the same time.

Guilt induced Julia to offer to go with Matt, which earned her a look that almost reminded her of the much more likable boy he'd once been.

"You'd *hate* that movie," he said.

She grimaced. "Probably. Still, if you want company…"

He remembered he despised her and sneered, "Sure. My mother. Yeah, thanks but no thanks."

Knowing she should feel rejected, Julia could only be relieved.

After the kids left, she tried to convince herself that she was blissfully happy alone and wouldn't even notice if Alec didn't come home right after work. Or came home only to change clothes because he had a date.

Of course, every time she heard a passing vehicle, her head came up. She hadn't quite memorized the sound of his SUV yet.

She couldn't miss it when he pulled into the driveway so close by, though, and only a minute later her doorbell rang. Her pulse accelerated even though she'd half expected him.

He had already shed his suit coat and tie. The cuffs of his white shirt were rolled halfway up strong forearms. He looked tired, she saw, but smiled when he saw her. "Hey. You and the kids want to go out for pizza or something?"

"It so happens the kids have already gone out for burgers and a movie." She paused for effect. "Without me."

One eyebrow tilted up, giving his face a wicked cast. "A fairy godmother?"

"Andrea."

He knew about Liana's new friendship, but still looked surprised. "Did you hog-tie Matt or drug him into compliance?"

She told him the arrangement for separate but equal movies. "He'll probably sit at a separate booth at McDonald's or wherever they went, too, but Andrea seemed to understand. I haven't started dinner yet, but if you're okay with something simple—"

"I vote we go out," he said. "Someplace decent."

"You mean someplace the kids would boycott?"

She loved his smile. "You got it."

He suggested Chandler's Brew Pub, owned by the mayor. There was a live band scheduled, but he thought not until later in the evening. Julia quickly changed, had second thoughts over her choice and would have started over if she hadn't been so aware of Alec waiting.

When he saw her wearing slim-fitting black pants, heels and a shimmery tunic-length sleeveless sweater, his eyes had a glint that raised heat in her cheeks. It wasn't the first time she'd seen that expression on his face, but she hadn't decided what to make of it. If he was attracted to her, he obviously didn't plan to act on it. Maybe he was only being politely appreciative.

"You look about twenty-two," he told her. "No one would believe you have a kid Matt's age."

"That makes you a dirty old man to be giving me the once-over," she suggested lightly.

He laughed. "It's been quite a few years since I've looked over a girl that age with anything approaching serious intent."

She felt a small burst of pleasure. Was he implying he had serious intent where she was concerned?

But when he stepped so ostentatiously aside to let her exit ahead of him, ultracareful not to brush against her, the thrill died as if he'd dumped cold water on it. No, of course not. He thought of her as a sister. What else?

Oh, God, she was so pathetic. Foolishly in love with her brother-in-law.

She had to be sure he never knew. For the hundredth time, at least, she reminded herself that of course she should be glad he didn't feel the same. His indifference reduced any temptation on her part, and yes, that was good.

Alec was steadfast with her and the kids in a way Josh had never been, that was true. But in one essential way, he was too much like his brother. She'd always known that. She'd listened to the two of them talk so many times, voices laconic as they casually exchanged stories of terrifying exploits, but the excitement they felt seeping through.

Yes, but are they really so much alike? asked a voice in her head, one she'd heard more often lately. *Alec made a decision Josh never would have, didn't he?*

But he could still regret it. He could still go back.

And while he called himself a desk jockey now, she saw the way his head turned as they walked to his Tahoe, his expression flat. Julia knew he was conscious of everyone and everything within a block radius, down to any shadow of movement passing behind the reflected sunlight on windows.

Once a street and vice cop, always one.

Please don't let him be too bored.

Yesterday had been the Fourth of July. Since fireworks were shot off the crater rim of Angel Butte, they had been able to put lawn chairs on Alec's small patio and watch from there. Liana had oohed and aahed while Matt, predictably, appeared bored. The show *wasn't* as spectacular as some they'd seen, but they also hadn't had to fight crowds, spend ages searching for parking and walk miles for a good spot for viewing. To Julia, this felt…magical. All of them together in the dark, in their own yard.

All the neighbors were outside, too. After the fireworks show, people started lighting their own smaller ones. Andrea and Sophie came over. While the girls swooped across the lawn waving sparklers, Matt and Alec set off fireworks Alec had bought, murmuring together and laughing. Watching them, Julia had felt the sting of tears in her eyes from, oh, a complicated mix of gratitude and joy, and sadness, too.

Talking about last night carried her and Alec through the short drive to downtown. The police department had gotten the predictable complaints, there'd been a few minor injuries but no serious ones and he was pleased at how his officers had handled the holiday.

He found street parking less than a block from Chandler's. On a Friday night like this, the sidewalk was busy. He stepped around her to be sure he was walking on the curbside, and actually went so far as to lay a hand on her back. The warmth of it burned through the thin knit of the sweater. She was kept from feeling flattered, though, by his expression, which was oddly distant as he kept watch around them, much as he had between her front door and his SUV.

Had he always been so…protective? Funny, she

didn't remember ever noticing until recently. If he hadn't been edgy in L.A., she couldn't imagine why he'd be so here. Surely she was imagining things.

He held open the door to Chandler's. They'd barely stepped in when she heard a groan, almost but not quite beneath his breath. She looked at him, surprised.

He bent so his mouth was close to her ear. "Chandler's here. Thank God, it looks like he's well into his meal, so neither of us will feel obligated to suggest we make it a foursome."

The handsome and absurdly young man serving as host greeted Alec as Chief Raynor and ushered him and Julia straight to a table that had just been cleared by a busboy. The route took them close to the booth where a man she recognized from that television news interview sat with a beautiful woman with pixie hair and intriguing earrings that shimmered in the light when she turned her head.

Alec's hand splayed on Julia's back again and he steered her over to the booth. "Chandler," he said with a polite nod. "Cait. I'd like you to meet my sister-in-law, Julia Raynor. Julia, our mayor and my boss, Noah Chandler, and his fiancée, Cait McAllister."

In a surprisingly gentlemanly gesture, the mayor slid out of the booth and rose to his feet. He took Julia's hand in his much larger one. "Good to meet you. We've all been hearing about you."

She laughed. "Hmm. I think I'll refrain from asking what he had to say."

Noah Chandler was an intriguing man, she realized. She remembered the word *tough* coming to mind and even thinking he was kind of ugly, but in person…he was really a very sexy man, if big enough to be alarming to her. And the smile on his fiancée's face was genuine and warm.

"We didn't know if you'd arrive in time or not," Cait said, "but Alec has an invitation to our wedding and we hope you'll come, too."

Julia returned the smile. "I'd love to come. You should have made the wedding on the Fourth, and you could have had a fireworks send-off."

Noah's grin was downright rakish. "Oh, there'll be fireworks."

Cait laughed, rolled her eyes and blushed all at the same time.

The host was politely waiting to one side, clutching menus, so Alec excused them and they allowed themselves to be seated by the window.

Not until they were alone did she laugh. "Okay, why the groan? He seems nice enough."

"*Nice* isn't the word that comes to mind to describe Mayor Chandler," Alec said drily. "He's improving on acquaintance, though." He glanced their way. "I did tell you about Cait getting kidnapped and Noah rescuing her, didn't I?"

"Yes, sort of." Her forehead wrinkled as she thought back. It had all happened during her last few days getting herself and the kids ready to leave Los Angeles. As she remembered it, he'd said they "had some excitement here in Angel Butte."

"But I hadn't met anybody you were talking about, and mostly I was having a quiet panic attack because our handpicked town didn't sound nearly as safe as I'd imagined it. So tell me again."

"Let's choose our meals first, before the waiter shows up," he suggested.

Since she'd had it with pizzas and burgers, she went with an interesting-sounding wrap, while Alec ordered a steak. Once they had their salads and a Cabernet from a Willamette Valley winery, he told her the story in more detail.

She had also seen Cait McAllister's brother during that news clip. He was the police captain who was running for county sheriff, the one the mayor admitted having blacklisted for the job of police chief. Cait had lived in Angel Butte as a child, but hadn't been back since she was ten years old. Only recently had she moved here to be near her brother. Within days of her arrival, impulsive words spoken to a barely remembered acquaintance made her the target of a killer. She'd eventually remembered as a child seeing two men burying something, and one of the two was the man she'd spoken to.

"After they filled in the hole back then, they poured a concrete patio over it," Alec told her. "Once Cait pointed us to the right place, we broke it up and, no surprise, found bones." He grimaced.

"In a bizarre twist of fate, the dead man was Chandler's father. Solved what had been a mystery in his life."

She listened, intrigued, as he told her more about Noah. He owned two more restaurants besides the one here in Angel Butte, but evidently had enough energy left over to have decided to run for mayor.

"Consensus is, the last mayor was known for turning a blind eye to a lot of shady practices, while Chandler may be an SOB but is scrupulously honest." Alec shrugged.

Their salads arrived, and they both picked up their forks.

"Back to the story," he said after a moment.

Cait had survived one murder attempt, after which her brother and Noah both had done their damnedest to keep her safe, according to Alec. Watching anyone 24/7 was next to impossible, though. Perhaps inevitably, she'd been left alone for the few minutes that allowed the killer to grab her.

It was Noah who had rescued her, at high cost to himself. The bullet had come close to killing him.

"Gutsy thing Chandler did," Alec conceded. "He's barely back at work."

She smiled at his air of grudging admiration. "Come on, you like the guy."

He grinned crookedly. "Like I said, I'm warming to him."

She laughed, studying him across the table. Noah Chandler definitely had sexual charisma that would have any woman giving him at least a second glance, but as far as she was concerned, so did Alec…times ten.

There were moments when her heart caught at his resemblance to her husband, but more often she would wonder why he *didn't* look more like Josh. Both men had the near-black hair of their Italian mother as well as her rich brown eyes. Josh had been an inch or two taller and definitely broader, although some of that might have been because of the conditioning he had to maintain as a navy SEAL. His face had been wider, his features less sharply defined. Alec had a lean, greyhound elegance his brother lacked. Josh in general had been more physical, less thoughtful. He always wanted to be doing something. He'd drag one of the kids out to kick the soccer ball or practice pitching. He'd started teaching Matt to surf. Evenings, he and Matt would retire to Matt's bedroom, where she'd hear them hooting and groaning as they played video games. Josh was so competitive, it had become a joke between them—but what was funny when she was twenty-two had become less so as the years went by.

Alec, she thought, was more subtle. He was hard to read; it was rare to catch naked emotion on his face. She suspected he, too, liked to come out on top when it came to the important things, but he was relaxed about the little everyday moments that to Josh were all a contest. The irony to her was that, as a SEAL, Josh had needed to be able to take initiative, but in a more cosmic sense he was always following orders. What if he disagreed with the politics behind a military action? she would ask, and without fail he'd deal the patriot card. Meanwhile, she'd watched Alec steadily rise in the hierarchy, accepting the loss of action so that he could gain command and the ability to make the decisions.

For the first time, she identified the key difference between the brothers. For all that he was a warrior, Josh had remained boyish in his motivations. *Boyish* was not a word that would ever occur to her in relation to Alec. He was all man, and had been for a long time.

Part of what made him a man was his unwavering sense of duty. For all she knew, he didn't even like her. But, by God, she was his brother's widow, her kids were his niece and nephew, and so he would take care of them.

What scared her most was to think that he might stay single because of a commitment to her, when he didn't love her at all.

Oh, dear God. I should have said no. I should have taken the kids and gone home to Minnesota, she thought, the squeeze of panic stealing her breath. *I shouldn't have let him make such a huge sacrifice for us.*

"Do you hate your job here?" Her voice came out thin, and under the table her fingernails bit into her palms.

He stared at her. "What brought that on?"

"I don't know." She fought to recover her poise, to keep him from knowing how close she sometimes was to a complete breakdown. "Belated second thoughts, maybe?"

"You think you forced this on me." Those dark eyes read her too well.

"I didn't mean to, but—" she closed her eyes briefly before she could finish "—I think I did."

"No." The one word came out harsh. "Damn it, Julia! I didn't know you were still thinking like this. If you'd taken the kids and gone back to Minnesota, I'd have gotten hired as police chief there whether you liked it or not. I'd have followed you."

"Because you think that's what Josh would expect."

Now she really couldn't tell what he was thinking.

"No," he said finally, calmly.

It was her turn to stare. Was he implying…? But he couldn't be.

"I used to lump you and Josh together, in a way," she heard herself say.

A flicker of some emotion passed through his eyes. "Except that you were married to Josh," he said after a moment.

She flapped her hand. "You know what I mean."

"No, I don't."

"I thought you were both addicted to taking risks. That you'd chosen the careers you did because parachuting in the dark under gunfire or kicking in a drug dealer's door gave you the ultimate high."

His jaw bunched. "You mean, you thought we were a pair of adolescents."

Julia bowed her head, unable to hold that intense gaze. "Not quite, but…I suppose I believed there was an element of that in both of you."

"Did Josh know you felt that way?"

"Yes," she said softly, trying not to remember that last, terrible fight and the things she'd said. She had to live forever with that memory, but she didn't have to tell anyone else about the end of her marriage.

"It didn't occur to you there was any idealism in our career choices?" Alec asked. "To you, we were just a couple of cowboys out for a good time?"

"I said an element!" she shot back, shaken to realize he was angry. "I understood how dedicated Josh was. And you, too. I just—" She couldn't go on.

"What, Julia?" he asked inexorably.

She shook her head.

To her shock, he laid his hand over hers. "Tell me," he said, his voice gentler.

"I started to resent it." Not wanting to see his expression, she looked at his hand, so much larger than hers, broader across, at the thickness of his wrist and the dark hairs dusting his forearm. "At home, all he did was kill time. I could tell he was waiting for a mission, for his real life. The kids loved him, but he was more like a playmate than a father." Finally she lifted her gaze to meet his dark eyes. "Don't get me wrong. I was proud of him. Somebody has to do the job he did. He worked hard to do it well. He was courageous. I know that." Her voice broke and she had to take a moment to collect herself. "But I came to realize we weren't nearly as important to him as that job was. And call me petty, but the day came when I resented having to be a single parent while he was always off saving the world."

She saw understanding on Alec's face, but also something more indefinable. He removed his hand, and she saw his fingers curl into fists on the table-top.

"So that's why you were so shocked when I suggested we all move together." He sounded careful, as if he wanted to be sure he understood how she saw him.

"Yes!" She glared. "Do you blame me?"

Again those muscles gathered in his jaw, before he moved his shoulders and the tension visibly drained from him. "No, I guess I can't. I thought we knew each other better than that, but I realize Josh couldn't talk about what he did, and it never crossed my mind that you were very interested in what I did all day."

"Of course I'm interested."

One corner of his mouth turned up in a half smile that didn't touch his eyes. "Then I'll start talking. To tell you the truth, there are times I'd like nothing better than being able to lay ideas out or vent to someone who doesn't have a horse in the race."

"Unbiased."

He dipped his head without taking his gaze from her. "Yeah."

"Then I won't do." She felt her smile wobble. "Because I *am* biased. I'm on your side."

"God, Julia." His voice was hoarse, his emotions momentarily unguarded.

Her heartbeat did some wobbling, too.

The waitress appeared with their entrées, probably a fortunate interruption. Julia noticed that Noah Chandler and his fiancée were leaving, Noah pausing only to nod at Alec, who did the same. She wondered what they'd conveyed with that very restrained exchange.

"Men don't always understand what women need," Alec murmured, momentarily confusing her. Then she saw the amusement that lightened the depth of emotion they'd both been feeling.

"I have noticed," she responded.

He laughed, although she sensed he might be forcing it. "When you need something from me, tell me. Otherwise, I won't know."

Your heart. I need you to love me.

He would tell her he did. Like a sister.

"Anything," he added, sounding husky.

They looked at each other for an uninterrupted stretch that had warmth rising in her cheeks as she wondered crazily what he meant.

Anything.

"I never suspected," he said after a moment.

"Suspected what?" She didn't sound quite like herself, but if he noticed he gave no indication.

"I assumed you and Josh were completely happy."

"Don't you think any marriage has tensions?"

"Maybe. I don't know. I've never tried it."

"Why not?" she asked. "Have you ever come close?"

He shook his head. "I love my parents, but I wouldn't want what they have."

She nodded her understanding. Norman Raynor was a tense, rigid, demanding man who both dominated and dismissed his wife. Even Josh, not often given to self-reflection, had talked some about his father's expectations for his boys and his contempt for women. At the time, Julia had thought to be grateful that Alec and Josh didn't have a sister. She had blamed Norm for his sons' choice of careers, too; he had been a firefighter who thought men should be men. Mostly he and Rosaria had been great with the kids, but Julia hadn't been enthusiastic about her children spending a lot of time with their grandfather as they got older and more conscious of things like gender roles.

"I feel sorry for your mother."

"She made her bed." Apparently realizing how harsh that sounded, Alec shook his head. "I don't mean that. No matter how bad the marriage is, she'd never leave him. If nothing else, her faith wouldn't let her. But it's more than that. I'm not sure she even notices how he treats her anymore. I remember from when I was little how happy she was. Laughing and singing all the time." His mouth crooked up and his expression softened. "Good smells from the kitchen, fresh flowers from her garden on the table, an Italian tenor bellowing from the stereo." He grimaced. "Of course, the music went off when Dad walked in the door, and if Mama was lucky, he'd grunt his appreciation for amazing food. The change in her was gradual. She'd listen to music less and less often, smile less. By the time Josh and I were in high school, she'd lost any gift for happiness. I don't know if she'd recover it even if he dropped dead of a heart attack tomorrow."

Julia couldn't help herself. She touched him, only fleetingly, her fingertips to the back of his hand, but it was enough to draw a startled, somehow riveted stare from him.

"Were their feelings hurt that we moved away?" she asked, as much to distract him as anything. His parents hadn't said much to her, but she'd never been sure how they felt about her anyway.

As a distraction, her question worked. Alec gave a grunt of his own. "Couldn't tell with Mama. Dad thought me quitting my job was asinine. I'd be a captain before I knew it, maybe rise to chief of the LAPD. *He* knew how to bring Matt into line, and it didn't involve pampering the kid or uprooting the whole damn family. 'My belt's still good for something,' he said."

Julia shuddered. They were both silent for a moment.

"I always thought I might be more like him than Josh was," Alec said unexpectedly. "Josh was more…happy-go-lucky, for lack of a better term. I internalize everything."

Yes. She'd seen that.

"I was thinking something like that," she admitted. "The only thing is, Josh was only happy when he was in motion. Eventually I started wondering if he had an attention deficit disorder, but surely he'd have had to be patient, I don't know, crouched somewhere waiting for the bad guys to make a move. I know he was smart, but he almost never picked up a book. Even TV bored him. He could sit down for about the length of a meal, then he'd get twitchy and leap up and need to do something."

"Yeah, he had some trouble in school. Far as I know, he was never diagnosed, but—" He put down his fork and seemed to mull that over. "Actually, I don't know if that's true or not. Dad would probably have given hell to any teacher or school administrator who tried to lay the blame for Josh's issues on some problem in his brain when obviously *they* were lacking. He limped through graduation, but he enlisted the minute he graduated.

Never crossed any of our minds that he might go on to college."

Somehow the conversation drifted after that. First Alec and she exchanged their own experiences in higher education. She shook her head over her idiocy in dropping out before getting her degree, Alec telling her his father had belittled his own determination to get his.

"'Why waste your time?' he'd say. 'You should have gone straight to the police academy. Think of the street experience you'd have by now.' He'd shake his head. 'You've been to school for thirteen years already. Why would you want to write a paper about Robert E. Lee's military mistakes or the fact that some damn philosopher tried to prove himself wrong?'"

"Some damn philosopher?" she queried.

"Descartes. He was determined not to be smug in his beliefs."

"So he tried to prove he was wrong."

"Right." Alec shook his head. "Funny Dad should have chosen that paper to disparage, because I take Descartes's theories about self-doubt seriously. Whenever I go too far out on a limb, I think, hold on, remember Descartes, and take the other side. Sometimes I actually do convince myself I was wrong."

"I'm impressed," she said, smiling. "You actually demonstrate the value of those college classes on a day-to-day basis."

He smiled, too. "I told you, I internalize everything."

She had been so wrong about him, Julia thought as they finished dinner and returned to the Tahoe. Why hadn't she ever noticed how different he was from her husband?

Of course, she knew the answer in part. While she was married, she hadn't let herself dwell on any feelings in particular for Josh's brother. And later—it had taken her a long time to emerge from the grief and the guilt, and by then she was consumed by her children's needs. For all the time she and Alec had spent together, most of their conversations had to do with the kids, Matt in particular. It alarmed her a little to realize that this evening, she and Alec had been, for possibly the first time, only a man and woman. She couldn't help wondering if he'd made any discoveries about her.

She was more self-conscious than usual when they got back to the duplex. The kids weren't due back for another half an hour. *I could invite him in,* she thought, but had the unsettling thought that doing so might be dangerous. She didn't dare betray her feelings to him, not if she was going to continue to depend on him the way she had been. She'd be foolish to misinterpret the expression in his eyes when he'd said, *When you need something from me, tell me.*

So she thanked him for dinner, made her excuses and shut the door firmly on the man standing on her doorstep. The one whose voice had become husky when he implied he would give her anything at all.

Inside, heart thumping, she knew her greatest fear having to do with him was that he'd give what she asked, but for all the wrong reasons. Even the idea of that was unbearable.

CHAPTER FOUR

"You didn't follow instructions," said the hollow voice. It wasn't any more distinct than it had been during the previous phone call, but Alec was damn sure the speaker was the same man.

His phone had rung while he was waiting for a table at a deli near the police station and having the passing thought that he could have called Julia to see if she wanted to meet him. Of course, she'd probably have had to bring Liana, at least, which would have killed his fantasy of being alone with her, something he'd begun to crave.

Seeing the unfamiliar number, he had stepped back outside. Traffic noise wasn't a lot better than the buzz of a roomful of people talking, but at least he wouldn't be overheard. With his back to the brick wall, he gazed unseeing at passing vehicles. He'd trace the phone number, but he was betting on a throwaway.

The fact that he'd been thinking about Julia when this son of a bitch called to issue another threat roused all his protective instincts.

"Something you should know about me," he said. "I don't respond to threats or blackmail."

"One last chance," the muffled voice told him, and the call was over.

He brooded as he stowed his phone. The first call had come less than two days after Julia's arrival in Angel Butte. He couldn't see how her showing up could have triggered anything. Probably one had nothing to do with the other…but he'd been police chief here in Angel Butte since the first of April. Only now that he had family was anyone threatening him. Yeah, that made him nervous.

Today was July 12, which meant two weeks had elapsed since the first threat. That was remarkably patient of the caller, he reflected.

After a moment's thought, Alec dialed the mayor's mobile number. It only rang once.

"Raynor?"

"I just got a second anonymous call," he said.

"Threatening?"

He thought about it. "By implication. I'm told I have 'one last chance.'"

"Why aren't they calling me, too?" Chandler asked.

"Good question. I'm the new boy in town. Your support for McAllister has to have more impact than mine."

There was a pause. "Maybe, but could be they figure they undercut my support enough by getting the word out that I refused to hire him as chief of the department here in Angel Butte."

"That's possible," Alec conceded. A smile twitched at his mouth. "It's also possible your reputation precedes you."

"As a hard-ass?" Noah Chandler sounded amused.

"Something like that."

He chuckled. "You plan any action?"

"I don't think I'll bother with the campaign manager this time. I'm going straight to Sheriff Brock himself."

"Good," the mayor said. "You'll let Colin know?"

Alec agreed he would.

"Anything on Bystrom?"

The subject of the previous Angel Butte police chief was a sore one for Mayor Chandler. Alec was more accustomed to the slow pace of justice. One of the reasons arresting officers were so careful to document their every action and thought was that, by the time that arrest actually came to trial, assuming it ever did, they'd long since forgotten the details. He understood the mayor's frustration, though.

During what turned out to be an unrelated investigation last year, Colin McAllister had stumbled on evidence suggesting the former police chief was corrupt. With Chandler's backing, McAllister had gotten a warrant for Gary Bystrom's financial records, which showed a sizable second income from mysterious sources. Tracing the source of those deposits was something the federal Drug

Enforcement Agency could do better than a local police department. Angel Butte P.D. was part of a regional coalition of law-enforcement agencies, including the DEA, focusing on drug trafficking. They were all working right now on tying failed raids or other favors to the dates of some of those payments to the former police chief.

In the wake of Bystrom's resignation and the ensuing investigation, McAllister and now Alec had been forced to look hard at their own officers. Gary Bystrom hadn't been known as a hands-on police chief. Somebody would have had to tip him off to upcoming raids or other actions for him to have useful information to pass on. To date, five officers had been identified as having accepted bribes, some directly from Bystrom, some from the same sources who had paid off the police chief. All five had been fired. Alec was far from satisfied that the house was totally clean, but was starting to feel as if this had become more of a witch hunt than a dispassionate investigation. It had been weeks since he'd found anything that would justify further warrants. If the department harbored any more crooked cops, he could only hope they'd see the writing on the wall and look for jobs elsewhere.

"I left another message with the agent in charge" was all he could offer now.

Chandler grunted, wordlessly expressing dissatisfaction.

"You know it's going to be out of our hands anyway," Alec reminded him. "They'll want to file charges in federal court."

"As long as his ass goes to jail," Chandler said flatly.

Alec agreed. He hadn't met the man who'd preceded him in office, but that didn't mean he couldn't despise him. Alec had spent the past three and a half months untangling and fixing everything the son of a bitch had let go out of sheer laziness, never mind the elastic morals and the greed.

He and Chandler left it at that.

WHEN THE PHONE RANG, Julia pounced on it. "Alec?"

"Yeah." He sounded tired. "Sorry to have run so late. Have I missed dinner?"

Most nights he ate with them. She'd told him all he had to do was let her know, that he was always welcome but shouldn't feel pressured to give up every evening for them, either. As far as she knew, the couple of dinners he'd missed were because of work obligations.

"No, you're not the only one running late." She hesitated, not wanting to dump anything else on him right now, but he'd notice when he got here if Matt was still missing. "My darling son has also failed to appear, even though I told him what time I'd planned dinner for."

Alec's voice sharpened. "Do you know where he is? I can pick him up."

"Not a clue. After lunch when I asked where he was going, he said 'around.'"

She'd seen Matt's attitude deteriorating these past few days but hadn't yet said anything to Alec. She wanted desperately to believe she was imagining things, but now…she couldn't delude herself anymore.

"Do you want me to try to talk to him?" Alec offered.

She hesitated. They were already depending so heavily on him. "I don't want you to damage your relationship with him."

"Julia, I'm on your side, not his." He sounded implacable. "I may not be his father, but I'm the next best thing. The way I see it, you and I have to stand together."

She didn't cry easily or often, but hearing such a strong message of support had her eyes burning. "Thank you" was all she could manage to say, and that was with a thick voice. "I'm not used to having…" She stopped. Had he understood what she'd meant, telling him that Josh was more buddy than parent to the kids? The truth was, he *hadn't* been on her side. He'd gone so far as to undermine her authority, giving permission for Matt to do something to which she'd already said no, or chiding her right in front of their children for being too strict.

"I'll be there in five," Alec said brusquely and was gone.

She'd barely hung up when she heard the front

door open and close. Julia stepped from the kitchen. "You're late."

Matt's entire posture radiated rebellion. She didn't know whether she hated the slouch or the sneer the most.

"So?" He shrugged. "It's summer."

"You know I expect us to sit down to dinner as a family most nights."

"A family. That's a joke."

His tone was so vicious, it sent a shudder through her. "Losing your dad doesn't mean we aren't a family anymore."

"*Losing* him?" He looked at her in disbelief. "He's *dead.* He's not lost. Without Dad—" Matt choked. "We're just not, okay?" He whirled and raced for his bedroom.

"Dinner will be on the table in ten minutes," she called after him.

"I'll eat in my bedroom."

Julia didn't have much of a temper, but what she had suddenly sparked. She moved fast, planting her hand on his door before he could slam it. "If you plan to eat tonight," she told him with steel in her voice, "you will be at the table in ten minutes. Hands clean, prepared to behave politely. Is that clear?"

"I don't know why I came home at all!" he yelled and threw his shoulder at the door so that it closed right in her face.

Shaken, she retreated to the kitchen, where she

turned the burner on beneath the green beans she'd snapped earlier.

She heard the snick of a door and soft footsteps, so she wasn't taken by surprise when Liana said from right behind her, "Why is Matt so mad, Mommy?"

Julia turned and held out her arms. Liana catapulted into them. Hugging her hard, Julia bent to kiss the top of her head as she rocked her. "I don't know, sweetie. I wish I did." She paused, battling her conscience. Asking either of her kids to rat out the other seemed…wrong. She was getting desperate, though. "Does he talk to you?"

"Uh-uh." Her daughter shook her head hard. "He says I act like a baby and I wouldn't believe him anyway."

Believe what?

The doorbell rang. Liana straightened. "Is that Uncle Alec? Can I let him in?"

Julia laughed, hoping it sounded natural. "Of course you can."

Liana started chattering the minute she got the front door open. Julia heard the slow rumble of his responses. A minute later the two stepped into the kitchen, Alec's dark eyes going right to Julia.

A hand on his niece's thin shoulder momentarily silenced her. "Smells good," he said easily, but she could tell he knew something was wrong.

"Chicken cacciatore, and if you dare compare it to your mother's, I'll abandon you to open a can of soup for dinner tomorrow night."

He laughed, probably guessing the recipe was *from* his mother. "Have I ever complained about your cooking?"

"Says the man whose freezer is probably stocked with microwave meals." She turned to lower the heat beneath the furiously boiling green beans, mostly so he couldn't see her face while she went for casual. "Would you call Matt?"

She heard his footsteps going and his voice. A moment later he was back.

"He says he isn't hungry."

Did Mattie think he could sneak out here as soon as they were done and heat up leftovers? If so, he was in for a surprise. In fact, she might go so far as to balance a pan lid atop the refrigerator door in case he tried after she'd gone to bed. The clang should scare him and wake her up. Maybe her resolve to starve her son made her a horrible mother, but right this minute she didn't care.

Alec was pouring milk for himself and Liana, asking what Julia wanted, responding to some story Liana was telling about her day, and a minute later the three of them were ready to sit down at the small table. Julia ignored the unneeded place setting, although she saw both her daughter and Alec glance at it. His gaze moved from it to her face, where it stayed.

"There a problem?" he asked quietly.

"Matt yelled at Mom," Liana confided. She bent her head, her fine, silky hair falling forward to veil her face. "Sometimes he scares me," she said softly, sneaking a look toward the hallway.

Alec's eyes met Julia's, just a quick look, before he laid a hand on Liana's nape and squeezed. "Hey," he said. "He's a teenager. They can be butts. It's hormones run amok, you know. It'll happen to you, too, kiddo."

Liana looked up, her expression patently relieved. "Uh-uh. *I'd* never yell at Mom."

He grinned at her. "Famous last words."

Her forehead creased. "What's that mean?"

As he explained, Julia admired his endless patience with the kids. How was it he hadn't married and had children of his own? He never seemed bored with hers, never gave them anything less than his complete attention. Liana visibly bloomed with him.

We are so lucky, Julia thought, for at least the hundredth time. Then, *But he might* get *bored. Or— what if he already is, and is just hiding it?*

He told a few tall tales about his own and Josh's teenage years that had her and her daughter both laughing. Oh, she hoped that for once Matt had taken the damn earbuds out and was eavesdropping on his family. Let his stomach be rumbling, too, she thought vengefully.

Liana declared herself stuffed and decided to save her blueberry cobbler for later. Apparently she'd promised Sophie she'd come over right after dinner, so could she please be excused?

Within moments, she'd whisked out the front door, Alec following. Julia was clearing the table when he came back.

"She got there safe and sound," he reported.

Julia smiled at him. "You didn't think she would?"

His dark lashes veiled his eyes, making her wonder for a fleeting instant what he hadn't wanted her to see. No, she had to be imagining things. He was always cautious with the kids.

Without answering, Alec took plates from her, their hands brushing. She'd let him get closer than she usually did. Afraid color was rising in her cheeks, she reached for a serving bowl.

In the kitchen, she covered the bowl with plastic wrap. Alec set dishes in the sink.

"*I'd* like blueberry cobbler." He looked hopeful and even boyish, unusual for a man with a face so very male and enigmatic more often than not. "Especially if you have vanilla ice cream to go with it."

She smiled at him. "You know I do. Ugh. I can't keep cooking like this or we'll all get fat."

His eyebrows crooked as he nudged the faucet on with his forearm and began rinsing plates. "You doing it for my benefit?"

"Maybe," she admitted, sneaking a look at him. "Partly." Mostly. The kids wouldn't care if she put macaroni and cheese in front of them three nights a week and rotated hamburgers, pizza and maybe spaghetti the other four. She enjoyed having another adult to cook for. "Think of it as payback."

She didn't realize she'd been seeing pleasure on his face until something like anger took its place. "Damn it, Julia, let's not go there. The three of you are family. There's no obligation here."

"How can I help but feel some?" she protested. "Especially after everything you gave up?"

Creases carved deep in his forehead. "Didn't you hear a thing I said the last time we talked about this? Exactly what is it I gave up? Do you think my job was glamorous? Fun?" He sounded exasperated.

"You chose it." For the first time, she felt uncertain. "You seemed to love it."

He let out a breath and moved his shoulders as if loosening tense muscles. "I chose law enforcement. I'm still in law enforcement."

"Oh, right," Julia scoffed. "This is a town that had, what, two or three murders last year? Compared to something like one a *day* in L.A.?"

He shook his head. "Less than one a day. And do you know how much we'd lowered that rate these past ten, fifteen years? That's my goal—preventing crime, not cleaning up after it. And yeah, working Homicide was interesting, but so is understanding what a smaller city needs from its police department and making sure we deliver. I don't know what this fixation you have is, but I'm liking this job, Julia."

"But…" Momentarily flummoxed by what sounded like sincerity, she stopped. "I'll bet you sit in front of a computer all day, don't you?"

"I do some of that, but I sit through a lot of meetings, too." His frown had relaxed. "Yesterday I worked out with the SWAT team. Today I spent a couple of hours in the crime lab listening to a compelling pitch for new equipment. Day before I rode along for a few hours with a patrol officer fresh out of training." Vibrancy rang in his voice. "Last week I had breakfast with half a dozen other police chiefs in the region, sharing issues, concerns, solutions. Got some damn good ideas. I've met personally with every single member of the city council in the past couple of weeks, and I think I've got the votes to approve hiring an additional fifteen officers spread across the department, plus a civilian-crime analyst, which apparently was a new concept to them."

"You're a busy man."

"Yes, I am, and I feel damn lucky to be able to shake free long enough to sit down to dinner with you most nights."

She threw up her hands. "We love having you here, but don't feel…"

Alec's eyes narrowed. "Don't you dare say the word *obligated* to me one more time."

Her relief was so profound, Julia had a peculiar, weightless feeling. "Okay. I'll consider it verboten." Even her voice sounded light. Darn it, she'd planned to skip dessert, but decided she'd splurge tonight. She took the ice cream out of the freezer.

"Good." For a moment, the skin beside his eyes

crinkled with a smile that didn't have to touch his mouth to make her knees weak.

She had to give herself a stern talk while she dished up the cobbler. He'd notice if she kept reacting like this. Surely she'd become…inured, with him around so much.

When she looked back at him, it was to find his expression had become more somber. "What's the deal with you know who?"

Sanity returned with a rush. Thinking about her son was a surefire cure for this idiotic giddiness. Keeping her voice low, she told Alec about Matt's latest outburst and her insistence that if he wanted to eat at all, he'd do it at the table with the rest of his family.

"That sounds fair enough to me," Alec agreed.

With the ice-cream scoop in her hand, she went still, not looking at him. "He scares me sometimes, too."

"Are you scared for him or of him?" he asked after a moment.

"Both." Impatient with herself, she scooped out the ice cream, then returned the carton to the freezer. "Oh, not really for myself. It's not that I think he's going to go out and get a gun or anything. It's just…" Which of her darkest fears did she need to share?

Alec took one of the bowls from her hand and nudged her toward a chair.

She sat, still brooding. "What do I do if he completely defies me? I mean, so far he more or less complies if I tell him to go to his room or whatever. But I can see in his eyes sometimes that he's thinking about refusing. It's not that he's huge, but neither am I. And anyway, do I really want to try to physically restrain him?"

"No." Alec held up a hand before she could finish. "Hell, no! You call me, is what you do."

Julia gave herself a little shake. "Oh, I hope the situation won't arise."

"Promise." He sounded completely serious, even grim.

After a moment, she nodded. He held her gaze as if he wasn't sure he believed her, but finally he, too, dipped his head, then started eating.

The cobbler was fabulous, if she did say so herself. She'd spotted a sign for Blueberry Acres and was handed a flat and allowed to pick to her heart's content. She'd frozen plenty of berries for half a dozen or more cobblers and pies. She happened to know that Alec had a special weakness for blueberries.

He didn't say anything else until he'd cleaned his bowl and sat back with a replete sigh and a "Damn, that was good. Thank you." A moment later, he said, "He'll come around, Julia."

She tried to smile. "I hope so."

"Listen. That damn wedding is coming right up. The invitation says no gifts. Do you think they mean it?"

She had a feeling he'd changed the subject deliberately, but went along with it. A little of Matt went a long ways these days.

"I'd assume so. Do you have any idea whether either of them are involved with a charity? It might be nice to make a donation in their names."

"Hey." Alec looked relieved. "That would be good. Yeah." Some nameless emotion crossed his face. "We have a battered-women's shelter in town. I think that might be appropriate."

Julia opened her mouth to ask why, but could tell from his face that he wouldn't answer. She imagined the laughing, assured woman she'd met and couldn't envision her as a victim, but... You never really knew, did you? And Cait McAllister's interest—or was it Noah Chandler's interest?—might have to do with a mother or other female relative instead. Although, if that was the case, how did Alec know about it?

"Why don't we both do that, then?" she said. "If you like, I'll pick up two cards, one to go with the donation and one for the bride and groom."

"Thank you." He stretched and groaned. "I suppose I should go beard the lion in the den."

"You don't have to."

"Yeah, I do." They carried their bowls to the sink. As she rinsed them and put them in the dishwasher, he leaned a hip against the counter. "The wedding is Saturday, but what would you think about all of us doing something Sunday? Matt is starting that orienteering thing next week, isn't he?"

She made a face. "In theory. If he doesn't balk at the last minute. The first session of swim lessons for Liana and Sophie starts, too."

"Lucky we could put off having you start working," Alec remarked.

Julia felt a funny squeeze of emotion at the way he so casually linked them. *We* could be a powerful word, she'd discovered.

"I've heard Elk Lake up by Mount Bachelor is especially beautiful," he went on. "Probably jampacked with tourists, too, but what the hell. We could take lunch, swimsuits, have some fun. What d'you say?"

She smiled. "Liana and I say yes."

Muscles flexed in his jaw, shadowed with an evening growth of beard. "Oh, Matt'll be coming, too, like it or not." He made an impatient sound. "Wish me luck," he said, but didn't wait for it.

ATTENDING A WEDDING with Julia at his side sure as hell beat going on his own.

She'd been in town almost three weeks now, but except for the dinner out at Chandler's, this was their first public appearance as a couple. Alec was very conscious that people were checking them out.

He had also, until they were safely inside the church, been conscious of being exposed in a way he didn't like—and of conceivably placing Julia in danger simply by having her with him.

Given that the latest threat had been made only two days ago, Alec had worried about the fact that it had to be commonly known he'd be attending Noah Chandler's wedding. He couldn't imagine anything like a bomb, given that plenty of the area's movers and shakers were bound to be present, too, including some who were Brock supporters. Still, he'd hustled Julia from the parking lot into the church fast enough to earn him a startled glance or two from her, and hadn't been able to completely relax until they were seated.

The church was full, but the wedding party itself was small, just a matron of honor and a best man, bride and groom. It was almost a family group, entire unto itself—the bride's brother gave her away, and his wife served as her matron of honor. The only nonfamily member was the best man, a guy named Eric Henson, whom Alec had been told was a civil engineer.

Alec watched with some amusement as Noah Chandler waited at the altar, his gaze fixed on the church doors with a desperate intensity that Alec suspected hid his terror that Cait would fail to appear. At one point his best man murmured something that either went unheard or disregarded; the friend smiled and clapped a hand on Noah's shoulder.

Noah in a tuxedo looked about like he did in a

business suit—subtly wrong. Maybe the build was too bulky, maybe the face too homely.

He was saved when the organ music changed from lulling to traditional, the doors swung open and Nell McAllister started down the aisle, face solemn. She took her place and the bride appeared on her brother's arm.

"Ooh." Julia sighed. He glanced over to see her rapt face, her lips parted with pleasure.

Damn, she was beautiful.

So was the bride, he'd concede, even if she didn't stir anything special in him. Noah, though, looked as if he'd died and caught his first glimpse of heaven. Alec doubted he breathed during her procession.

Cait had chosen a simple dress with crisscrossed seams that made the thin ivory silk slide over her body in a way that fully justified her groom giving up oxygen. She wore a diamond at her throat. No veil, only bits of sparkle and a few pearls somehow scattered in her feathery hair.

Alec faced the front when everyone else did. He used the moment to steal another look at Julia, who as it happened was looking at him right then. He couldn't quite decide what he saw on her face, but the tide of pink in her cheeks suggested she hadn't expected to be caught peeking at him.

He had served as best man at her wedding. He had a bad feeling that, even then, he'd watched her walk down the aisle with the same hungry gaze that had been on Josh's face and that he now saw on Noah's. The difference was, he'd done his best to hide it, as well as to talk himself out of believing the constriction of his chest meant anything. All he was thinking, he'd told himself, was that Josh had gotten lucky. Man, Julia Lydersen—about to become Julia Raynor—was pure class. Someday, Alec wanted a woman to look at him the way she looked at his brother. That was all. He was feeling a pang of envy, one step removed. Not that he wanted *this* woman.

In the years that followed, he'd once in a while thought, *If I were meeting her somewhere and she was unattached...* A few times he'd wondered if Josh knew how lucky he was. Josh had always seemed more casual about his wife than Alec thought he should have been. She and his brother had been ten years into their marriage before Alec had admitted to himself that his sister-in-law was solidly in the way of any of his relationships getting serious. Not that he wanted *her,* he'd told himself—but none of those women measured up. And by then he'd started thinking, *That idiot doesn't deserve her* or *his kids.*

The only blessing had been that they lived in San Diego, while he was in L.A. He'd get down weekends sometimes, mostly when Josh was in town but, as time went on, increasingly often when Josh was overseas. Even then, he'd been filling in for his brother.

Just not quite ever letting himself think how much he wanted to fill in permanently.

Good thing, too. He'd have had a hard time living with the guilt if he had, in full awareness, coveted his brother's wife. As it was, he could live with the friendship that had grown between them, the tight relationship he had with Josh's kids. What they'd had already made sliding into something closer yet after Josh's death more possible.

Now, so aware of her in the pew beside him that he felt her every soft breath, Alec also felt crushing pain as he watched the simple ceremony.

He would give damn near anything to be making those promises to the woman beside him and to gaze into her eyes as she made them to him.

Ask her. She might do it.

Only thing was, he needed more than the promises. More than her in his bed.

He needed to know he wasn't a fill-in. Second best. Second husband was okay, but he needed to know she loved him.

And that seemed as likely as them going home after the reception to find a sunny-natured thirteen-year-old boy eagerly waiting in hopes Mom would play a computer game with him, and, oh, by the way, he'd met this really great guy today who had invited him to go fishing with him and his dad, and could Uncle Alec go, too?

The crushing pain became something a whole

lot bleaker. *Repeat to self: At least they need you. At least she talks to you.*

"Do you, Noah Chandler, take this woman…"

The minister's voice washed over him.

Julia had blushed. He wondered what that meant. Glancing down without turning his head, Alec saw how close his loosely curled hand lay to her thigh and to her slender hand spread on it. He could move his, just a fraction of an inch at a time, and his knuckles would graze the silky, peach-colored fabric of her skirt. Or he could stretch a little, casually, and lay his arm on the back of the pew behind her, maybe smiling apologetically.

"I now pronounce you man and wife." The white-haired minister smiled benevolently at the two people gazing into each other's eyes. "You may kiss your bride."

With a huge grin, Mayor Noah Chandler swept his bride into his arms and kissed her passionately and at length.

Alec turned his head and met Julia's green-gold eyes—and she blushed again. He took a chance and reached for her hand. She returned his clasp.

CHAPTER FIVE

"I've never been to a wedding," Liana complained from the back of Alec's Tahoe the next day. "I wish I could've gone."

Julia smiled over her shoulder. "But you've never even met the two people who were getting married. I didn't see any other kids there, did you, Alec?"

He glanced in the rearview mirror. "Maybe a couple of older ones. Don't worry. Sooner or later, you'll get stuck going to some weddings. Most of them are pretty boring."

Julia poked him with her elbow. "They're not!"

His grin lit his lean, dark face. "You ever been to the kind with eight bridesmaids all in hideous purple dresses? And vows the bride and groom wrote themselves?"

She chuckled. "Well, no."

"I *like* purple," Liana declared.

"We know, sweet pea," her uncle said, a smile still playing at the corners of his mouth. "I'm betting your swimsuit is purple."

"It is! It's new, too. Mommy and I went shopping Friday. 'Cuz I'm starting lessons tomorrow, you know, and my old one stunk. Plus it was getting kind of small."

"It wouldn't have stunk if you ever remembered to rinse it out when you shower," Julia suggested. "But it doesn't matter, because it was definitely getting too small. You're growing, kiddo."

"I wish I'd grow faster," she said, sounding momentarily discontented. "I'm always the shortest kid in the class."

Matt, beside her, hadn't said a word during the drive. Predictably, he wore his earbuds, which emitted the deep thud of the bass notes. Julia had no doubt he was listening, though. If she could wish for a growth spurt for either of her children, it would be for him, not Liana. Being short was way harder on a boy than a girl. By eighth grade, a few of the boys would already have started shaving, she thought. They'd mostly be skinny and gangly, but reaching for their adult height. Except for the sullen expression and the clothes, Matt could have been going into sixth grade like his sister.

Was that his problem? she wondered. Or even part of his problem? Or, heaven help her, would puberty make dealing with him even tougher?

When they reached the lake, the water was brilliantly blue. Mount Bachelor reared impressively over the forested landscape. It still held a cap of snow even in July; apparently the snowpack had been deeper this past winter than in recent, dryer years. Alec had learned about a resort where they could rent kayaks or stand-up paddleboards if they wanted. There turned out to be a lovely, sandy beach and a small store where they could supplement the food and drinks they'd brought in a cooler. By the time they carried their paraphernalia to the beach, even Matt looked interested.

They found a good spot off to the side to spread their blanket and shed clothes.

"Swim before lunch?" Julia asked.

"Yeah!" her daughter exclaimed, already toeing off her flip-flops.

Matt glanced around with elaborate casualness before pulling his T-shirt over his head and baring his scrawny chest. Julia ached with sympathy.

"Suntan lotion," she said brightly, handing each kid a tube.

Matt, of course, rolled his eyes, but possibly recalled the time last summer when they'd gone to Malibu Beach and he had refused to put any lotion on. Alec had kidded later that they could have roasted their marshmallows over him. Matt had thought that was funny because *Alec* said it. It would have been different if she had, of course. He'd suffered, though.

She peeled off her T-shirt, but hesitated before removing her shorts. It wasn't as if Alec hadn't seen her in a swimsuit before; they'd gone to the beach half a dozen times in the past year. But it had been a while, with Alec living here in Angel Butte since

March and she and the kids still in L.A. And—she'd become increasingly conscious of *his* body lately.

He, of course, stripped without the slightest hesitation. The body revealed was not scrawny. In fact, he was more muscular than he looked dressed, when the effect he gave was long and lean. He was laughing at something Liana had said, leaving Julia to watch him unobserved. Dark hair dusted his chest and formed a line down his washboard stomach to the low-hanging waist of his board shorts. Muscles in his back flexed as he tossed his shirt aside, then made a mock lunge at Matt, who was surprised into a rare laugh. Julia felt a squeeze of astonishing, bittersweet joy at the sound.

Alec looked back at her, an eyebrow raised. "You're dawdling."

She rarely bothered wishing for a body she no longer had, after carrying and raising two children. Resigned, she unzipped her shorts and stepped out of them. Alec gave her one almost covert head-to-toe appraisal. A muscle jumped on his jaw and his eyes darkened, holding hers for a moment.

Then they all walked to the water, Alec's arm lying across Matt's shoulders. "Last one in's a coward," he declared.

Julia dipped a toe and squeaked at the icy temperature. "I'm a coward. Feel free to go ahead and leave me behind."

He laughed and advanced on her. She retreated, Liana giggling and even Matt looking…normal. A plunge into freezing waters was worth seeing that expression on his face.

Even so, she bolted and ran, making it about three strides before Alec caught her. He swept her up and waded into the lake.

"Don't do this," she begged. "Don't…"

The hard arms released her. The flash of his white teeth was the last thing she saw as she sailed through the air.

"Aaah!" she screamed and hit the water. Her whole body curled in a spasm of horror. This was a high mountain lake, formed by snow runoff.

She exploded back out of the water, but found herself nearly waist deep. Furiously splashing Alec, who was still laughing, she yelled, "I'll pay you back for that! I swear I will!"

Her son was laughing like a loon, her daughter trying to contain more laughter with a hand clapped over her mouth. Both barely had their feet wet.

Alec turned and grinned at them. "Laugh, will you?" He made the face of a horror-movie villain and waded toward them. "I've only begun."

Matt dived in, emerging with the same expression Julia had no doubt had on her face. "It's freakin' *cold*."

Julia smiled evilly. "You get numb."

More gently, Alec chivied Liana in. At least the day was hot. The contrast felt blissful after a few minutes. Mostly egged on by Alec, they dived and played tag and floated until Julia noticed Liana was shivering. Matt, too, she realized. Neither of *them* had any body fat.

They sprawled on their blanket, sharing chips and dip and each taking the sandwich prepared to suit his or her individual tastes. Julia renewed her suntan lotion and urged it on everyone else, too. Matt, seeing that his uncle accepted a tube without hesitation, followed suit.

Alec sprawled on his back, taking up more than his fair space. "How about a nap?" he suggested.

"No!" Matt protested. "You said we could rent a kayak or something."

Alec groaned and laid a forearm over his eyes.

"Tickle him," Liana said, looking inspired.

"Yeah!" Brother's and sister's eyes met in a rare moment of accord. The next minute Alec was fighting his way out of a two-pronged attack. He reared to his knees, Matt in a headlock and Liana dangling from beneath one arm. Laughing, Julia whisked food leftovers and drinks out of danger.

"*We* could rent a kayak," Liana suggested daringly. "You could nap."

"I want Uncle Alec to go," Matt insisted. "I'd have to do all the paddling if I went with you."

"Uh-*uh!*"

The battle was joined. Alec throttled the combatants into breathless, giggling defeat.

"All right, you've woken me up. Julia?" He looked at her. "Kayak or paddleboard?"

"I wouldn't mind trying a paddleboard," she

decided. She'd been watching people a distance away standing on what looked like surfboards, but paddling. "It looks like fun."

"You'll get dumped," Alec warned.

"Yes, but I've kayaked before. I want to try something new."

Her son frowned. "When have you kayaked?"

"At home in Minnesota. It's the land of ten thousand lakes, you know."

His forehead crinkled. "How come we never did it when we were visiting Granddad and Grandma?"

"We've mostly gone for Christmas, remember? The lakes were frozen."

"Oh. Yeah." She could see him trying to decide whether his mother had knowingly deprived him of a coveted experience. Apparently unable to decide, he turned back to Alec. "Well, *I* want to try it."

"Fair enough." Alec ruffled the boy's spiky, half-dry hair. "I think we can leave our stuff, don't you?"

They split up after renting two single kayaks and two paddleboards, the guys disappearing for forty-five minutes or more along the lakeshore, Julia and Liana struggling to master their less-than-efficient new mode of transport. Both wore bright orange flotation devices, as did Matt, who'd been insulted but reluctantly acquiesced to the rental requirement for youths under eighteen.

Eventually man and boy returned and exchanged

kayaks for paddleboards. Liana and Julia didn't go far, though, as Liana's skinny arms had to be tiring.

Turning her head so that she could see the other three, Julia had a moment of happiness so sharp, it almost brought tears to her eyes. Alec, tall and strong and kind, was laughing at Matt, who had just taken a tumble and was climbing back aboard, his hair seal-dark, water streaming off him, his face transformed with a grin. Liana giggled as she awkwardly tried to do a U-turn.

Competing memories, all bad, surged through her head. The fight with Josh. The doorbell ringing and her, unaware of how quickly life could shatter, answering it to find three uniformed, sober-faced men on her doorstep. Telling the kids, seeing Liana withdraw and Matt react with rage. Then, only days later, the first time he turned savagely on her.

Why can't it be like this all the time?

It was Alec she couldn't look away from as she held her paddle suspended over the water. *My children are happy because of* him. That was only part of why she loved him, but, oh, God, it was an important part. And she had never loved him more than she did right this minute.

She felt as if she'd frozen the moment, and now action resumed. The clutch of acute emotion eased; sound was restored. She wished the day didn't have to end.

The sun was dropping in the sky, though, and

they were all tired. They turned in their kayaks and paddleboards and PFDs, had ice-cream cones all around and finally packed up to go home. Julia could tell from the heat in her shoulders and face that she'd had too much sun, but she couldn't regret it.

Both kids became quiet soon after they started the drive. For once, Matt didn't turn on his iPod, instead craning his neck to look at the lake.

"Maybe we should think about buying kayaks," Alec said, glancing in the rearview mirror. "There are plenty of lakes right around Angel Butte. I could get a rack for the Tahoe to carry them."

Matt's face was stunningly open and hopeful. "Could we?"

"Don't know why not." Alec looked rueful. "What with the lawn mower, I already can't park in the garage. We'd have room to store them."

"Cool," her son said.

Julia smiled at Alec. Not until she heard the muffled sound of music from the backseat did she say, "You're a nice man, Alec Raynor."

His eyes had a glint. "Some men would consider that an insult, you know. Cops aren't supposed to be nice."

"Pooh. Nice is one of the greatest compliments there is."

He reached across the space between the seats and squeezed her thigh. "Then I'll take it," he murmured, his voice a little huskier than usual.

Her heart gave a thump, and that happiness sharpened again. "Thank you," she murmured.

"What for?" he asked, sounding genuinely puzzled.

She nodded toward the backseat.

In the next instant, the relaxed warmth of his face was gone, lost in one of his enigmatic expressions. She absolutely could not tell what he was thinking when he nodded and took his hand away.

ALEC KEPT WAITING for the other shoe to drop.

One last chance.

How was he going to be made sorry? No—the voice had said *very sorry.*

He couldn't guard Julia and the kids around the clock, much as he'd have liked to. He still didn't even know whether the threat involved them in any way. He himself had gotten hyperaware whenever he was walking in the open or driving, from the minute he backed out to the street in the morning.

His conversation with Sheriff Eugene Brock hadn't reassured him. Alec had dropped by the sheriff's department to see Brock in person, waiting politely while the guy's PA spoke in hushed tones on her phone, after which the door to the inner sanctum opened and the sheriff himself came out.

"Raynor! Good to see you." He was all bonhomie. He offered coffee, which Alec declined.

Alec had been here before and now made a lightning assessment of an office furnished with an enormous desk that had to have been designed to intimidate. The huge leather chair behind it appeared adequate to cradle the sheriff's bulk.

Eugene Brock was fifty-eight years old. The campaign photos mostly showed a younger and fitter sheriff. In some he was garbed in SWAT-team black or wore a Kevlar vest and cradled a weapon. In one he stood in front of a snapping American flag, wearing full-dress uniform and looking square-jawed and solemn. In person, he had to heave his big belly into place as he settled behind his desk. He'd acquired an extra chin or two, and his eyes now appeared beady in a fat face. He was not an attractive man, and he was one hell of a poor example to his officers.

He was campaigning on a platform of long experience and wisdom. He boasted endorsements from some local groups who'd likely benefited from "you scratch my back, I'll scratch yours" policies. The police union had come out in favor of Colin McAllister, which must have rankled with Brock.

That day, Alec had settled into a chair opposite Brock, sat back with casual ease and said, "Gotta tell you, Brock, I don't appreciate threats."

The shock on the sheriff's face looked genuine. *Shit. It's not him,* Alec thought in dismay.

"What the hell are you talking about?" Brock blustered.

"Your campaign manager didn't tell you?"

"He said you claimed you'd gotten some kind of

phone call you were trying to blame on us. Sounded like a prank call a teenager might've made."

"This wasn't a teenager. And his demands were real specific. I was to publicly withdraw my support for Colin McAllister or I'd be sorry."

The chair creaked as the sheriff sat back. To his credit, he looked perturbed. "Wasn't us," he said flatly. "Even assuming I believed in dirty campaign tactics, why would I bother? That brouhaha with McAllister dropped him like a rock in the polls."

Alec didn't bother mentioning that Captain McAllister had begun to rebound almost immediately.

"I had a second call," he said. "I'm told I have one more chance."

Brock chewed that one over for a minute. Literally. Alec began to wonder if he had some chewing tobacco tucked in his cheek. "I'll talk to my manager," he said finally. "Have him ask around, be sure we don't have some loose cannon working on the campaign. But let me say again, it wasn't me."

Alec nodded, stood and looked down at Sheriff Brock. "Just so you know," he said, "something happens to me or a member of my family, the investigation will be looking at you anyway."

Brock slapped meaty hands on his desk, outrage transforming his face. "You threatening me? If you go to the press, I'll slap a lawsuit on you so fast—"

"No press," Alec said flatly. "Just be sure you pass on that message, too. I want whoever is making

those calls to get it. I don't submit to threats, and if
he tries to carry them out, *I will come after him.*"

He'd walked out on a blustering man, confident
his point was made, but afraid he hadn't made it to
the right person.

If not Eugene Brock, who?

Since then, his worries had stayed at a low simmer. He wished the damn election wasn't still more
than three months away. In the meantime, he was
relieved that Matt had gone to the first day of the
orienteering class and come home, if not enthusiastic, at least not sullenly proclaiming he'd never
go again. Alec didn't want either of the kids on the
loose and unsupervised, and there was no way Julia
on her own could corral Matt the way Alec would
have preferred. Liana he was less concerned about;
Julia kept a close eye on her and her buddy Sophie.
He was still convinced she wouldn't do anything
much differently if he told her about the two phone
calls. But he knew she'd stew about them, and he
wanted to save her that.

He spent Tuesday night that week with his two
police captains, going over the data they'd gathered and refining the pitch he would make next
week to the city council. He would be sorry to lose
McAllister come November. There was no one else
in the department he could see who was qualified
to replace him. Alec would have preferred to pro-
mote from within, but this time they'd have to go
outside to hire a new captain of investigative and

support services. At least he was safe on the other sid—Brian Cooper, in charge of patrol, was solid, ethical and content with his job. When Alec had asked once why he hadn't applied to be chief when the position was open, Cooper had shaken his head and said, "I'm, what, ten years at the most from retirement? No, thank you. I have enough headaches where I am."

After they broke up and Alec was home, stripping for bed, he grimaced at the knowledge that it had been all he could do not to cancel the blasted get-together so he could have dinner with Julia and the kids.

Here he was living for the time he spent with them, and she seriously thought he would put his job ahead of them. He was getting to the point where he'd be pissed off, if he didn't have enough memories of the strain on her face every time Josh had up and disappeared to who knew where and who knew when he'd be back. He kept remembering how many nights when Josh was *in* town that Alec answered his phone and could tell from background noise that his brother was in a bar. Or he'd talk about surfing, or conditioning, sometimes the kids but rarely his wife.

Yeah, she had reason for her fears, so he tried not to take them too personally.

Wednesday after dinner, she cleared the table, then spread out flooring samples and glossy pictures of stock cabinets and sinks and faucets and half a dozen ceramic tiles. "I've been thinking," she said.

He tried to hide his consternation. She didn't want his opinion, did she?

"Okay," he said cautiously.

"What if we redo your kitchen first? You're mostly only eating breakfast there now, so it'll be less disruptive than when I have this one torn out."

"That makes sense. Then you'd have a decent kitchen to work in while this one is gutted."

"Yes!" She beamed. "Which means you have to make some decisions."

He wondered if she had any idea how beautiful she was when she was happy. God help him, he wished there was a better way to keep her happy than to pretend interest in poring over these squares of vinyl flooring that all looked alike to him.

"I put it in your hands," he reminded her.

"Well, I assumed you wouldn't want to prowl Lowe's or Home Depot with me, but I also don't want to find out after the fact that you detest a color I've chosen or a particular style of cabinets."

"Julia," he told her with complete sincerity, "you've put your stamp on every place you've lived, even that crappy first apartment you and Josh had. I always think, huh, what'd she do to make this place look so classy and, I don't know, homey? Wave your magic wand over my kitchen. I promise I'll like it. Picking out flooring for the bathrooms just about killed me."

"Okay." She looked earnest. "Bear with me and I'll tell you what my first choices are."

"Thank God," he muttered.

She laughed, but said with all seriousness, "I don't want to make the two kitchens identical, although I suppose it wouldn't matter."

Alec hoped not, since the bathrooms on both sides of the duplex were identical.

"So, here's what I'm thinking for your side."

She gave him a choice of two cabinet styles. One had crisper lines. He laid his finger on that photo. White sink or stainless steel? He went with stainless steel. Faucet? Whatever. Flooring, he leaned toward a vinyl that had enough color and pattern he guessed it wouldn't show the dirt as much.

"That's good," she murmured. "We can pick up that hint of rust—or, hmm, maybe the blue—with a tiled backsplash."

"Great."

Suddenly she was laughing at him again. "You should see your expression. Pure desperation."

He grinned. "Caught."

"I'm amazed at how beautifully you dress, considering how much you hate shopping."

"I put shopping for a new suit in the same category as I do picking out a new handgun or bulletproof vest," he explained. "It's part of the job and has enough of an impact on how people react to me that I consider it in the nature of a weapon."

She looked flummoxed. "You're serious."

"Damn straight."

"How come Uncle Alec can say *damn* and I can't?" Liana asked from behind him.

His mouth crooked up, he turned and held out an arm. Still a little girl in looks and in his eyes, she came and leaned trustingly against him.

"Ask your mom," he suggested.

Mom made a face at him. "He's a big boy. I can't wash his mouth out with soap."

"You've never washed mine out with soap." Liana pondered briefly. "Or Matt's, either, and *he* says bad words."

"He's trying to sound grown-up," Julia said. "Teenagers do that."

The ten-year-old's face brightened. "You mean, as soon as *I* turn thirteen, I can use any words I want?"

"Over my dead body," Alec told her. He gave her hair a tug. "You can't turn thirteen. Or if you do, at least promise me you won't look twice at any boy."

She giggled. "There's kind of a cute boy in Sophie's swim class." She looked shyly at her mother. "Did you notice him? He's got brown hair and, I don't know, he's *tall*."

Julia rolled her eyes Alec's way. "I noticed him."

He laughed. "Show Liana what you're going to do to my kitchen."

It turned out she'd happily accompanied her mother on the forays into home-improvement stores and had her own opinions. She wasn't pleased that he liked those *plain* cabinets. Still, she conceded it was his kitchen before disappearing again to her bedroom.

He and Julia already had keys to each other's sides of the duplex. She promised she'd keep him apprised of dates when workmen would be in and out.

"You don't leave guns out, do you?"

"I have a gun safe."

"Oh. I guess Matt mentioned that once."

As far as he knew, she'd never seen any of his bedrooms. He'd mostly made a point of closing his bedroom door when they were over. He hadn't thought it through in the early days, but knew on some deep, instinctive level that he didn't want to be able to picture her there.

Now…damn. Now he wanted nothing more than to have her in his bedroom. To be in there with her, the door closed, the kids nowhere around. To be drawing her toward the bed.

His body responded predictably to so little, the fleeting beginning to a fantasy. He couldn't quite suppress a groan.

"Is something wrong?" Julia asked, looking surprised.

"No." Nothing new, anyway. "How long is this work on the kitchen going to take?"

"Oh…in theory, two or three weeks. As long as, when they tear out the flooring and old cabinets, they don't find damage we don't know about. If all the subcontractors show when they promised, finish their part on time, none of them make a mistake…"

He imagined sleeping with the smell of sawdust and paint and grout for months on end. Yes, but he could think of it as a kind of perfume trailing behind Julia, who was masterminding all the work on *his* kitchen. He could live with that, he decided.

"No rotting floors when they did the bathrooms, so we can hope." His erection had subsided and Julia was gathering up her samples. Time for him to go, little though he wanted to.

"I'll stick my head in Matt's room and say goodnight," he said, rising to his feet.

Julia's head came up. He thought there was something anxious, or maybe only hopeful, on her face. "Tomorrow night?"

"Tomorrow night," he confirmed. He took a chance, stepped forward and kissed her cheek, soft and giving. "Thank you. I'm getting spoiled."

She smiled, color rising to make her look more sunburned. "Haven't eaten so well since you left home?"

He patted his belly. "I'll have to watch it or I'll start looking like Sheriff Brock."

She rolled her eyes. "I saw your stomach Sunday. No danger there."

Alec cocked his head. "Looked, did you?"

"In envy." But her eyes shied from his. "I'm lucky women can wear swimsuits that cover their stomachs."

"There is nothing whatsoever wrong with yours," he told her. "You have a hell of a body. You can't tell me you don't have men hitting on you regularly."

"Don't be silly," she said, but not convincingly.

Going to say good-night to the kids, Alec was struck by the realization that in the next couple of months Julia would be dealing with all those construction subcontractors. Potentially being alone with each for hours, if not days. They were bound to be primarily male.

That night as he lay in bed, hands clasped behind his head, staring at his dark ceiling, he faced a fear he hadn't let himself acknowledge in a while: that one of these days, Julia would fall in love with someone else. Maybe get married, provide her children with a stepfather. Leave him on the sidelines— if he was lucky to be that close.

Alec muffled a sound of anguish. He didn't know if he could live with that. But what were his options?

For the thousandth time, he calculated the risk-versus-loss ratio and came to the same conclusion as always. The chances were staggeringly high that he would lose everything on the mere chance that she would welcome a sexual advance from him, of all people. This, though, was the first time he let himself realize, with hollow certainty, that he would lose her anyway if he did nothing.

CHAPTER SIX

JULIA STUCK HER HEAD in her son's bedroom Thursday morning. "Rise and shine. Breakfast will be on the table in ten minutes."

"I'm not going today," Matt mumbled.

"Of course you're going today," she said in her best cheerleading voice.

"It's stupid. All we do is stand around."

"Matt…" she said weakly, then gave herself a mental slap. She couldn't afford to sound ineffectual. He'd run right over her. "You can't spend your summer doing nothing. I want to know where you are."

"You know where I am," he said disagreeably. "I'm in bed." He yanked the pillow over his head.

"Ten minutes," she repeated, leaving his door open. Retreating to the kitchen, she dumped the already-beaten eggs into the frying pan she'd left heating and began stirring.

What if he ignores me?

The eternal question. Alec was long gone to work. She could not call the police chief begging him to come roust her kid out of bed, for heaven's sake. This defiance wasn't that flagrant. Matt hadn't called her one of the horribly obscene names he had before, the ones Alec hadn't heard. Matt was a teenage boy. Teenage boys were quite likely, she suspected, to reject the idea of organized activities designed to keep them busy and out of trouble. Maybe the orienteering *was* boring. Who knew whether the instructor was really an expert or was any good at teaching?

Should she let it go?

Could she afford to surrender even a small battle with Matt without losing ground she'd never recover?

Was it losing if she agreed he had the right to opt out of a summer activity? School, now, that would be different.

And, truthfully, she had a sneaking sympathy for him. She and her friends had run wild summers. In such a small town, it hadn't occurred to their parents that they needed organized supervision. She'd loved summers.

She hugged Liana when she appeared and handed her a plate. "Eat up, kiddo. You want to digest before you go swimming."

Her daughter thumped herself down at the table. "Matt's not up."

"He's bored with the orienteering thing. He doesn't have to do it if he doesn't want to." Julia dished up for herself.

"He doesn't?" Liana sounded amazed.

"You don't have to do swim lessons if you don't want, either." Julia mentally crossed fingers as she sat at the table, too.

"Well…I like to swim."

And there was a cute boy to be watched.

"Riding camp starts on the twenty-ninth," Julia reminded her.

"That will be so cool." Liana gave a little bounce in her chair. She ate a couple of bites, then tore her slice of toast in half. "I wish I was going to be in Sophie's class when school starts," she said in a smaller voice.

"I know." Julia gave her a hug. "But look how quickly you made a friend. You'll make more."

"I kind of like Jenna in my swim class. *She's* my age, and she goes to the same school I will be." She frowned. "I guess Lauren does, too, but I don't like her that much. And there's a couple of boys I might end up in a class with, but yuck."

"How about the cute boy?"

She scrunched up her face. "He's twelve. Soph says he's mad his mom made him take swimming lessons, except he guesses it might be okay 'cuz he thinks he'd like to be on the swim team."

"Boys do improve by middle school," Julia conceded.

"You're just going to let Matt *sleep?*"

"I guess I am." Julia smiled to hide her self-doubt. "He can't get in any trouble that way, can he?"

He still hadn't put in an appearance when it came

time for her to drive the girls to the pool. By the time they got back almost two hours later, she knew without even looking that he was gone. The loaf of bread sat on the counter, drying out with the bag left open. He hadn't put the jam or peanut butter back in the refrigerator, either. Or wiped the counter. None of which was a big deal, but damn it, where had he gone?

She checked his bedroom, and sure enough it was empty, bedcovers thrown back, pillow hanging half off the mattress, yesterday's laundry strewn on the floor.

She'd long since given up on the clean-bedroom rule. If he wanted to wade in dirty clothes, let him. All she insisted on was that he return dirty dishes to the kitchen and not let food rot in his room. So far, he'd cooperated that much.

The doorbell rang, and she found the cabinet guy wanting to talk about the fact that the corner wasn't square in Alec's kitchen and what he thought they should do about it. Julia was still amazed that his kitchen had not only been gutted already, but the new cabinets were being installed within days of her order. It turned out the store kept some of the more popular cabinets in stock, and Alec had chosen one of those styles. Remodeling *never* went this smoothly. Disaster would strike, she was sure. Maybe this was the first sign.

She went to take a look, but relaxed when she saw that the problem wasn't as severe as he'd implied. They agreed the gap could be covered with a strip of oak, and the countertop could be cut slightly askew to match. Of course, the countertop guy might not be so compliant. Another strip…? What would that do when it came to tiling the backsplash? Ceramic tile wasn't forgiving.

She'd worry about it when the time came. Windows and doors were never plumb, she knew that, corners never square, especially in cheap construction like the duplex. As Alec had said when she reported on various small holdups, so far, so good.

Disaster was probably waiting to strike when the work started on *her* side of the duplex.

Perhaps an hour before dinner, she heard the front door open and close so quietly she guessed Matt was trying to sneak in. Moving just as quietly, she intercepted him.

Alarm flared on his face, and all she had to do was breathe in to know why. He'd been smoking marijuana. His eyes were red, too, and he swayed slightly.

"You're stoned."

"You don't know what you're talking about," he said rudely.

"Where did you get the marijuana?" She barely recognized her own hard voice.

He sneered, "So now the truth comes out— Mommy dearest was a pothead."

"Where?" she snapped.

"Like I'd tell you."

"It doesn't mean anything that your uncle is police chief in this town."

"Right. Use Uncle Alec." While she smoldered, he added, "Smoking weed is legal in Washington."

Her anger nearly choked her. "We don't live in Washington. And I'm betting it's not legal there for minors, anyway. Matt, you are thirteen years old. No matter what kind of brat you're being, I will not allow you to abuse drugs or alcohol."

"Brat." His laugh was long and disturbingly high. His expression was even more disturbing when he quit laughing. "Bet you can't stop me."

Julia couldn't rid herself of the shock. This boy wasn't her son, Matt. She didn't know who this was. "What is *wrong* with you?"

Ugliness transformed him. "*You* know. Don't pretend you don't."

"I have no idea."

"You're a liar!" he screamed and barreled past her, knocking her sideways into the wall. His bedroom door slammed and she heard a scraping sound. He had to be pulling his dresser across the floor to block the door.

Julia stood where she was, rubbing her shoulder and shaking. Why, oh, why, was Matt's rage still escalating? Had she done or said something so terribly wrong? Or had he found new friends who brought out the worst in him?

Dear God, what was she going to *do?*

"Damn it, Matt." Alec stood in the hall, arms crossed, aware of Julia watching from the kitchen. "If you don't open this door, I'll break it down. And you know I can do it."

"*She* can't come in," his nephew said from his bedroom.

"It's just me. I doubt your mother wants to talk to you."

He waited through a pause, although his muscles were locked as tight as if he was preparing to smash through a door on a drug raid. He had a flash of picturing it—wearing black, bulletproof vest covered by a police windbreaker, heavy boots on his feet, weapon in his hand. The tension of knowing he might have to kill or be killed in the next minute or two. He summoned the ability he'd learned to block out all distractions, all doubts, all fears, to operate coldly and professionally until it was done.

This was a thirteen-year-old boy on the other side of the door, not armed dealers. A boy he loved.

The long scraping sound made him wince, thinking of the just-refinished hardwood floors. A moment later, the door opened a crack. Alec planted his hand on it and pushed, making Matt fall back.

No smoke hung in the air, but Julia was right; the kid stank of marijuana.

"What in the hell are you thinking?" Alec asked, closing the door behind him. Yeah, scratches marred the finish near his feet. Part of him was thinking they might buff out, even as the rest of him was grimly focused on a boy who seemed determined to self-destruct.

Matt hunched his shoulders, but his jaw was set defiantly. "Like you've never smoked weed."

"I did in college," Alec agreed. "Didn't much like it."

"Well, I do."

"Where did you get it?"

"You think I'm going to rat some guy out to my uncle Alec, the police chief?" Matt asked incredulously.

Alec shook his head, letting it go. "You know there'll be consequences for this."

"You're not my dad!" All the rage Alec had heard the first time Matt yelled that at him was in his voice again. This had to be all about Josh in some way Alec couldn't understand.

He tried to keep his posture loose. "What do you think your dad would say about you smoking pot?"

Matt hung his head.

"I'm not Josh, but you and I both know he'd want me to be standing in for him when he can't be here."

The boy's head shot up. "Can't be here. That's a good one."

Alec tossed out a trial balloon. "He didn't choose to die."

"*She* said—" Eyes wild, he balked.

"What did your mother say?"

He only shook his head.

"Matt, you have to talk to us. We can't fix what's wrong if you clam up like this."

His nephew only stared back, mouth clamped shut, eyes blazing.

"You're on house arrest," Alec said flatly. "We'll talk in a week if you don't try to sneak out, if you've done all the chores your mother asks of you and if you act like a decent human being. I had a good time kayaking Sunday. I was hoping you were interested in making a new start, but apparently not."

Matt shrugged.

Alec toed the scrapes on the floor. "Whatever this costs to fix, you'll be working off. Don't move furniture again without precautions."

He walked out of the room and went to the kitchen, shaking his head.

Julia looked stricken. There was utter silence from Liana's bedroom, where she was no doubt huddled in fear of being splashed by the acid of her brother's hate.

Weary, Alec pulled out a chair and sat at the kitchen table. "Is it me? Does he resent me for trying to take Josh's place?"

She stood backed up to the counter, arms tightly crossed as if she could hold herself together that way. "It's not you. It's me. I just have no idea what I did."

"It'd be one thing if you and Josh had a screaming fight and he'd gone tearing out onto the freeway and hit an abutment at eighty miles an hour. Then Matt might blame you."

Something ghosted over her face, moving too quickly to be identifiable. It was enough to catch his attention, though, and he asked himself for the first time whether she suspected what was going on with Matt. But...what could it be?

"Josh died on the job," Alec said more slowly, watching her. "Didn't he ever talk to Matt about how risky some of his missions were?"

"I don't know."

"Maybe it's Josh he's really mad at, but Josh isn't here. You are."

She gave a broken laugh. "I don't think Matt has ever in his life been mad at Josh. It was always me. I was the one who set the rules, the one who enforced them. Dad was the good-time guy who encouraged Matt to break them."

Alec was silent for a moment, a frown pulling at his forehead. "You're kidding," he said finally.

"No. I could never understand it. He was a navy SEAL. He *had* to understand discipline. Would he have encouraged a young sailor to break the rules?"

Thinking back to the boy his brother had been, the sometimes-wild teenager, gave Alec a partial answer, one that made him uncomfortable. "I think he knew he needed discipline that came from outside himself. Growing up, most of us internalize the concept of getting things done because there'll be consequences of some kind if you don't. Josh, though, he didn't bother with assignments if a teacher went too easy on him. He never listened to Mom. It took Dad, who'd pull out the belt if either of us didn't follow orders."

Julia made a helpless sound. "Thus Josh chose the military."

"Maybe."

She blew out a long breath and then tipped her head back. "I hate to say it, but that makes sense. It might have been sort of a disability."

"I wish I'd known what he was doing."

"Why?" She pinned him with those extraordinary eyes. "What could you have done?"

"Talked to him. Tried to make him see what he was doing to you."

"To me? Don't you mean to Matt?"

Alec shook his head. "It was you he was being unfair to. Matt and Liana had you to fill in what was missing. Two years ago, they were both great kids, whether Josh was a good parent or not."

"So you're saying…this doesn't have anything to do with Josh."

He shook his head again. "No, it has to do with Josh. But what?"

He watched carefully, but now she lowered her head and stared down at her bare feet, as if riveted by her toes. Her hair slid from behind her ears and partially veiled her face.

She was hiding from him. *Hell,* he thought. She did know something. Or feared something.

Or—maybe not. He had no idea how much grief she still carried. She'd implied that it was less than he had feared, because the marriage hadn't been as solid as he'd believed. That might almost be worse, though; weren't ghosts said to linger because something important was unresolved? Could grief be like that?

Huh. It occurred to Alec that the same explanation could be applied to Matt. What if, the last day or so before Josh went wheels up, Matt had been angry at his father? Angry at the absences? Oh, hell—the issue could have been anything. Fathers and sons fought. But in a kid's head, if Dad died, could he blame himself? Or Mom, by extension, because she was the grown-up and maybe it was really her fault if Dad let Matt down?

I am reaching, he admitted. But—maybe.

The alternative was to think that Julia had a secret, too, and the possibility hurt.

Why? Wounds could be kept private. He'd never been entirely open with anyone, including her. *He* had a huge secret—he was in love with her.

The silence had been long enough she was sneaking looks at him. Suddenly the timer dinged, and she jerked.

"Oh, no! I haven't even cut up the broccoli!"

He must have made a face, because she gave him the same chiding look she'd give one of the kids, then half laughed. "Oh, why bother? Liana doesn't like it, either. Salad will do." She hesitated. "Do we invite Matt to the table?"

"Stoned? Hell, no."

After a moment, Julia nodded and grabbed a pot holder. "Why don't you call Liana?"

Whatever was in the oven smelled good, but he had a suspicion none of them were as hungry as they should be.

He shook his head, passing Matt's door and rapping lightly on Liana's. The day at Elk Lake, the Matt he knew and loved had been present again. Had something happened since? Or had he been angry at himself for succumbing to the temptation to have fun with his family—even, God forbid, with his *mother?*

Alec had a suspicion that an everyday, average punishment like restriction wasn't going to work on Matt. Whatever drove him to this furious behavior festered deep. Try counseling again? But when Julia had, back in L.A., Matt had refused to talk. *You can lead a horse to water...*

He was a kid. He'd crack eventually, and the poison would all pour out. Then they could do something to help.

The cracking part, though, didn't sound like a lot of fun.

FRIDAY MORNING, JULIA was surprised to get a call from Nell McAllister, married to the Colin McAllister, who was running for county sheriff. They had talked at the wedding, and now she suggested they have lunch.

"If you can get away from the kids. Or you can bring the kids."

Julia imagined Matt a happy fourth at the table and said hastily, "Any chance we can make it tomorrow or Sunday?"

"Tomorrow would be great. I'm off, and I think Colin is working."

Alec only raised his eyebrows when Julia told him that evening after dinner about the invitation. "You talked to her at the wedding reception, didn't you? She seems nice enough."

"Are you working tomorrow?"

He grinned. "Are you asking me to babysit?"

She made a face at him. "Boy-sit, actually. Liana will be fine at Sophie's."

"Matt hasn't tried to jump the tracks yet, has he?"

"He's hardly said a word, but he hasn't left the house today, if that's what you mean."

"I vote we stick to the weeklong restriction, but I was thinking of giving him a, er, temporary parole." He gave a half shrug. "If you agree."

"What kind of parole?"

"I thought he and I could do something. Go for a hike, maybe. I keep thinking I can get him to talk."

Julia didn't even hesitate. "Yes. Please. He's been quiet, but..." She didn't know how to describe her uneasiness. What was Matt thinking as he lay brooding in his room?

Alec's dark eyes met hers, but all he said was "You need to make friends. You might like Nell."

Saturday morning, Alec and Matt left long before Julia did. They'd decided on a hike and she had packed them a lunch, which they stowed in Matt's old day pack, which showed serious wear after a year of being banged around full of schoolbooks.

"Oh, Lord. Back-to-school shopping," she said, and they both gave her identical looks of startled alarm as they went out the door. She smiled once they were gone. She could suggest to Alec that clothing Matt was a form of arming him, as much as those beautiful suits Alec wore were for him. Shopping with *her,* Matt would make every decision with a goal of horrifying her or defying her. Maybe Alec could make him see some sense.

It was the first humor she'd found in anything in days, imagining herself pushing them out the door to go clothes shopping.

She and Nell met at the Kingfisher Café, owned by Nell's high school friend Hailey Allen. At the wedding, Julia had met Hailey, plump, buxom and mischievous, and liked her.

She brought over their soup and ended up sitting at their table for a few minutes. "Alec tells Colin you're an amazing cook," she said.

"He said that?" Flattered, Julia laughed. "That's because he's getting home-cooked dinners every night instead of fast food or something from the freezer. I doubt his standards are high. Although," she added in fairness, "his mother really can cook. Traditional Italian. That's probably why he's so thrilled with my meals. I got most of her recipes."

Hailey's eyes narrowed in interest. "I've never done much Italian. Can we get together and swap secrets?"

"I'd love to," Julia said with a warm smile. "Can you escape from the restaurant long enough to join us for dinner one of these evenings and try out one of Rosaria's recipes?"

"I'm closed on Sundays and Mondays," she said promptly. "Cool. Will Alec be there, too?"

Julia's heart bumped. "You're interested in him?"

Hailey snorted. "Not that way. A cop who has that stone-cold thing going? No. Anyway, I'm seeing someone." Her grin at Nell had a sly cast.

Nell cast her eyes upward. "My brother. Who is *three years younger.* Not to be a traditionalist or anything."

"You wouldn't think it," Hailey murmured.

Julia laughed. "Was he at the wedding? Did I meet him?"

Nell shook her head. "Felix has barely met Noah or Cait. He just finished his law degree at Willamette and is doing a three-month internship with the Department of Justice in D.C. Then he's considering job offers in Portland and in Bend, thanks to Hailey."

Bend was the biggest city in central Oregon, not that far northeast of Angel Butte.

"Not just me." Hailey's smile was soft. "He missed you, Nell. He really wants time with you."

"Ohh," Nell breathed, seemingly struggling with emotion. "I didn't realize—"

Julia recalled the story Alec had told her about the fifteen-year-old Maddie Dubeau vanishing one night, escaping her captor with a head wound and amnesia and remaking herself as Nell Smith, who had come back to Angel Butte only last November. Of course her brother thought her reappearance was some kind of miracle.

"Oops!" Hailey said, jumping up. "Frantic hand signals from the kitchen. Enjoy your lunch."

In her wake, Nell asked politely, "Do you have siblings?"

"An older brother." Julia felt a pang, remembering the expression on Colin's face when he'd walked his sister down the aisle to meet Noah Chandler. "We were never close. Ten years apart in age, which was maybe too much. My parents were…quite stern. Home wasn't as happy as it could have been."

"Mine, either," Nell said, her eyes shadowed. "I realized later that was one reason I didn't try harder to recover my memory. I didn't want to come home."

Julia nodded, able to understand even if her childhood hadn't been that bad. "I take the kids to their grandparents' every few years for Christmas, but…" She shrugged. "The minute we walk in the door, I remember why I went so far for college."

"Makes sense to me." Nell smiled. "So, tell me about your kids."

Julia's laugh was weary. "Are you sure you want to hear about them? You don't have any yet yourself, do you? I don't want to scare you off."

"No, although we're thinking pretty soon…" She touched her belly in an unconscious gesture any woman would have recognized. "I'm only twenty-nine, but Colin is thirty-five. He doesn't want to be too old when our kids get to be teenagers."

"Oh, he definitely doesn't," Julia agreed, more heartfelt than she'd intended.

Nell's eyebrows rose. "Your boy is…?"

"Thirteen." She hesitated. "Let's say Matt hasn't handled losing his father well."

"As in…depressed?"

"As in Jekyll and Hyde. Is it Jekyll who's the evil one? I can never remember."

"No, I think it's Hyde."

"That's my boy," Julia said with a sigh. "I don't know how Alec and Colin feel about each other, but I'm here to tell you that, no matter what Colin has told you about him, Alec is a saint to take us on."

"Is that what he did?"

Julia found herself talking, and talking, as sandwiches replaced the soup then pastries arrived with a wave from Hailey. Julia hadn't realized how much she had needed a friend. She didn't think she was making too much of an assumption, either; they segued into Nell talking about her troubled relationship with her parents, and a little about the years of living without the memories most people took for granted as a foundation for their personality.

"You'll like Cait, too," she said. "She's as mixed-up as all the rest of us."

Julia laughed. "Bless you. I really needed this."

Nell insisted on paying for lunch. On the way out, she asked where Matt was today. "I suppose you can't exactly call it child care, given his age…."

"I called it boy-sitting when I stuck Alec with him." Her mood got flatter as she thought about going home. Had the day gone well for Alec and Matt—or been a disaster?

Please, she begged silently, *not a disaster.* Matt needed *someone.*

She thanked Nell and they parted ways, Julia to shop for groceries on her way home. She was a little uneasy at how important feeding Alec had become for her. She had a bad feeling she was pretending he was hers and setting herself up for heartbreak.

Why did life have to be so complicated?

CHAPTER SEVEN

ALEC DIDN'T START the day with big plans. Urban Southern Californians that they were, neither he nor Matt had ever done much in the way of hiking. Alec had taken up Nordic skiing after arriving in Angel Butte in late March. Living here alone, what else was there to do? He'd considered alpine skiing, but the idea of breaking bones didn't much appeal to him. The kids were younger; he guessed they'd want to try it. Him, he was happy gliding through silent, snowy woods.

"This is a short hike," he said as they pulled away from the duplex. "About three miles. Circles one of the lakes, crosses a couple of streams. I'm told it's pretty."

Beside him in the Tahoe, Matt shrugged. Par for the course—he hadn't been unpleasant yet, but he wasn't brimming with enthusiasm, either. Alec hadn't expected that he would be. Polite, now, that he did expect.

"Maybe next week we can go look at kayaks," he suggested.

"You mean you'll let me out of the house again?" There was a sneer in the voice.

"When the seven days are up. If you've done what I asked of you." He paused. "If you want to skip the kayak idea, that's fine." He thought about threatening to take Liana or Julia or both with him instead, but canned it. No, he and Matt needed things to do together that were *theirs*. Julia would understand that.

"Kayaking was cool," Matt finally mumbled.

"You been up to the top of Angel Butte yet?" Alec asked on impulse, seeing the turnoff.

"I didn't want to ride my bike up."

Or push it, more likely. The road that circled to the crater rim was steep. Alec was a runner and challenged himself to go to the top one or two mornings a week. He'd been disconcerted to learn that the mayor did the same. He and Chandler met each other coming or going every now and then.

"Let's drive up there," he said.

Matt didn't object and even looked mildly interested.

They emerged at the top and Alec pulled into the small parking lot. When he opened his door, Matt hopped out, too. There were a couple of other cars up here and a pickup with a camper. A family stood reading the historical-designation placard that told the story of the angel that gave the butte and town its name.

"She's been here since 1884," Alec told Matt

as they walked along the paved path that led to the marble angel atop the base he'd been told had been added not that many years ago to boost her so she could see over the top of the scrubby trees growing out of the cinder sides of the butte. "This was the Wild West then. Supposedly the guy who ran the stagecoach stop and trading post was involved in cattle rustling. A bunch of the ranchers decided to hang him, no trial required. He claimed an angel appeared to protect him. Scared the vigilantes away. He'd evidently made a silent vow, because next thing people knew, a huge crate arrived on a wagon, and what was in it but a marble statue of an angel, carved in Italy. There wasn't any road up to the top in those days." He contemplated the eight-foot-tall angel with her tucked but delicately incised wings. "Can't imagine how they got her up here unbroken."

Matt stepped off the path to look up at her face, weathered into a serenity that might or might not have been there originally.

"Think what that must have cost," Alec said thoughtfully. "Makes you wonder where he got the money, doesn't it?"

Matt cackled. "Stealing cattle."

Alec's mouth tipped up. "Probably."

He stood to one side and watched as his nephew climbed the three broad steps of the base and then jumped down, circling until he stood behind her.

"She looks kind of like the sister I had for third grade," Matt said.

Alec had forgotten the kids had gone to a Catholic school in San Diego. He and Josh had, too, for a few years, although both had switched to the public schools by sixth or seventh grade.

"None of the nuns I had for teachers looked like her," he said. "They were an aging bunch."

"Sister Regina wasn't. She was, well, kind of pretty. Although it was hard to tell with the, you know." His hands shaped the wimple and Alec nodded. "But she used to fold her hands in front of her like that, and she always stood totally straight and with her head high, and she never missed *anything,* even when she had her back turned, like when she was writing on the board or something."

"Eyes in the back of her head."

"She could see even through all that cloth."

Alec laughed. "Could be. Hey. Let's get going before the day gets too hot."

The angel seemed to have eased the tension. The drive wasn't ten miles northwest to a small campground and parking lot at one end of Osprey Lake. The campground appeared to be pretty well full. When he looked both ways, bright colors caught Alec's eye where fishermen on rocky promontories cast lines into the deep lake waters.

Alec offered to carry the pack, but Matt, displaying outraged pride, insisted he could. Alec didn't force conversation as they set out on the dusty trail.

They nodded at a few fishermen in passing, but otherwise, despite this being a weekend, he and Matt found themselves mostly alone. In the quiet they could hear birdcalls and see chipmunks and squirrels darting up trees and then pausing to peer around the boles or from high branches at these two intruders.

"Doubt we'll see any larger wildlife," Alec commented, "but if you'd like we can get higher in the mountains on another trip or head east into the desert. We should probably both get outfitted with hiking boots, though, if we're going to do much." He risked an add-on. "Maybe your mom and sister, too."

"We used to walk a lot on the beach," Matt said after a minute. "This is different." Another pause. "It smells different from home."

"I've noticed." They stopped on a short timber bridge that led over a small, rocky rill. The forest surrounding them was still the dry ponderosa and lodgepole pines, from what Alec had been told. He'd noticed from the first how distinctive the air smelled around here, clean and tangy. He didn't know whether it was volcanic soil or trees or just the lack of smog, or all three, but he liked it.

Matt jumped down to cross and recross the stream, balancing on rocks, then clambered back up to the trail. Moments like this, he looked so young, not like an angry boy whose father had died violently half a world away not so long ago.

Partway around, they settled on a big rock extending out into the lake to eat their lunches. Alec had hoped Matt might want to talk, but instead he lay on his stomach, dipping his hands in the lake and watching minnows dart like pale shadows beneath the sparkling surface.

Alec enjoyed the silence. He had to be guarded most of the time—on the job it was automatic, with Matt he had to watch what he said and with Julia… oh, hell, that was the hardest, fearing how easily he could give himself away. This, lounging here with his head tipped to the sun, made his muscles grow lax and his eyelids heavy. He could, quite contentedly, have sprawled on the rock and napped.

But after a while Matt said in astonishment, "You aren't going to sleep, are you?" and Alec groaned.

"Given half a chance."

"You can't! That's boring. Only old people and babies take naps."

He pushed himself up, wadded his lunch leavings and poked them into the day pack, pleased Matt did the same with no argument. They both trod a few feet off the trail to take a leak, then ambled on around the trail.

On this side of the lake, they passed only a lone fisherman, who either wasn't aware of them passing or didn't want to bother exchanging greetings.

Matt whispered, "Do you think he's catching anything?"

"Wouldn't be so many of them trying if there

weren't some decent trout in the lake," Alec suggested. "That's probably what they're all planning for dinner tonight."

"I've never had trout." Matt sounded doubtful. "I don't know if I'd like it."

Alec hadn't either, come to think of it. "If you like fish, fresh trout is supposed to be the best."

The stream at the head of the lake was livelier, draining from the mountains. They could hear the burble as they approached. Alec wasn't sure it was safe to drink from; he knew you could get giardia or the like from some mountain water. Matt was disappointed but shrugged.

Most of the way they'd been deep in forest that grew to the rocky lakeshore, but circling toward the campground, the trail suddenly opened in a meadow that in May or June would have been scattered with wildflowers, judging from the seed heads.

"Oh, look." Matt suddenly crouched.

Crack.

Jesus. That was a gunshot. Alec threw himself atop the boy, flattening them in the tall grass. Was some idiot *hunting?* He risked raising his head slightly.

Crack.

He heard the thud of the bullet striking a tree trunk too close to them.

Swearing, he flattened himself again. If this was hunting, he and Matt were the prey.

"Let's scrabble to the trees," he said and lifted himself enough to let Matt squirm out from beneath him. As Matt kept going, shivering the grass, Alec contorted to pull the small .38 caliber he kept in an ankle holster. He'd feel better to have his big SIG Sauer in his hand, but this was better than nothing.

Smaller and lithe, Matt was better at the squirming, snakelike system of propulsion. Alec had to half crawl, exposing more of himself. Prickles traveled up his spine and raised the hair at his nape at the consciousness of having his back to the enemy.

Matt reached the first puny pine tree and stopped. Looking up, Alec saw the fresh white wound scored by the bullet. That gave him a direction.

"Keep going," he ordered, voice harsh. "Quick."

He half rose and threw himself behind the first larger tree trunk he saw. "Keep down," he told Matt, who turned a scared face up to him.

Weapon in hand, Alec eased around the tree far enough to look along the shore toward the campground, then to scan the woods beyond. A flash of color made him jerk, but it was one of the fishermen, who was crouched behind the thin growth of huckleberries as if they could protect him.

Nothing.

Alec let a couple of minutes tick by.

More nothing.

"All right," he said quietly. "I want you to stay right here, Matt. I suspect the shooter is long gone, but I'm going to work my way around and find out. I'll come back for you. Got it?"

"I'm scared," Matt whispered.

"You should be. Somebody was shooting at us."

The boy gulped. "At *us?*"

"Looked that way." Alec moved fast, crossing an open five feet or so, then paused behind the narrower bole of another pine. "Stay," he said again.

Ten minutes later, he'd reached the campground, where he found a terrorized group congregated behind an RV. Scared gazes riveted on the small Colt in his hand. He extracted his badge, which he'd stowed out of habit in the back pocket of his khakis.

"Anybody see who was shooting?"

Headshakes all around, then the predictable babble, one voice running over another.

"You see or hear any vehicles leaving the parking lot?"

"Yes!" Eyes still rolling like a spooked horse's, a woman said, "Just now. I think it was a pickup."

"Yeah," an older man agreed. "Or maybe an SUV. White."

"It was silver," insisted one of the fishermen. "I heard the door slam. Thought someone was taking off because, shit, those were gunshots."

"They were," Alec said grimly. "All right. I'm going to call for reinforcements."

No, damn it—he'd put his phone in the day pack,

left behind with Matt. He borrowed someone else's and reached dispatch for the sheriff's department. A woman assured him a unit was on the way. He thanked the teenager who'd lent him the phone, then returned through the woods, not on the trail, for Matt.

By that time, Matt was gibbering with excitement and the aftermath of adrenaline. "Is anybody *dead?*" He sounded torn between dread and ghoulish hope.

"Not that I've found so far. I think those shots came closest to us," Alec said.

"Do you think somebody didn't see us there?"

It was possible, of course; people too often were idiots when they had a firearm in their hands. Or when they didn't, come to think of it. But Alec's every instinct whispered, *No.* This was no accident. Somebody had been trying to kill him.

Or Matt, he thought with a chill. He was the one who'd crouched before the sound of the gunshot. Alec had still been standing there, a perfect target.

He wouldn't be sorry if he were dead. But if this boy he loved had been bleeding at his feet, Alec would have suffered.

The lingering adrenaline made a fine starter for rage like nothing he'd ever felt before, a spark in dry grass. Threatening him was one thing. But his family?

Whoever they were, those bastards would pay.

"WHAT?" JULIA STARED in shock at Alec. Matt slouched beside him. The two looked back with those dark eyes, so much alike.

"You heard me." Alec sounded grim. "Only two shots, but those bullets came damn close to us. I think it had to be deliberate."

"But...why?" Her brain wanted to stutter to a halt. What if one of them had been killed? She could not lose anyone else she loved. She couldn't. "I don't understand," she faltered.

"Matt." Alec barely glanced at her son. "Go to your room. I need to talk to your mother."

Matt reared back. "But I was *there!* Why can't I stay? I'm not some little kid."

"You're not an adult, either. There are things she needs to know that I don't want you to hear."

His mouth opened and worked. Julia saw the moment he translated adult dismissal into rejection.

Matt whirled and ran. His bedroom door slammed so hard it vibrated the few framed pictures she'd hung in the hall.

"That...might not have been smart," she suggested.

Alec said a word he never had around her before, paced away and swung back. "Did you want him to hear that I think somebody tried to kill him today?"

Shock bumped her again. "Him?"

"I could be wrong. The shooter might have been aiming at me. But I don't think so. We'd stopped momentarily and I was a bigger target. Just before I heard the gunshot, Matt dropped down suddenly to look at something on the ground."

"But…that makes no sense!" she cried. "He's thirteen! Why would anybody try to shoot him?"

"Happens all the time in L.A."

She dismissed that with a shake of the head. "Drive-bys. Gangs. This was different."

"Yeah," he conceded. "It was." He let out a long breath. "Let's sit in the kitchen. There's…something I haven't told you."

He grabbed a can of soda and all but drained it in one long drink. Enveloped by this feeling of unreality, Julia watched him, his head tipped, throat working. His shirt was open a couple of buttons, and sweat sheened his face and neck and chest and made dark circles under his arms. After setting down the can, he wiped a bead of cola from his chin.

Julia sat across from him, her back straight, her hands clasped, feeling rather like she had this past year in the too-frequent school conferences where she was braced to hear from a teacher or vice principal the latest outrages perpetuated by her son. Ashamed, as if all this was her fault.

As it might be, she reminded herself. *In a way.*

Alec eyed her with a look she could only interpret as wary. "Let me say first," he said, "that it's possible this was nothing but stupidity. Who knows?

A teenager out shooting for fun. Neither of us is wearing as bright colors as maybe we should have."

She nodded; his shirt was olive-green and he wore khaki pants. Matt's shorts were khaki-colored, too, and today's T-shirt was a faded navy.

"The sheriff's deputies who showed up didn't want to believe this was a deliberate assault." His jaw muscles spasmed; he hadn't liked being patronized. "Of course, they work for Eugene Brock."

She sat back, eyes widening. "Explain."

"I'm getting there." He sighed. "I've been threatened a couple of times recently."

Her breath left her.

"You saw the newscast that night at the hotel when I expressed strong support for Colin McAllister in his run for sheriff," Alec continued.

Julia nodded.

"I was told to withdraw that support publicly or I'd be sorry." He paused. "When I didn't follow instructions, a couple weeks later, I got another call offering me one more chance."

She somehow convinced her lungs to draw air and pushed away the image of a bullet slamming into Alec's broad chest, of blood blossoming and him staggering, then folding and going down as his life drained out. It was horrifyingly vivid. She'd imagined Josh's death a thousand times.

He reached across the table suddenly, grasping one of her hands. "Julia…" he said in an altered tone.

"But that means they'd be trying to kill *you*," she said, her voice rising. *They.* Faceless, inimical.

"That's what I thought. It's why I didn't tell you."

Her shock turned to anger and she bristled. "What does that mean? You didn't think a threat to you was any of my business?" She was distantly aware she was yelling. "That, hey, you go down in the line of duty, it's nothing to us?"

"Ah…no." Looking more cautious, he let go of her hand and sat back. "I know how to take care of myself, Julia. I've been extra careful. I only meant that I didn't think you needed to take any unusual precautions with the kids or in your own activities."

She jumped up, unable to sit any longer. Crossing her arms tightly, Julia paced across the kitchen, then swung to face him. "Don't alarm the little woman, right? How…how *Josh* you sound."

Alec's eyes narrowed. "Don't use that brush on me. I face threats on the job. I don't have to bring them home."

Her chin jutted out. "But this time you did."

She could see him clench his jaw. He dipped his head. "Yeah. I'm afraid this time I might have."

Hearing something like agony in his voice, she felt her anger falter. Alec would never willingly do anything to endanger her or the kids, she knew that. She had no doubt he would give his life for any of them. For Liana or Matt, anyway.

She closed her eyes for a moment, then went back to the table and made herself sit again. "Okay. Ex-

plain why you think someone who is mad at you
might have taken a potshot at Matt."

"Two potshots."

That sent a shudder through her. One stray shot
was an accident; two was a whole lot more sugges-
tive. "Two," she echoed.

"I could be wrong," he said again. "Even if he
was aiming our way, the guy might just have been
a lousy shot. Though both bullets came closer than
I like," he added reflectively. Seeing the gathering
storm on her face, he seemed to shake that off. "I
was reminded of the way the threat was phrased.
'You'll be sorry.' The thing is, if what they really
want is me to throw my support behind Sheriff
Brock, or at least to embarrass McAllister by yank-
ing that support from him, killing me won't achieve
the goal. With Matt wounded or dead, I'd definitely
be sorry. They might think that would do the trick."

She wanted to kill someone, if only she knew
who. Then panic hit her and she leaped up, turning her head until she spotted her phone lying on
the counter. "I have to be sure Liana is at Sophie's."

Sophie's mother, home from work, confirmed
that the girls were there. Julia managed to calm
herself before she resumed her seat, where she ven-
tured, "Could the miss have been intentional? To
make the threat more real?"

"That might be," he agreed. "Either way, we need
to keep the kids under close watch. Preferably inside. I'd like a good, solid fence around the back,

the sooner the better. One somebody would have to scale to see over. I'll make some calls Monday."

"Then…you won't do what they want."

"Is that what you think I should do?" His tone was entirely neutral, stripped of all opinion and emotion.

Would he if she asked? She didn't want to know the answer. After a moment, she shook her head. "I'm scared, but…of course not. If this Brock person would use tactics like these to win an election, he's the last person who should be in office. Especially heading a law-enforcement agency! Anyway, your ethics are too important to you."

"Not as important as you and the kids."

She smiled shakily. "Thank you for saying that. And for offering, if that's what you were doing. But no."

Alec nodded, his relaxation so subtle she wouldn't have seen it if she hadn't known him so well. "All right. I don't really expect an attack in town. You should be safe enough in a crowd, say, at the pool. But we can't let Matt take off on his bike the way he has been. Good thing he's on restriction. The orienteering class would have been out, that's for sure. Horseback riding should be okay for Liana. They'll probably mostly be in an arena. And you'll be there."

She nodded, but said, "They'll be taking some trail rides the second week."

"Huh." He rubbed a hand over his jaw. "Can you go along?"

"It may look a little odd, but I'll insist."

"Uh…do you know how to ride a horse?"

"I've done it before." Twenty years ago, but she couldn't imagine they'd be galloping. She could sit on a placid horse for hire plodding along behind others. "Somebody could still take a shot at Liana."

The way he was watching her, she wondered if he was thinking, *Or at you.* But, of course, an outsider would have no way of guessing she mattered much to Alec.

If she did.

No, she knew she did, even if it wasn't necessarily the way she wanted.

"That's a couple weeks away. I may have answers by then."

"All right. But…what do I do with Matt? He's not going to like any of this."

He sighed. "No, he won't. And…I don't know. Let me think about it."

"I'd better work on dinner."

"And I need a shower. Hey." His expression grew lighter. "You enjoy lunch?"

"I really like Nell. I think we can be friends. She says I'll like Cait, too. Oh, and Nell's friend Hailey, who owns the restaurant we went to, sat with us for a bit. I'm going to invite her to dinner someday. She covets your mother's recipes."

Alec laughed. "Does she? I suspect Mom will be flattered if her food lands on a restaurant menu."

She frowned at him in sudden speculation. "You are calling home, aren't you?"

For a moment he looked as sheepish as a kid. "Not in a while."

"They lost Josh, and you know they love you."

"Even if my father's way of showing it was taking his belt to me?"

"Even if."

He grimaced. "Yeah. I know even Dad loves me. And you're right." His mouth quirked. "As always."

She smiled. "Stick your head in and talk to Matt on your way out. We'll see you in about half an hour?"

"Perfect." He sniffed. "What are we having?"

"Pot roast. As I'm sure you could guess."

Laughing again, he headed toward the bedroom. Snapping green beans, Julia heard him knock on Matt's door before opening it.

Not two minutes later, Alec was back, his expression grim. "Matt's gone. Out his window. I checked the garage, and his bike's gone, too."

CHAPTER EIGHT

LEAVING JULIA TO DO what she could to preserve dinner for later, Alec drove around town. Up one road and down the next, scanning cross streets, searching for one skinny kid on a mountain bike. Anxiety warred with a desire to strangle him.

The bad news was that Julia and he had talked for quite a while, giving Matt plenty of time for his getaway. The good news was that the shooter or any confederates were unlikely to be watching for this opportunity; they'd surely expect Alec to have placed a guard on the kids.

Assuming, of course, that the shot hadn't been intended to kill him instead.

Alec kept his phone sitting on the seat beside him. He checked in with Julia a couple of times. No Matt.

In two-plus hours, he had plenty of time to swing between guilt—he shouldn't have sent Matt to his room like a naughty little boy—and fury at the kid's stupidity as well as his willingness to scare the crap out of his mother. Alec didn't want to think Matt derived pleasure from that aspect of his escape, but had to suspect he did.

He was about to give up the search as a lost cause when his phone rang. Julia.

Pulling to the curb, he snatched up the phone. "He's home?"

"No." Her voice was oddly flat. "Alec, he's been arrested. He was allowed one call from the store where they caught him. Not just shoplifting, but filling his pack with stuff. I spoke to an Officer Wilson."

Jim Wilson was a stolid, competent officer with no apparent ambition to rise beyond patrol. Had Matt told him who his uncle was? Probably.

"In other words, he set out to hit us both where it hurts."

"Yes."

"Do you want to deal with it, or shall I?"

"Which would you prefer?" she asked.

"I may be hard on him, but I'd rather handle it if you'll back me."

Her hesitation was brief. "Go for it. Nothing I've tried has done any good."

"All right. I'll let you know what happens."

The drive to the corner grocery store where Matt was being held didn't take long. A squad car still sat out front, he was glad to see.

When Alec walked in, an older, balding man was behind the counter. Alec nodded and said, "I'm here for the boy."

The guy's expression darkened. "Father?"

"Uncle."

"Officer's got him in the back room."

"Thanks." Alec went down the center aisle and saw a door marked Employees Only. He knocked before going in.

Square, middle-aged, with salt-and-pepper hair, Jim Wilson half sat on a scarred oak desk, one leg braced on the floor. He faced Matt, who looked even smaller than usual, dwarfed by the big, rolling oak desk chair he sat on. His feet didn't come close to touching the floor and his head was hanging until he flashed one look up at Alec. It brimmed with so much anger, Alec could barely see the fear.

Wilson didn't look surprised to see him, which meant Matt had told him Uncle Alec was the police chief. Probably with malicious glee.

"Chief," he said. "Figured you'd want to take the boy home."

"Tell me what happened," Alec said without looking again at Matt.

Wilson did. He'd responded to the usual call. The store owner had seen the kid stuff a bag of candy in his backpack. When he yelled, "Hey!" the boy bolted. The proprietor had been able to grab him before he made it out the door.

"He says when it's something like a candy bar or a soda, he calls the parents. But this time, when he looked, he found the pack almost full. Said he'd had a run of business and hadn't been paying as much attention as he usually would to a lone kid. Take a look." The officer nodded at Matt's pack, sitting on the desk.

Alec stepped closer and did. Hell. It was stuffed. He poked inside. There was a liter of soda, but also a six-pack of beer. Chips, candy bars, a bag of gumdrops and a tin of chewing tobacco. *Really?* he thought in disbelief. Even more disturbing was the package of condoms. Did Matt imagine he had a use for them, or was he intending to give them away in an attempt to win friendship from whatever older boys had given him the marijuana?

Alec grunted. "Take him in. Charge him. He needs to go to juvie."

Matt's head shot up. *"What?"*

"You sure?" Gary Wilson asked.

"I'm sure." Alec gave his nephew a stony look. "I'll see him there in the morning."

As he walked out, Matt was screaming, "You can't do that!" to his back.

JULIA FLINCHED WHEN he got back to her place and told her what he'd done.

"You left him to spend the night in *jail?*"

"Juvenile hall."

"Still." Her voice was smaller.

"We've bailed him out." Alec's jaw flexed. "Over and over. This time, we can't even say he was under the evil influence of a tough crowd of kids. It was a deliberate act. I don't know that he consciously hoped to be caught, but I think that's exactly what part of him wanted to happen. 'See what you made me do?' Another year, he'll be in high school. Once he starts school here and kids get to know him, patterns will be set. He has to suffer consequences before he can decide whether the behavior is worth it. Now is our best chance to stop this before it's too late."

It was a long, long moment before, to his relief, she nodded.

They were in the kitchen. Weren't they always? That was where he most often found her and where she automatically led him when he arrived. In the case of the duplex, it gave them the best chance of going unheard by the kids in their bedrooms.

"Liana?" he asked.

"I called Andrea and asked if Liana could spend the night. She dashed home and packed a bag. I walked her back over there."

All he could think was that *she'd* then been exposed out front, lit by streetlamps in the dusk. But what was he going to do, ask her never to step foot out of the duplex?

He'd thought he was leading these people he loved to safety in Angel Butte, and instead he'd introduced new danger into their lives.

Maybe. There was still the possibility of an idiot with a gun. Alec wished he could believe in that explanation.

"I saved some dinner for you," Julia said, suddenly brisk. "Let me warm it up."

"Did you eat anything?"

Refrigerator door half-open, she went still. "I don't know if I can."

Emotions roiled in his chest. "You eat, I'll eat."

"All right," she said after a minute. Not until she'd reheated the pot roast in the microwave and served them both did she ask whether Matt would have gotten dinner.

Alec wanted to lie to her, but tried not to. "Probably not. He won't have been processed until long after mealtime. I've got to tell you, the idea of his stomach rumbling a little tonight does not fill me with sympathy."

Julia bowed her head enough he couldn't read her expression. "No," she said even more quietly.

They ate in near silence, him keeping a surreptitious eye on her. Had he done the wrong thing tonight, coming down hard on Matt, who was, after all, her son and not his? She'd given her consent—but she hadn't known what he had in mind. Unless Matt was referred for diversion, he would now have a juvenile record. The cop in Alec thought, *It's past time.* That didn't mean the uncle didn't hurt for the eager, happy boy he'd known until this past year and a half. The boy who had briefly reemerged the day at Elk Lake.

"This wouldn't have happened if I hadn't sent

him to his room so damn brusquely," he said into the silence.

"No, it wouldn't." Julia's ready agreement was like a slap. Until her eyes met his and she said more slowly, "Instead, it would have been the next time either of us made him mad or hurt his feelings. Which we wouldn't be able to help doing. His instant rage is not normal. I wish I understood it. What I do know is that we can't, oh, tiptoe around him. I think I've been doing too much of that. I've let him become a bully, in a way. He takes pleasure in terrorizing me, and even Liana sometimes."

She sounded so troubled, Alec desperately wanted to make it all better. The intensely protective part of him didn't like knowing that so far he had failed.

"It would be easier if I didn't know the anger comes from pain," she continued. "But I can't fix that if he won't talk about it."

"No." Alec had to clear his throat. "I keep thinking—"

Eyes steady on his face, she prompted, "You keep thinking?"

"That sooner or later he's going to break and it will all spew out. He's a kid. How long can he hold in whatever's bothering him?"

She gave the saddest laugh he'd ever heard. "It's been a year and a half and counting."

"But he's getting angrier."

"Yes. It's like a poison, spreading through him."

Julia gave herself a little shake. "That's melodramatic. Don't listen to me."

"I always listen to you," he said hoarsely.

She looked at him, startled, and for the longest time they only stared at each other. Alec was suddenly excruciatingly aware that they were alone, as they so seldom were. Not just alone as they'd been that night in the restaurant, but alone as in no kids, no people at the next table, no bustling waiters. Alone as in her bedroom was thirty feet away.

"Julia…" His voice was still…not his usual. A rasp.

He'd swear she hadn't blinked. Her eyes seemed huge, dominating her face, the color never richer or more mysterious.

"What?" she whispered.

He shouldn't do this. Couldn't stop himself. It was as if he'd run to the end of his endurance. Or maybe he'd broken, the way he hoped and feared Matt would.

"Do you think of me as a brother?"

Now she blinked a couple of times, quickly. "A brother? Not…exactly."

"Do you see Josh when you look at me?" His voice turned harsh with this question, one that cut deep for him.

Tiny creases formed on her forehead. "No. I told you. I think I used to. I thought you were like him, but since he died I've been discovering how very different the two of you were."

"Physically?" God, what if she said yes?

"No." Her color had heightened, either at the implications of her admission or at whatever she read on his face. "You have the same coloring, but... no. Never." Her gaze dropped to his hand, fisted tightly on the table, then rose back to his face. She swallowed, but also lifted her chin. "Why are you asking?"

"You haven't guessed?" He was afraid if he moved he'd fall on her like a starving animal. He should have done this more smoothly. *Have an exit strategy, remember?* Instead, God help him, he'd boxed himself in. "I've been afraid I've given myself away a hundred times."

"You...haven't."

He couldn't remember the last breath he'd drawn or that he'd seen her draw. *She* might be afraid to move, too. What did that mean?

"I've wanted to kiss you for a long time." He turned his gaze away for a minute, afraid to see horror on her face. But when he looked back, she was still staring, and her lips had parted slightly.

"Me?" she whispered.

"Yeah. Damn it. I didn't—I *don't*," he corrected himself, "want to jeopardize..." He ran out of words. Groaned.

Her teeth closed briefly on her lower lip. She closed her eyes, then opened them again. "I want to kiss you, too."

"I was determined not to pressure—" Were his ears ringing? "What?"

Suddenly she looked shy. "Don't make me say it again."

Dumbfounded, he was probably gaping. "You've been thinking about me that way?"

She nodded, still shyly.

"Julia." Alec shoved back his chair and stood, holding out a hand to her.

She stared at his hand as if it were a stick of dynamite, but after a moment she rose, too, then hesitantly reached out. His much larger hand engulfed hers, fine-boned and quivering slightly. He gently drew her toward him, his gaze never wavering from hers.

She came to a stop a few inches from him. He gazed down at her face, eyes downcast, the fragile skin of her eyelids increasing his awareness of her vulnerability. He would give anything not to hurt her. Was this a terrible idea? But then her eyes met his again, and he was lost.

He bent his head, slowly, giving her time to back away if she was going to. But to his astonishment, she lifted her hands to his chest and flexed them, just a little, but enough to send a shock of pleasure through him.

"Julia," he said again, low and husky, and touched his lips to hers.

The kiss was as gentle and unthreatening as the one a mother might give a child. He lifted his head to see her holding very still, eyes closed now, face raised as if to the sun. Alec made a sound and covered her mouth with his again, this time more urgently. He licked her lips and they parted. His tongue stroked inside, tasting dinner and her, sliding over her tongue. Distantly, he was aware that she'd risen on tiptoe and her hands had crept up, one to grip his nape. His arms had closed tightly around her. He lifted her higher, finding the perfect fit, reveling in the slender body and subtle curves he'd wanted to touch for so damn long. His hands seemed to have a mind of their own; one tangled in her hair while the other stroked up and down her back. God, he wanted her. It took an extreme effort of will to keep from rocking his hips against hers.

Take it slow. The kiss was a gift, a dream. He didn't want to blow it.

He had no idea how long it lasted, only that he never wanted to let her go. Even so, he eased back on the throttle, gentling his mouth, nibbling on her plump lower lip and touching his tongue to the dip in her upper lip, nuzzling her, finally separating their mouths entirely but resting his forehead against hers.

He felt—God—better than he'd ever felt in his life. But something else threatened his exultation, an emotion he didn't want to acknowledge. Fear of the damage he might have done?

Or shame?

Ridiculous.

"That was a long time coming," he murmured.

Her "Yes-s" came out as a sigh, a breath he felt as much as heard.

Finally, he had to lift his head and look at her. All he could think was how beautiful she was, with her fine-textured skin that didn't seem to tan beyond a hint of gold, a fan of lashes only a little darker than the maple-syrup shade of her hair and those amazing eyes. He'd noticed before how the color seemed to change depending on emotion; when she was angry, the gold predominated. Right now, gold striations only accented a green more vivid than he remembered seeing. She appeared dazed, slumberous.

Unguarded, they stared at each other. He couldn't help wondering what she saw on his face. *Please, not Josh.* Hell, what if she was *comparing* them?

She'd said she was long past that, but…how could she help it, when he was her dead husband's brother?

The disturbing reminder allowed him to step back. Confused emotions formed an indigestible wad in his belly.

"I'm not going to push you." That sounded loud and abrasive. He frowned and lifted a hand to run his knuckles over her cheek. Her skin was so smooth, almost childlike. How she'd kept it that way under the often brutal Southern California sun, he'd never know. "I want you, Julia. It's been killing me to know you and the kids weren't really mine."

Now she looked startled. "You mean—"

"Yeah." His throat closed. A kiss was one thing. Admitting how much he wanted beyond that, that was something else. He did anyway. "I mean."

Her eyes dilated. "All this time?"

He could tell he'd shocked her. "Not while you were married. I never let myself think like that." He hesitated, seeing emotions chasing each other across her face, some that echoed what he was feeling. "Let's go sit down. I think we'd better talk."

"All right."

This time they went to the living room. She chose one end of the sofa and curled her legs under her. Alec sat on the coffee table, close enough that his knees almost bumped hers.

Her expression was fascinated, hopeful and, yeah, perturbed.

Talk, he told himself. No pressure, but he had to get it right.

"I thought Josh was lucky," he said abruptly, "that's all. The past few years, I started feeling angry at him. He didn't treat you the way I thought he should."

"What do you mean?" Her forehead crinkled.

"Some of what you've said. I could see he took you for granted. When I was over, you'd put fantastic food on the table, lay a hand on his shoulder before you sat, as if he was the center of your world, and he hardly acknowledged you. Did he ever do anything romantic for you? Take you out to dinner without the kids, just because? Suggest a weekend in Cabo?"

Lips compressed, she shook her head. "In the early years, we were too poor. And then, well, maybe it went both ways. By the end, I wasn't sure I even liked him." Her eyes had darkened with remembered pain. "Maybe he didn't like me, either."

Alec shook his head, resisting the urge to touch her. "He never said anything like that. My take is, he was happy." Appalled, he wondered what he was doing. Selling Josh as the perfect husband to her? But he wouldn't lie to benefit himself, either. "You know our parents. It wouldn't occur to my father to do anything to let my mother know he appreciates her. Maybe Josh thought that was normal."

"Maybe."

"I need you to know I never thought of you as anything but Josh's wife, until he was gone." He made sure she saw and heard how serious he was. He even thought he was speaking truth.

Thought—but wasn't 100 percent sure. How could he be, when so soon after Josh's funeral he had found himself thinking he didn't have to find a woman who could measure up to Julia—because Julia herself was now available? Had the hunger for her been there all along?

Was that where this curdling sense of shame that was souring his joy—*I kissed her! She let me!* She *kissed* me!—came from? If so—damn it, that was irrational. Josh was long gone. Nothing would bring him back. Was it so wrong to love the same woman his brother had loved?

No. Of course it wasn't. His qualms…were just something he had to get past. He hadn't even known he felt any such thing.

Julia searched his face and finally nodded. "I need you to know *I* never thought of you as anything but a brother-in-law then, too. I'm not sure I was capable of…developing feelings for anyone else. I was too caught up in the kids and a marriage that was disintegrating."

"That bad?"

"Yes. We wouldn't still be married." Julia sounded very certain.

She'd implied as much, but Alec hadn't really thought about the ramifications. How much of a role could he have taken in her life and the lives of the kids if she'd been his brother's ex rather than his widow? Oh, damn—another reason to feel guilty?

He made himself nod in acceptance.

"Something else you need to know. Whatever you decide to do about this—" he gestured, encompassing them both "—about me, won't affect my commitment to you and the kids. Okay?"

After a moment she nodded, but then shook her head. Was that temper glinting in her eyes? "What *I* decide? Anything between us is…is mutual, surely."

"I started this." *I love you.* "I could tell I took you by surprise." She had to decide what she felt for him.

"You know it's more complicated than that. Gee, do I want him or don't I?" She pretended to think. "Yes! I do. But that doesn't mean there aren't other factors to consider. The kids. Especially Matt. What would he think? Your parents, and…" Her voice fell. "What would Josh think?"

That hurt and he couldn't help lashing out. "Your defense against every decision."

"What?" Looking offended, Julia stared at him, chin so high it would have poked him if he'd leaned forward. "I shouldn't take into account what Matt's father would have wanted for him?"

"The man you were ready to divorce?" he said harshly, before his brains kicked in. "Julia…"

She drew herself back, her spine stiffening. "That's a low blow. Maybe this isn't a good time to talk."

"No! Damn it, listen to me." He leaned forward. To his shock, she scrunched against the sofa cushion, almost as if she was afraid of him. He held up both hands, palms out, and very slowly sat back. She looked almost as shocked as he felt. It was a minute before he could speak. "You're right," he made himself say. "I've…let myself feel jealous. I guess I was petty enough to wish it wasn't Josh you wanted with you. But Liana and Matt *are* his kids, not mine." However much he'd been pretending they were.

Her whole body sagged. "No, it's not like that, Alec! I don't want Josh here, not the way you mean.

He never *was* here, when it came to making tough decisions about the kids. Until you, I was always alone in that. It's… I suppose I was protecting myself. When I reminded us both of Josh."

"Protecting yourself?" he echoed, not understanding.

"From feeling too much for you." Her gaze slid momentarily from his. "From counting on you too much. I suppose I was, oh, reminding myself that they aren't your kids, that however nice you were being you didn't have any obligation for the long haul."

"Yeah," he said very softly, "I do." He risked reaching for her hand, moving slowly enough she could evade him if she wanted.

She didn't. She gripped him as if she was afraid he might let go. "Is that what we are?" Julia sounded halting. "An obligation?"

Oh, man. He had the worst case of heartburn he'd ever imagined. "You know better than that."

"Yes." She smiled shakily. "I suppose I do."

"I meant what I said. I *am* in this for the long haul, no matter what happens between us. I don't know how many times I have to repeat myself. There's no obligation on either of our sides. Got that?"

Her head bobbed.

"Okay." He squeezed her hand and let go. With seeming reluctance, she did the same. "We both have a lot to think about." He hesitated, then made himself say it. "Maybe we should leave it at that for now."

Alarm flared in her eyes. "You're sorry—"

"No." He swallowed. "No, Julia. Never. I've wanted more from you for a long time. I still do, but only if you're sure." With a grimace, he added, "I recognize that we have to think about the kids. Although I've got to tell you, Matt's tender feelings are pretty low on my scale of priorities right now."

"He's my son. I can't dismiss him so easily."

Alec made himself smile, if crookedly. Half rising, he bent forward and kissed her cheek, restraining himself with an effort from nuzzling in for more. Standing and looking down at her, he said, "You know I don't mean it, either. I didn't enjoy walking away from him tonight."

Her eyes shimmered and he greatly feared she was battling tears. "I know, Alec. Someday he will, too."

"Maybe." He backed up, bumped the coffee table and stepped sideways. "I'll call you in the morning as soon as I've talked to him."

She stood, too. "Do I... Do we need a lawyer?"

Her faint emphasis on *we* smoothed out some of the rough spots in his mood.

"No. We let the judge slap his hand and, I hope, scare him a little. And we let him know that we're always there for him when he really needs us, but we won't be saving him from trouble he brought on himself anymore. If he's old enough to commit the crime—"

"He's old enough to do the time?" she finished, with a weak attempt at humor.

"Something like that."

"I think you're right. And Matt does love you, you know."

"He's confused, that's all." He didn't dare let himself kiss her again. Or hold her, however lost and vulnerable she appeared right now, arms wrapped around herself. He had to leave while he still could. "Good night, Julia."

Somehow he got himself out the front door and waited until he heard her lock it behind him. Then he scanned the yards and street in each direction, searching for any hint of movement, any wrongness. It was late enough now that most people had gone to bed. He heard a dog barking in the distance, saw the flicker of light around drapes and window blinds that told him some people were still watching TV. The window next door that he knew was Sophie's was dark. Didn't mean the girls were asleep, but Andrea was trying to move them that way.

He crossed the short distance between Julia's door and his own and let himself in. Once inside, he stood in the small living room, looking at nothing, unable to take the simple steps required to get ready for bed.

I kissed her. She kissed me back.

The sweetest kiss of his life. The one he'd waited

for the longest. He wanted it to be that simple. They were both single, free and clear. Alec didn't even think his brother would mind, if he could know. He'd want his family taken care of.

But Julia was right that a relationship between them *wasn't* simple. In fact, it would be complicated as hell. They did have to think about other people. Deal with memories.

Alec was willing to do all that. A ragged sound escaped him, close to a laugh but not quite. All that? He would do anything, overcome any obstacle, to make Julia his.

Julia *and* her kids.

She obviously didn't understand when he told her that what happened was up to her, but he'd meant it. And discovered now how much he hated having no control over her decision.

Eventually he took a shower, bracing his hands on the wall and holding his head under the beat of water as he tried not to remember Matt's face when he realized Uncle Alec wasn't going to rescue him. Remembering instead the crack of gunfire, the moment when he'd plastered Matt to the ground and known this boy might have been the target. *My fault.* The feel of Julia's hands on his body, the dazed wonder in her eyes when he lifted his head and looked down at her.

Hell of a day, he thought, aroused, uneasy and, yeah, still exultant. No wonder sleep was elusive.

CHAPTER NINE

MATT WOULDN'T SO MUCH as meet Julia's eyes when she went to pick him up.

First thing that morning, she'd dropped the girls at the big park by the river where the Parks Department was having a track-and-field day. Julia helped them sign up for the events they wanted to participate in, gave them money to buy lunch at the concession stand and made them promise, cross their hearts and hope to die, that they would not wander away from the group. She spoke to a couple of mothers and a Parks Department employee, all of whom promised to keep an eye on Liana and Sophie.

Then she went home to wait.

It was midmorning before Alec called to say that Matt was being released. As mad as she was at her son, Julia raced out of the house so quickly she realized she'd forgotten her purse and had to go back for it.

At juvenile hall, she had to sign some papers, after which a uniformed guard went to fetch him. Maybe this wasn't jail, but it felt like it. The guards were expressionless, leaving her feeling judged.

And why not? If her son's anger and pain weren't her fault, who was to blame?

She sat in a plastic chair, waiting, her eyes on the door through which the guard had disappeared. It was heavy, closing with the solidity of an air lock. The upper glass inset had wire mesh embedded, making it unbreakable. When the door swung open finally, Julia leaped to her feet, her heart hurting at the sight of Matt, head hanging, grubby clothes the same he'd worn yesterday when he set out for the hike with Alec. The guard's beefy hand rested on Matt's shoulder. Gently, she thought, but it probably didn't feel that way to a boy who'd been arrested yesterday.

She wanted to hold out her arms, but he just stood there, stiff and waiting, still looking at the floor. "Let's go home," she said instead.

He shuffled beside her, not once meeting her eyes. As she unlocked the car, she said, "We need to talk, but let's wait until we get home."

He maintained his stubborn, stony silence.

If only Alec were here, too.

At the duplex, Matt tried to bolt for his bedroom.

Tough love, she reminded herself. *Don't make Alec the bad guy.*

"Matt," she said sharply. "Stop."

He did, with his back to her. She couldn't help noticing how shaggy his hair was, curling on his neck. How skinny that neck was. She had to take it on faith that he would grow into a man's body as impressive as his dad's or Alec's.

"Have you had breakfast?"

He mumbled something.

"You may go take a shower and change into clean clothes. Then come to the kitchen. Understand?"

His shoulders hunched, which she chose to take as acquiescence. He trudged toward his room.

He must have been at least a little chastened, because not long after the shower shut off, he did appear in the kitchen, wearing a pair of the excessively baggy pants and an equally sacky shirt she hated. He looked at her at last, but so expressionlessly it gave her a chill.

"Are you hungry?" she asked.

His mouth lifted in the faintest of sneers.

Tough love.

"Fine," she said. "I'm having lunch. You don't have to. Sit. I'll be with you in a minute."

She made a sandwich she wasn't sure she could choke down, but carried it and a soda to the table, where she chose the seat directly across from him.

"Did Uncle Alec talk to you this morning?"

His thin shoulders lifted in a sulky shrug.

"Answer my question," she snapped, a little shocked at how hard she could sound.

His eyes lifted momentarily to hers, and Julia saw that he was surprised, too.

"Yeah."

"All right." She didn't touch either her drink or

sandwich, only looked at her son. "I don't know if I'm telling you the same thing he did or not, but here goes."

Matt cast her another wary look. She rejoiced in it because his usual defiance and hate had been tempered, even as she grieved the necessity of making her oldest child afraid of her.

"Things will be different around here from now on. You can hate me if you want. I can't stop you. But you *will* do what I tell you to do. You are thirteen years old. I'm your mother, and this is your home, whether you like it or not. You're on restriction for the foreseeable future. There will be no more disappearing. If we do something as a family, you'll participate and you'll be pleasant. You won't talk to me the way you have been. You were caught red-handed stealing from that store. You'll be going to court, and you will be convicted. You *deserve* to be convicted. I'm only sorry I didn't let it happen sooner. I should have told Mr. Santana to call the police instead of going and picking you up myself. In future, the consequences of your behavior will be all yours to bear. Do you understand?"

He plucked at the woven place mat with his fingers and didn't answer.

"Do you understand?"

"Yes!" he yelled, dark eyes flashing.

"Fine." She nodded with outward serenity. "You may go to your room. You may *not* go anywhere else. Is that clear?"

"Yes."

"I can still make you a sandwich if you're hungry."

"I'm not."

Julia didn't believe him, but let him go. Her own stomach was churning and she was repelled by the mere sight of the food on the plate in front of her.

If he hadn't hated her before, he would now.

But what else could I do?

What if he went out the window again? Did they look for him? Report him as a runaway? Wait until he was arrested again and hope he was sentenced to serve time? It was horrible to be encouraged because he looked scared. She wanted to believe Matt wouldn't push them just to find out what they would do.

She sat there long enough, her stomach finally settled and she was able to eat half the sandwich. She wrapped the other half and put it in the refrigerator.

When her phone rang, she leaped for it and fumbled to answer when she saw that Alec was the caller.

"Hey," he said, sounding so gentle her knees wobbled and she sank to the chair. "How did it go?"

"We had a come-to-Jesus talk. He's now sulking in his bedroom. Probably starving, but he's too proud to admit he's hungry."

Alec chuckled. "He and I had one of those talks, too. Mostly one-sided."

"Ours was, too." Already she felt better. "Although—" she lowered her voice and glanced toward Matt's closed bedroom door "—I started wondering what we'd do if he did take off again."

"You get the impression he will?"

She frowned. "Um…maybe not right away. I do think he's frightened."

"Good," Alec said heartlessly. "That's a step in the right direction. Aside from anything else, I hope he stays that way until I get answers on the shooting."

She felt a strange, disorienting blip, like when the DVD player was acting up and the image on the screen momentarily broke up then re-formed. Oh, dear God—had she actually, in all the other stress since, *forgotten* that someone might have tried to kill Matt?

"How will you ever find out?" she asked.

"I'm on my way to talk to Eugene Brock again. I called and told him to have his campaign manager there, as well. I expect them to open a serious investigation."

"Did those deputies even canvass the campers up at the lake to find out if they saw anything?"

"Yeah, and I talked to some of the people myself. Apparently nobody saw anyone with a rifle. Unless the shooter was one of them, it almost had to be the driver of the pickup or SUV that took off right after it happened. The silver one, or maybe it was white," he said drily. "Our witnesses were useless."

It was a moment before she could say anything. "I'm scared, Alec." She didn't say, *I'm just as scared that someone is trying to kill* you.

"I know," he said in that same tender voice. "There's something else, too." Now he sounded... unsettled. "But it'll have to wait. Nothing urgent, I promise. I'm here at the sheriff's department. We can talk tonight, okay?"

"Yes, okay." Nothing urgent, but he hadn't sounded happy about whatever it was he thought she needed to hear. "Dinner?" she asked.

"I'll be there."

That had to be good enough. But now she'd piled on a new worry—*something else.* Just what she needed.

But she had to block out all her worries, tell Matt where she was going and head back over to the park to watch over the girls.

ALEC LEFT THE SHERIFF'S department no more satisfied than he'd been the last time he'd come here, and just as uneasy. Neither Brock nor the campaign manager, a small-time professional who'd last handled the campaign of a state senator from this side of the mountains, seemed like good liars. The manager, a middle-aged guy named Carl Rumsey, had looked especially horrified at Alec's barely veiled accusations. Alec had introduced the possibility that the sheriff's department had some bad apples in it, one of whom had taken the potshot at him.

"You know if he wins, Colin McAllister is going to be taking a hard look at the integrity of every single officer in this department, just as we've been doing in Angel Butte. Gives some of those officers plenty of motive for trying to derail his campaign any way they can." He'd stood up, giving them a cool look. "I can't say I was real impressed with the diligence of the two deputies who responded to the report of the shooting, either."

Brock's face flushed purple, but he didn't defend their conduct, either.

Alec hadn't been at the police station five minutes when Colin appeared in his office. He didn't bother with a hello. "You weren't planning to tell me that somebody followed through on those phone threats?"

Alec tugged to loosen his tie. "I was going to tell you."

His captain listened to a description of events, including Alec's fear that the shots had been aimed at Matt and not him at all. Alec also shared the impressions he'd gained when talking to Sheriff Brock and Carl Rumsey.

"You're convinced they didn't know anything."

"Reluctantly, I am."

Colin grunted, understanding him. "There's nothing uglier than a law-enforcement officer willing to kill an innocent to cover his own ass."

"You've already run across one who was willing to."

Lieutenant Duane Brewer had headed the major-crimes division and had, Alec gathered, been a mentor to Colin. Brewer had been minutes away from killing Colin's wife, Nell, when Colin took him down.

"He was hiding more than minor corruption," Colin pointed out. Which was true enough; in fact, it had turned out that, behind the persona of a dedicated cop, Brewer had hidden the hideous reality that he was a pedophile and serial killer.

Alec leaned back in his desk chair, watching Colin pace. "What about Ronald Floyd? A deputy district attorney who murdered twice to protect his reputation and that nice little second income he was enjoying. *And* was ready to kill again."

Floyd was dead, shot by two responding officers, but he'd left a mess. Alec had no doubt the current district attorney would have liked to bury Floyd's crimes as deep as his body, but the fact that he'd shot the mayor of Angel Butte and been trying to kill Colin's sister made national headlines. There was no keeping any of it quiet. Noah Chandler was still pissed about the story making *People* magazine.

Colin scowled at him. "You've made your point."

"I don't like it any better than you do."

Colin's expression changed. "Heard about your nephew, too."

Alec grunted. "He was out to embarrass me."

"He's the reason you took this job." At Alec's grimace, Colin continued, "You said he's rebellious."

"He took his father's death hard."

They both knew that explanation was inadequate. Colin didn't comment, though, only nodded.

"I don't have any problem with it if you want to back off on your support for me," he said abruptly. "You can't risk the kids."

"Even Julia doesn't want me to do that."

The other man stared at him. "You're not thinking," he said after a minute. "No election is worth risking their lives."

"It's…not that simple." Alec nodded at a chair facing the desk. "Sit down for a minute."

Colin eyed him, then complied.

"If this is really about Brock's reelection campaign, what happens if I back down? Will that knock you down far enough you won't be able to climb back up, given how far away the election is? People in Angel Butte are getting to know me, but they don't vote for the sheriff. Outside the city limits, how many voters know who I am or care? Why is my endorsement so important?"

"You're suggesting if these tactics work, they'll try them again."

"That's what I'm afraid of," Alec said. "If they aren't already."

Colin was shaking his head. "Nobody has scrambled yet to withdraw their support."

"So maybe I'm the test case. After me…what about those county councilmen who've come out in favor of you? Don't they have wives and children, too? Noah's got Cait to worry about. What's his name—the head of the local bar association—he'd be on the list. We could go on. Where would it end?"

"With Eugene Brock sweeping to victory," Colin concluded grimly.

"Who better than me to take a stand?"

"I'm the one who should be taking it."

"By removing yourself from the race? You know none of the other candidates has a prayer. Are you going to give this bastard what he wants?"

"Crap!" Colin finally said explosively.

They stared at each other, two strong men who didn't like admitting there were no good options. Alec felt sure he wasn't the only control freak in this room. Most cops leaned that way, especially ones who rose to running the show.

"All other issues aside," Alec said slowly, "I can't hold the job I do if I ever give in to something like this. We've seen what happens when someone leading a law-enforcement agency lacks a solid sense of integrity. It's not somewhere either of us wants to go."

Colin growled his agreement, slapped a hand hard down on Alec's desk, then pushed himself to his feet. "You'll keep me up-to-date?"

"I will."

Colin nodded and left.

Alone, Alec stared, unseeing, at the closed door. Did he have the right to make this decision, even if Julia had agreed? What if *they*—faceless and malevolent—got to Matt or cheerful, innocent Liana? Or—and the thought filled him with horror—Julia? God knew he'd made morally ambiguous decisions as a police officer. Right and wrong were too often gray. But this… Could he live with himself if taking the high road resulted in one of the people he loved dying?

No.

And yet…

His breath gusted out, and he scrubbed a hand roughly over his face.

If any more bullets flew, they'd damn well better have *his* name on them.

DINNERTIME WAS SO STRAINED, Julia had no appetite, despite the fact that she hadn't eaten much all day. She wasn't alone; Liana, too, was quiet, her face pinched and the assessing glances she sneaked at everyone else anxious. She answered Alec's questions about her day in monosyllables and pushed her food around on her plate just like Julia did.

Matt had nothing at all to say. Alec appeared preoccupied and occasionally lapsed into silences during which she had the feeling he'd forgotten the rest of them were there. And yet, both males at the table were still somehow able to ingest large quantities of food despite their moodiness.

For no known reason, that made her mad. Usually she *liked* feeding them. Tonight, she wanted to dump Matt's dinner on his head, and maybe Alec's, too, just to vent the turmoil that made her feel like a teakettle about to scream.

Admittedly the past two days had been upsetting, but she'd had plenty of upsetting days these past couple of years. She was *used* to them. Worse, she couldn't even identify most of the emotions tumbling inside her, far less understand them.

Well, except one—anger. Most of which was aimed at her son, but she was startled to discover she harbored some for Alec, too. What she couldn't figure out was why she was mad at him. She knew he was doing his best for them. He was the one on *her* side.

But—oh, God—she had to blame *someone* for the disaster their so-hopeful move to small-town America was turning into, didn't she? And tonight she felt petty enough to hold him and his job responsible.

When Julia couldn't stand it for another minute and judged they were all close enough to done anyway, she ordered, "Liana, you clear the table. Matt, your turn to clean the kitchen."

"Why do *I* have to?" he burst out.

She stiffened. Oh, he so shouldn't have chosen now to challenge her. "Did you cook?"

His glare bounced off the force field of her anger.

"Spend the day earning the money that puts food on the table?"

He flicked a glance at his sister. "*She* didn't, either," he said spitefully, then mumbled something.

Julia hid behind a veneer of calm. "What did you say?"

He sneered. "You're not working, either."

Alec had kept silent until then. Now his dark eyes narrowed on Matt's face. "Watch it, buddy."

"It's true!"

Her simmer heading for a full boil, Julia held up a peremptory hand before Alec could say anything.

"And yet somehow I've managed to feed and clothe you and pay for your sports equipment and your allowance and your baseball cards…" Her voice was rising and she didn't care. "And your iPod and your video games and your—"

Alec's hand on her arm stopped her. She was shaking. Even Matt looked alarmed.

"Do what I asked you to do," she snapped and left the table, marching into the living room. Right this minute, she hated that the duplex was so small. She wanted to get a whole lot farther away from her son than the cramped quarters allowed.

Alec followed her.

"You might want to leave me alone right now," she warned him.

He had the gall to laugh. "A smart man would."

The look she turned on him should have seared his flesh. He kept smiling. His eyes were so kind, her anger began to deflate. She huffed and turned away from him, crossing her arms tightly around herself.

"Let's go next door," he suggested.

"Do we dare…?"

"Why not?" He raised his voice. "Kids, your mom and I need to check out the work on my kitchen. We'll be back in a little bit."

There was grumbling, which she was able to ignore.

Some of the tension tightening her skin eased the minute they stepped outside.

"Maybe we should consider adding an interior door between our units," he suggested.

Julia blinked. "That would look a little strange when we start renting the duplexes."

"We'll make it a sturdy one that locks from both sides. It might be a selling point to friends or family who want to be side by side the way we do."

She did like the idea of having him even closer, in a way. "Maybe," she said.

He nodded. "I hope you don't mind me not consulting you, but I hired a fencing company today. They'll be out here to start day after tomorrow. We're going with a solid, six-foot cedar fence. Right now, I won't have the backyard split in half, but we can do that later to get ready for renters."

Julia nodded. "I'll feel better when the kids are outside if they can't be seen from the street."

"That's the idea." He unlocked and let them into his side of the duplex. "Coffee?"

"Not for me."

He gestured at the leather sofa, one of the few pieces of furniture he'd bothered to have moved from his condo in California. After a minute she sat down.

Still on his feet, he asked, "What's up, Julia?"

"What do you mean, what's up? This has not been one of my all-time great weekends."

"No, but I've seen you a hell of a lot calmer when things were as bad or worse." He still sounded patient, but unless she was imagining things, some exasperation was nibbling at that patience. He'd taken up a stance with his back to the brick fireplace.

She opened her mouth to ask what could be worse, but snapped it closed. Being told her husband had died overseas and would be returned to her in a flag-draped coffin, that had been worse.

"I had such hope!" she heard herself burst out. "I can't believe everything's gone so wrong."

"Matt packed whatever was bothering him and brought it along," Alec conceded.

"But somebody shot at him!"

Alec's lashes veiled his eyes. "Is this about my job?"

She tried to stifle her anguish, but it leaked out anyway. "Of course it is! The families of insurance agents or…or doctors or carpenters aren't endangered because of their jobs."

"I take responsibility," he said so woodenly she

couldn't tell if he was hurt, mad or what. "I told you there's more," he added after a distinct pause.

She'd almost been able to block out his mention of *something else*. "What?" she asked, apprehensive.

"I had a call this morning from Pete Henderson of the U.S. attorney's office."

All of her other fears receded, leaving this one standing in stark relief. "In California?"

"Yeah. You know I'm going to be one of the principal witnesses against Roberto Perez."

Her heart drummed. She nodded. Roberto Perez was believed to head a major drug cartel that spanned the Mexican-American border. He was being tried for conspiracy to commit murder, however, not drug trafficking. Alec had been the arresting officer. At the time, he had been a sergeant in Homicide, not yet promoted to lieutenant. The delays had become so chronic, she had almost forgotten Alec's warning when they moved to Oregon that sooner or later he'd have to go back to testify. She knew vaguely there were a couple of other trials he'd have to appear for, but this was the biggie—and the one that scared her. Which was why she'd blocked it out. Without Alec's testimony, Perez might well walk, and he had plenty of resources to eliminate one inconvenient man.

"They're finally dragging the thing to trial. It opens the first week in August. They're guessing they'll need me down there three weeks from Monday."

"Oh, my God," she whispered.

"We knew it was coming." Lines dug into his forehead. "I shouldn't be gone more than a week or two."

"Tell me they'll protect you adequately." She narrowed her eyes at him. "And don't you dare tell me you carry a gun and that's plenty of protection."

His fleeting grin suggested she'd taken the words out of his mouth. "I'll be met at the airport and kept in protective custody. The U.S. attorney's office has wanted Perez for a long time. They value me."

"Good." Protective custody sounded safe, didn't it? Except— Her breath came short. "Oh, my God! What if someone is trying to kill you *now,* before you can be hustled away down there?"

He didn't so much as move and did that veiled-eye thing again. "The thought has crossed my mind."

Julia stared at him, aghast. "And you didn't say anything?"

"Seems more logical that the shots went with the phoned-in threats."

"But…" She had to think about that. "Could those be, I don't know, a misdirection? You said Sheriff Brock seemed genuinely bewildered."

"That possibility, too, has occurred to me," he admitted. "So far, I've gone with the odds."

"The odds are Roberto Perez wants you dead!"

"Maybe." He waggled a hand. "Maybe not. If

I were assassinated right now, you think the FBI
and damn near every other federal law-enforcement
agency wouldn't be on him and his outfit like stink
on shit?" He grimaced. "Sorry. I don't have to be
crude."

Julia shook her head. She didn't care about crude.
"But you'd still be dead, and from what you've said,
he'd likely get off."

"Temporarily." He frowned at her. "Damn it,
Julia, don't look at me like that. What I think is
if Perez was behind this, I'd be dead. People who
work for him go for quick and dirty. Car bombs." He
shrugged. "This duplex isn't impregnable. Someone
could walk in in the middle of the night and put a
bullet in my head before I so much as opened my
eyes. What's happening doesn't feel professional to
me. That's why I'm leaning toward believing it's got
to do with the election and not the trial."

How could he sound so matter-of-fact when he
was talking about his own death? Julia found she
was shaking. *Not Alec. Please, not Alec.*

His expression changed. "Julia?"

Her fingernails bit into her palms. "You're scar-
ing me even more."

"Oh, damn." He crossed the room in a couple of
strides and crouched in front of her. Taking both
her fisted hands in his, he squeezed. "I'm sorry. I
wasn't thinking. God, I'm sorry."

I love him. The desperate thought was followed
by another. *He's not a* safe *man to love.* How could

she possibly have done this to herself a second time? He wasn't Josh, he wasn't *like* Josh, but Alec would never compromise to protect himself, either.

"I wish you didn't have to go."

"Yeah. I don't like leaving you and the kids." Those dark eyes wouldn't let her look away. "But you know I have to do this."

Her head bobbed. She did know. Because she loved him, she would never ask him to compromise his integrity. Catch-22.

"Have you told anyone here about the trial?"

"In a general way, when I hired on. I haven't told them the date has been set."

She gripped his hands. "You should have everyone in your department watching out for you. They need to know."

Again the lines in his face seemed to deepen, giving her an idea what he'd look like in ten years. *If he survives that long.* "You're right," he said finally, slowly. "I'm used to keeping my own counsel. But this is a case where more eyes are better."

"Promise."

"I promise."

"I can't lose you," she said, a catch in her voice.

"Julia." He said her name again, husky and raw, then stood, drawing her to her feet.

She flung her arms around his neck and met his kiss with all the passion and fear and desperation in her.

CHAPTER TEN

FROM THE MOMENT their mouths touched, Alec knew only sensation and Julia. He was stunned to awareness that he'd held back the first time he kissed her; this time he couldn't, not after the way she had flung herself at him. The other kiss had been a too-brief sample, a teaser. *This* was the real thing.

After all the long months of believing he would have to live his life loving her but unable to touch, having her in his arms like this damn near broke him. He lifted her against him, tried to meld her petite, supple body into his even as he devoured her mouth. The astonishing part was that she kissed him back with as much fervor, as though she was as starved as he was. Alec's hands were clumsy; one of hers dived into his short hair and, in holding on, pulled painfully. Their tongues tangled, their teeth bumped and, too quickly, his body was on the verge of combustion.

Julia made little throaty sounds that drove him to greater desperation. Twice he drew back only long enough for each of them to suck in air before he captured her mouth again, or let her capture his, he didn't know which.

Her hair, rich, smooth silk, flowed through his fingers as he learned the shape of her skull. Her breasts had to be flattened against his chest, the way they strained together. There was nothing gentle and quiescent in the way she kissed him. Her tongue stroked his, her teeth grazed his lip, her hips rocked with his.

Alec needed to be closer, to get inside her, as he'd never needed anything in his life. One hand had already found its way beneath her thin cotton shirt and stroked and kneaded her back, taut muscles and the delicate knobs of her spine. He wanted to enclose her breast but couldn't make himself back off far enough to squeeze his hand between them.

He lifted her, laid her back on the sofa. The glimpse he had of her face was intoxicating, the witchy swirl of gold and green in heavy-lidded eyes, lips swollen and damp from their kisses, color high over her beautiful cheekbones. Her head dropped back over his forearm, exposing the long, pure line of her throat. He groaned and first licked and then nipped, his teeth closing finally on the nerves and tendons between neck and shoulder.

Her back arched. She whispered his name.

The doorbell rang.

Alec already hated the damn doorbell, a trilling series of notes. This had him swearing viciously under his breath. His knee was planted on the cushion and his whole body ached to lower itself onto Julia, to wrap her long legs around his hips, to grind himself against her until he could somehow get their clothing out of the way.

The doorbell rang a second time.

Julia went stiff beneath him. "The kids!"

The first semirational thought he had was *Thank God we haven't put in a connecting door yet.* One that had been standing unlocked.

So aroused he was in pain, he levered himself off her and got to his feet, holding out a hand for her.

"Just a minute," he called, then took a good look at her.

"You'd better, uh, get in the bathroom and pull yourself together." His voice sounded—unnatural. Raspy. He cleared his throat.

She flinched and lifted her hands to her hair, in glorious disarray from his hands. He saw shock in her eyes. "Oh, no!" she whispered and fled.

Oh, no? Did she *regret* that kiss? Alec wouldn't let himself believe it. To be so powerful, it had to have been mutual. He couldn't have deluded himself into believing she wanted him as much as he wanted her.

Whoever was outside knocked.

Crap. He ran his fingers through his hair, hoping it wasn't standing in spikes, and started for the door. He willed his erection to subside. Liana wouldn't notice it, he convinced himself, but Matt might.

Which kid had come peremptorily calling? Or—damn—was this someone else altogether?

Not the bad guys—they wouldn't raise such a racket.

By long habit Alec looked through the peephole and saw the top of a head crowned by a high ponytail wrapped in some kind of neon pink elastic.

Liana, then.

He opened the door, keeping partially behind it. "Hey. You couldn't wait for your mom to come home?"

Her face was teary. "Why didn't you open the door? I waited and waited."

Because I was this *close to getting your mom naked.*

"We were talking." He nodded toward the short hall leading to the bedrooms and bath. The layout of his side of the duplex was identical to hers except in reverse, allowing their kitchens to back on each other. "Your mom's in the bathroom. Come on in."

She sniffed pathetically. "Matt's being *mean* to me."

Alec had to shake his head slightly, struggling to shift gears. From high emotion to patting a ten-year-old girl's hand.

Despite his dazed state, asking was automatic. "Mean, how?"

He'd had to fall in love with a woman who had two kids.

He loved them, too.

Most of the time.

"He says I act like I'm five years old and I still play with dolls and everyone at school will think I'm a *baby*." Her lower lip thrust out, making her look undeniably childish. Which Alec wasn't going to tell her.

Inwardly, he sighed. His body had conceded defeat. His tension hadn't subsided, though; he was too worried about what expression he'd see on Julia's face when she had to look at him after emerging from hiding.

He shook his head at her daughter. "You know he just likes to give you a bad time. Matt's probably worried because *he* doesn't look his age, and that's a bigger deal for a boy in eighth grade."

"Yes, it is." Julia's warm, reassuring voice came from behind him.

Bracing himself, he turned slowly. Her color was still high but she'd combed her hair so that it was smooth and glossy, tucked behind her ears. A memory of his teeth closing on one of those earlobes flickered. *Damn it*. Her eyes slid from meeting his, but he thought she looked shy, not appalled.

"Sophie's lucky!" Liana declared mulishly. "I wish *I* didn't have a brother."

"Seems to me you've had good times together," Alec remarked, going for mild. He wasn't about to categorically dismiss her feelings the way adults had a habit of doing. Matt had given her plenty of reason to wish she was an only kid. And, as big a

shit as Matt was being these days, no one in his
family was feeling real fond of him at the moment.

"And someday you'll be glad you have him, even
if it isn't until you're both adults." Julia hugged and
kissed her. "I promise."

Liana's disbelieving snort amused Alec, an emotion he was careful to hide.

"If you're so glad you have a brother," she challenged her mother, "how come we never see Uncle
Ray?"

Julia's eyes finally met the laughter in Alec's. Her
scowl was quelling. "Because he's ten years older
than me. We never did play together. By the time
I was a teenager, he was long married and away
from home. I suspect, when the time comes that
your grandparents are old enough that Ray and I
have to be making decisions about things like nurs-
ing homes, I'll be really glad I don't have to do it
all alone."

"Oh." Liana's shoulders slumped.

"Next time Matt says things like that," Julia suggested, "tell him you don't care what he thinks. And
that it doesn't matter anyway, because you're only
ten years old, *not* thirteen."

Alec tweaked her ponytail, darker than her
mom's hair. "Or you could get nasty and suggest he
worry about what the other kids are going to think
about *him*. You could say maybe in L.A. some of
the kids thought those baggy pants were cool, but
here they look silly."

"Yeah!" she declared.

Julia appeared undecided about whether going on the attack was a good idea. Alec had a feeling that Matt might pay more attention to his sister's opinion of his wardrobe than he would his mother's or uncle's. Especially if she claimed to have overheard some *older* girls saying…

"Can I stay here?" Liana asked. "Until you go back, Mom?"

Now Julia's eyes did meet Alec's. For a moment she let him see frustration to match his. He felt a jolt of renewed lust that had him gritting his teeth.

"You need me?" he asked, then had to clear his throat.

"Yes," she said as huskily. Their eyes held one conversation while Liana heard another. Then she smiled at her daughter while saying to Alec, "But not right now. Enjoy your peace."

He nodded. She wasn't ready yet to know that life on his side of the duplex was lonely, not peaceful. That, chaos, interruptions, sexual frustration and all, he wanted his home to be with her.

"Kitchen's looking good," he added, both for Liana's sake and because he thought Julia needed to hear it. What was more, it was true. He liked the cabinets, which had already been installed. Apparently, tearing out the old cabinets had revealed no rot, wet or dry. Even so, according to Julia the speed it had happened was akin to an emu leaping into the sky and flying.

After she and Liana left, Alec wandered back into the kitchen. A sample of what would be the countertop lay across an open drawer. It was a relatively inexpensive Formica, but he thought it was going to look good. The gray-blue was flecked with cream and navy and tan and rust, colors he vaguely recalled Julia saying she intended to "pick up" from the vinyl flooring he'd chosen. Boxes of four-inch ceramic tiles sat on the plywood floor, waiting to be installed on the wall behind the counter. Most of the ones he could see were a coordinating gray-blue, but he'd noticed one box that held navy blue ones instead. He couldn't imagine what the result would be, but had confidence in Julia's taste.

The plumbing seemed to already be in place, too, encouraging him to hope he wouldn't have to live with the disorder for long. Not that he wanted to cook, but he was looking forward to seeing Julia putting dinner together in his kitchen instead of hers.

He was pleased with the cool, neutral colors in here, which she had approved because they could be warmed—her word—with a splash of rust. *Splash* was her word, too. Alec was willing to bet, though, that Julia would use more vibrant colors in *her* kitchen and that he might be envious in the end.

If they got married, they could buy a house and start all over. He had a feeling she wouldn't mind. He'd live happily with red and fiery yellow and, hell, pink if she wanted.

His smile died as he returned to the living room, flipped through a TV schedule and glanced without interest at the book he was currently reading.

Another evening alone to fill.

As SHE WENT out one front door and in the other, Julia was buzzing, aroused, jittery and horrified at how close she and Alec had come to getting caught. Acting normal was a struggle. Thank goodness Matt had already shut himself in his bedroom. On the plus side, the kitchen was more or less clean. She rapped on his door to be sure he really was there and was answered with a surly "What do you want?"

"Letting you know I'm home," she said and went away.

Liana wanted to watch TV, a rerun of a silly family comedy. The laugh track alone sounded like fingernails on a blackboard to Julia. To escape, she had only a few choices—her bedroom, the kitchen or outside. Night was falling. What was she going to do outside? Sit on the too-small concrete patio in back and wait for bats to dart past? Since Matt and Alec had been shot at, she felt exposed every time she was outdoors. No, even if she left the light off, sitting outside wouldn't be soothing.

She wanted quite desperately to return next door, to Alec. Instead, Julia had to settle for her kitchen, where she took out the counter, tile and flooring samples she had checked out of home-improvement stores. She'd mostly made up her mind, but if either of the kids checked on her, she'd look occupied.

Finally alone, she thought, *Oh, my God.* She and Alec had come so close. One minute she'd been mad to the point of feeling steam coming out of her ears, the next she had wanted him as she'd never wanted anything or anyone in her life.

Naturally, that made her feel guilty. She'd be happier to believe she had truly loved Josh at the beginning.

The trouble was, she'd been so young. Too young. The only sexual comparisons she'd had were a few fumbling experiences in college. Her physical response to Josh had seemed marvelous to her at the time. It was possible he'd just had a better idea what he was doing than the boys who'd given her her limited experience. Now—well, now it was hard even to remember what she'd felt at the beginning.

Guilt came in infinite shades, she'd discovered. What was it Alec had said? That Matt had packed all his emotions and brought them along? Well, she had, too. Only…hers seemed to be stretching and growing, leaving less and less room for her heart and lungs to do their thing.

Because of how I feel about Alec.

Yes, but not entirely, she decided, frowning at an orange tile that was definitely on the discard pile. She was a mother; mothers felt responsible when anything at all went wrong for their kids. *I wasn't paying enough attention. I didn't say the right thing.*

If only I'd... It has to be my fault. The loop played through her head every night.

It was the Josh part she struggled with now. What if that last fight had left him too distracted to do his job safely? She'd give anything if there was some way to *know*.

Or...what if, in a way, he'd committed suicide because she'd told him he wasn't welcome at home?

No, she knew better than that. Josh had loved his kids, sure, but he had seen them only in spurts anyway. He was already the next best thing to a weekend father. Increasingly, Julia knew he hadn't loved her very deeply at all. What remained of their marriage had been...habit, on both their parts.

And really, he wasn't the kind of man who would ever have self-destructive inclinations. She couldn't imagine it.

Distraction, though, that might be possible.

But Alec was right that she couldn't have stayed married forever just so she didn't upset Josh on the chance he might be sent immediately out on a mission. She'd seen plenty of divorces among navy couples she and Josh knew. They went on the same way divorced couples did in civilian life, resenting child support, bitching to friends, trading kids back and forth, dating and sometimes remarrying.

Not my fault.

So why did it feel as though it was?

Timing. It was all timing. She'd laid down her ultimatum—and Josh had died.

Julia pushed aside the samples and put her elbows on the table. Finally, finally, she crept her way to her greatest fear—that she had already been attracted to Alec *before* she made that ultimatum. He insisted he hadn't thought of her that way, and she was certain she hadn't consciously thought of him as a man to whom she was attracted…but she had liked and appreciated him and looked forward eagerly to his visits.

What if she'd already been falling in love with her husband's brother?

She sat without moving, frozen, for too long. Until the burst of a soundtrack from the living room made her realize how late it had gotten, and she became Mom again, insisting the TV be turned off before Liana could get engrossed in the next show, one Julia didn't like her watching anyway.

There was still light under Matt's door when she went to bed herself.

AFTER JULIA AND LIANA left, Alec hadn't let boredom set in. He'd been needing to make time to reread his own notes in preparation for the long-awaited trial in Los Angeles, so why not take advantage of the empty hours stretching between now and bedtime?

The notes were from the investigation into the stabbing death of one Stanley, aka Skip, Brogan, simultaneously a midlevel drug runner and a police informant.

Roughly three years ago, Skip had let his long-time police contact—Alec—know that he'd overheard some juicy stuff about the big guy, Perez himself, but before they could meet to talk, Skip had been found in an alley with his throat slit.

Luck had produced an unusually observant witness who'd seen two men go into the alley and only one emerge. The witness was a then-fifteen-year-old runaway who had been huddled behind a Dumpster at the head of the alley. After the arrest, she had not only picked the killer out of a lineup, she had bravely agreed to testify at his trial. A known hit man for the cartel, Nolberto Rodriguez had cut a deal and agreed to testify that Perez had personally ordered him to take care of Skip Brogan. Unfortunately, despite the fact that Rodriguez had been moved secretly and under a new name to an Arizona prison, he'd still ended up dead, a crude handmade knife thrust with surgical precision between his ribs and into his heart.

The runaway was eighteen now and still living with the police officer and his wife who'd taken her in initially as a foster child. She had overheard Rodriguez tell Brogan that "Roberto says you have a big mouth and it's time to shut it." So far, Perez hadn't found her. Alec had been told the police officer had quietly adopted her and that using her adoptive name she would be leaving in August to attend Vassar in Poughkeepsie, New York. The skinny, scared teenager had come a long way. Alec almost wished she'd refused to testify. If she was killed and all that promise brought to an end, he'd be ready to kill Roberto Perez with his own two hands.

He spent the next hour reading and rereading notes he already remembered better than he did most from investigations he'd conducted that long ago. Still, the review brought back the sequence of interviews. He closed his eyes and recalled faces, smells, impressions. This was one conviction he wanted fiercely.

Eventually closing his laptop, which held the scanned pages of notes, his own and other people's, as well as depositions and signed witness statements, Alec brooded about more immediate problems. Who was responsible for the two phone threats and the gunshots?

Feet stacked on the coffee table, he tried turning everything he knew on end, but came back to the same answer: he didn't know.

What he did know was that Julia was right—he should be taking advantage of the police force of nearly a hundred men and women he commanded. He'd gained enough respect for Colin McAllister that he should long since have talked to him.

Yes, after taking the job in Angel Butte he'd initially had to hold himself aloof. McAllister and Noah Chandler had resented his hiring, and they weren't alone. But he'd passed that point ages ago without noticing. Although Alec boggled a little at the idea, he even thought it was possible he could become friends with the two men. They were both smart, tough and determined. Men he wouldn't mind having at his back.

His own laugh surprised him. Four months ago, he would have said that Colin and Noah were the two last men in the world he could trust. He shook his head. Live and learn.

And, hey, he had a feeling Julia would give him hell if he didn't follow orders.

His amusement didn't last long, not when he remembered her fear. But, in another way, the fear, along with tonight's kiss, did give him hope that she felt more for him than gratitude and an unwilling attraction. That there might be real hope.

MAYOR CHANDLER WAS the last to arrive, followed by Alec's PA, who handed out coffee for everyone.

He, Colin and Brian Cooper were already seated in the conference area to one side of Alec's office. Noah accepted his coffee with thanks to Robin and sat in an armchair with a grunt. Alec was reminded that he'd come damn close to dying not that long ago.

"How was the honeymoon?" he asked. This was the first time he'd seen Noah since the wedding.

Who knew that hard, ugly face was capable of softening like that?

"Good." Noah looked bemused. "Never saw myself as the lying-around-on-a-Caribbean-beach type, but I gotta say, I wasn't real eager to get back to work." He grinned wickedly at Colin, who was twitching a little. "We spent some time in our hotel room, too."

"You know I don't want to hear about you sleeping with my sister."

"It's legit now," Noah said cheerfully. "Even George Miller is satisfied."

"George Miller is never satisfied," Colin grumbled.

George Miller was nobody's favorite city council member.

"Speaking of." Noah turned penetrating blue eyes on Alec. "You ready for the council meeting?"

"Damn straight. In fact, we'll have the proposal and supporting information emailed to every city council member in the next day or two. You, too."

"It makes for good reading," Brian Cooper said, smiling with satisfaction. He'd been responsible for producing a goodly share of the relevant statistics about how understaffed the Angel Butte P.D. had become since the annexation. Alec had packed the pages with response times, citizen complaints, the necessity and risks of sending out inexperienced officers alone on patrol. Primed by Colin, Alec had been able to pull the numbers of experienced officers who'd quit in frustration and found jobs elsewhere, exacerbating the problems in Angel Butte. He had highlighted selective quotes from the exit interviews.

His goal was to hit the city council so hard in his

request for increased manpower, they'd go down at the first blow.

He'd already roughed out his talk, but with so many other distractions he was glad he still had time to polish it. And, while he might feel like an idiot, he intended to practice the speech aloud half a dozen times before the council meeting Tuesday.

Noah took a swallow of his coffee. "That what you want to talk to us about?" he asked.

"No. This is something else." He hesitated. "You all remember the threatening phone calls I received."

There were nods all around.

"While you were away on your honeymoon," he told Noah, "someone took some potshots at my nephew and me." He described the circumstances and the follow-up talk he'd had with the county sheriff and his campaign manager.

Colin's eyes had narrowed slightly. He hadn't altered his relaxed position, one ankle lying over the other knee, but Alec suspected he was bracing himself for an unwelcome announcement—say, that Alec had decided after all to withdraw his public support.

"There's something I haven't told you," Alec said abruptly. "Any of you."

They did know he was obligated to return to L.A. a few times to testify in court. But he hadn't mentioned the scale of the Perez trial.

He described the details of the investigation and

the prosecution's case, fresh in his mind now after his review. "Security will be tight once I arrive in L.A.," he said. "It already is for the other witnesses, of course. I'm in a different position than they are. I declined to go into hiding. Time has rolled on by. No rumors surfaced that I had a target on my back. I can't say it hasn't crossed my mind a few times."

All three men watched him unblinkingly.

He continued more slowly. "These threats sounded straightforward enough, so I mostly took them at face value. Why not?"

Colin stirred. "Because if you're blown up or shot dead in the weeks leading up to the trial, investigators were bound to look straight at Roberto Perez's organization. Unless, of course, they'd managed to set up a fall guy. Brock."

Alec shrugged provisional agreement. "That possibility has been at the back of my mind. If this is a case of misdirection, it suggests involvement by someone local who knows enough to make it believable, which is one reason I still think the Perez connection is unlikely. I've got to say, though, my talk with Eugene Brock and the campaign manager shook me a little. Their shock looked genuine."

"Perez is out on bail, I presume?" Noah asked.

"Unfortunately."

"How big is his organization?" Lines furrowed Noah's forehead. "Any chance the tentacles reach as far as the Northwest?"

Alec grunted at the unpleasant surmise. "A lot

of the product arriving in the area is coming from Latin America. We know that." He glanced at Colin. "Correct me if I'm wrong, but my sense is, it's mostly locals who have been arrested."

"A few pilots from out of the area. Otherwise, that's true."

"And yet," Brian reminded them, "the kind of money it took to buy Bystrom, Ronald Floyd and a bunch of cops, that's not local."

"No, damn it," Colin agreed.

"Shit," Noah said intensely.

"I guess what I'm asking is that you be aware of my problem," Alec said slowly. "Brian, I'd appreciate increased patrols by my house. I'm worried most about Julia and the kids."

"You considered sending them on vacation?" Noah asked. "Say, Hawaii?"

"It's crossed my mind. Trouble is, we all know disappearing effectively isn't easy. You can't get on an airplane without showing ID, for example. I could have someone else rent a house in Portland or Seattle…" He frowned, thinking about it. "A possible snag is that, at this point, I'm not sure I can trust Matt not to open his big mouth. He might do it just to be hurtful." It stung having to admit that. "Then there's the fact that, once they're out there, they'd be completely isolated. Here, there's some protection."

"That's a big plus," Colin said. "When we knew

someone was after Nell, we considered the same options. Ditto, later, with Cait."

Noah nodded his agreement.

"Here, you have your own police force as backup," Colin continued.

Noah grimaced. "Nothing is foolproof. We came close to losing both Nell and Cait. The kids make you even more vulnerable."

"Jane Vahalik knows everyone on the drug interdiction task force." Obviously, Colin had already been thinking. "I can set her to making phone calls, see if there's ever been a hint of a connection with this Perez's outfit."

Alec felt—not relief, that would have been premature, but something close. "I'll share everything I know about it. Names, known operations."

They asked about Matt: How did Alec intend to keep him corralled? Was the opening day for the trial certain? Any doubt about when his own testimony would be required?

"At least we have a limited time frame," Colin said. "Keep Alec's family safe for four to five weeks. If the motive has to do with the election, that's different."

"But I'd take it a lot less seriously," Alec said.

"I'm not so sure about that." Unexpectedly, it was Brian Cooper who disagreed. "Let's not rule out that possibility. Dirty officers in the sheriff's department have plenty of motive for wanting to keep Colin from taking the reins from Brock. Yeah, the chief here seems like a strange target, but what if he's right that he's just a test case? Scare him into compliance, move on to other local bigwigs."

Alec nodded. "I agree. Worst option, though, is something that we haven't even thought of."

For now, they had a plan, they agreed at last: try to determine if there was a local connection to Perez and his organization, and wrap Julia and the kids in as much security as possible.

Alec thanked them, trying not to sound embarrassingly fervent. Julia, he thought, had been right. To a man, they hadn't hesitated to offer ideas and support. More, they'd used words like *we* and *us*.

One for all and all for one. Wasn't that from Alexandre Dumas's *The Three Musketeers?* Yeah, he thought so. In one way it was a reassuring motto. In another way, not so much, since it suggested any one could be sacrificed for the good of all. Who would that be? The bright teenage girl who was so bravely willing to testify against Roberto Perez? Julia? God, one of the kids? How about somebody who worked for Alec?

He'd always taken for granted his own willingness to give his life to save another, just as he imagined Josh had. What hit him suddenly, disconcerting him, was the realization that now he wanted to live with a piercing hunger he had never felt before. He finally had real hope for the kind of future that had once seemed illusory, and, damn, he wanted it.

Hope and self-sacrifice didn't sit well together.

Alec made a rough sound, going back to his desk after showing the men out. He was getting maudlin, and that was something he couldn't afford.

A stray thought hit him. Maybe Josh couldn't have done the job he did if he let himself care too much about the people he left behind, over and over.

Alec's jaw tightened. Yeah, so Josh had made a choice—but it wasn't one Alec would or could ever have made. Did that mean he was a weaker man than his brother? He didn't know, but he wouldn't change who he was even if he knew the answer.

CHAPTER ELEVEN

WHEN HE GOT HOME Wednesday after work, Alec checked out the progress on the backyard fence and was pleased. Julia stepped out, too.

"They say they'll be done by the end of the week."

"The hard part is done." Workers had sunk the posts in concrete that already seemed to have set. Some of the crosspieces were in place. Pallets of six-foot cedar boards lay ready. There would be a gate on each side of the duplex. "We need to do some landscaping."

"We could at least get trees and a few shrubs in and established before the cold weather hits," Julia agreed, looking around. "I can't believe no one ever planted so much as a tree back here."

"If the landlord didn't, why would a renter bother?" Somehow the fencing emphasized the starkness of grass turned brown from summer heat. "We could either enlarge these patios or have decks built, too."

She smiled at him. "Not a do-it-yourself guy, huh?"

"I could do it in theory. Josh and I helped Dad

build that deck off the back of my parents' house. I'd rather take Matt kayaking."

"Do you dare?"

"I haven't decided. It depends where we go, I guess. The week is up, though. I thought I'd take him shopping for a couple of kayaks tomorrow, if that's okay with you."

"That would be fabulous." She eyed him. "It would be even better if you'd consider a little, er…"

He cringed. "Not clothes." Grinning, he dodged the sharp point of her elbow.

"You could disguise it by buying some hiking boots and, well…"

"Clothes."

She was still laughing at his resigned tone when the sound of the timer summoned them back in.

Once they were all seated at the dinner table and dishing up, Julia said almost casually, "I might have a possibility of a job."

Liana looked alarmed, Alec surprised. Even Matt quit shoveling food in momentarily, the fork halfway to his mouth. *He* probably wished she would go to work and leave him unsupervised all day.

Fat chance, she thought ungraciously.

"I didn't know you were looking yet," Alec said slowly, gaze on her face.

"This kind of came up out of the blue," she explained. "It's…well, you know how much I enjoy remodeling."

"Yeah." He glanced away. "Matt, please pass the biscuits."

Matt instead grabbed one from the basket and tossed it. Alec snatched it one-handed from the air and, without comment, split the sourdough biscuit open and began buttering it.

Eyes on her son, Julia opened her mouth, then closed it. Matt might have done that to be funny rather than snotty. And, face it, table manners were the least of her concern right now.

"Go on," Alec prodded her.

She told them that she'd borrowed tile samples from a store downtown that specialized in tile, blinds, flooring materials and wallpaper. "Naturally, their prices are higher than for the more basic materials at one of the big home-improvement stores, but the selection is way better, the quality higher and the staff is knowledgeable. They offer design services, too. I've been getting to know the woman who owns the store. I showed her pictures on my phone of our last house, plus what I'm doing to the two kitchens here in the duplex. I guess she liked what she saw, because she mentioned they're looking for someone else. It would mean working the sales floor, but also going out to look at people's homes, measure for blinds and so on, and help the homeowners come up with plans. I think I'd really enjoy the work."

Alec's smile grew as she talked. "Funny," he said,

"I'd been thinking of suggesting something like that. You talking with Hailey made me wonder if you might want to consider becoming a chef, but that has some drawbacks."

She made a face. "You think? Like really terrible hours?"

Liana asked what that meant, and Julia explained that most chefs worked lunch through dinner, which meant until a restaurant closed for the evening. "I suppose a pastry chef might not keep those hours, but they probably start at the crack of dawn instead. And...oh, I enjoy cooking for family, but I'm really not dedicated enough to do it as work. Besides, I'd have to get a lot more training before I could get any kind of decent cooking job."

"So—" Alec's gaze rested briefly on Matt "—is this a now-or-never opportunity?"

Realizing that Liana was listening anxiously, Julia smiled reassurance. "No. The woman's name is Clio Sinclair. She sounded like they could be really flexible. Late summer is a fairly slow time for them, except for work-through builders. Full-time residents are going on camping weekends, taking vacations, thinking about back to school if they have kids. They're not remodeling. According to her, summer people tend to have work done in the late spring or early summer, people with winter cabins in the fall. She implied I could cut back to part-time during school vacations, that kind of thing. She said if I'm interested we could talk."

"Talk," Alec said without hesitation. "It sounds perfect."

"I've thought about going back to school," she said tentatively.

"To do what?"

She laughed. "I have no idea. To figure out what I want to do with the rest of my life?"

His grin held both warmth and amusement. "You can do that, too, you know."

"Eventually."

"Who'd *want* to go to school?" Matt muttered.

Alec raised his eyebrows. "College can be an amazing experience. Exploring what interests you most. Hang on and you'll get there."

Predictably, Matt sneered. Because he wasn't looking, Julia rolled her eyes. Alec suppressed a smile she saw anyway.

"Okay, you've convinced me," she decided. "Or I've convinced myself. I'll at least have a serious talk with Clio. But I definitely don't want to start work until September."

Matt whined when once again she told the two kids to clean the kitchen, but Julia just said, "Drop it," and went to the living room.

"Getting tough there, lady," Alec said from right behind her.

She crossed her arms and faced him. She felt too restless to sit. "Did you talk to Colin?"

"And Brian and Noah." He told her about the discussion.

Listening, Julia had a suspicion he was holding back, but decided not to challenge him. At least he hadn't insisted on doing it alone.

"It felt good," he admitted. His mouth curved. "You were right. I was wrong."

"I'm glad," she said, "and I mean for you." She wrinkled her nose. "Not just because I like being right."

He chuckled, but sobered quickly. "What did Matt do all day?" he asked, voice low.

"Stayed in his room. I don't know. I wish I had chores I could insist on, but what?"

He shook his head. "I thought about having him take over mowing the lawn, but that would have him too exposed right now. The idea of him just lying in his bedroom all day brooding makes me uneasy, though."

"Me, too."

"Make him go with you when you take the girls for their swim lessons or do errands," he suggested.

"He'll hate it."

After a moment, Alec said, "A couple more weeks."

Her crossed arms tightened. "Longer than that."

He grimaced agreement. He wouldn't even be leaving for L.A. until something like the fourth or fifth of August, and then be there who knew how long. She imagined Matt as a seething ocean behind a crumbling seawall. She was running around heaving sandbags into place to shore up an inadequate defense. How could she hold it together?

Caught in the tension between her and Alec, she found it easy to tune out the background bickering from the kitchen and the occasional clatter that, in another mood, might have made her wince.

"I don't suppose you'll stay with your parents when you're down there," Julia said almost at random.

Alec shook his head. "No, I'll be spirited away somewhere behind armed guards. I probably won't even be allowed to tell you where I'm staying."

The idea of him simply disappearing like that filled her with dread. It wasn't only fear because she might need him and he wouldn't be here. She struggled to understand herself, not wanting Alec, watching her with those too-perceptive brown eyes, to be able to read her turmoil. Oh, Lord, she realized—he would be disappearing the same way Josh had. While Alec was gone, she would live with the same kind of strain she'd grown to hate.

Her throat closed. This might be worse. *Would* be worse. With Josh, his comings and goings had become routine—until he died during one of those disappearances—whereas Alec had become such a steady part of her life and the kids' lives she had begun to believe he would always be there. But also—the knowledge, painfully sharp, rushed over her—she loved Alec as she'd never loved her husband.

What did that say about *her?*

And what did it say about her that she wanted to beg him not to go? The words were right there. *Please. Please don't leave us.*

She could not let herself say them. For his sake, and for hers, she had to pretend she was stronger than she felt.

Praying that he hadn't noticed her breathing too fast, Julia went over and sank onto the sofa. "Your mother called today."

Alec swiveled, his eyebrows climbing, either at the abrupt change of subject or at the mere fact that she had talked to his mother. "Really?"

"Why so surprised?" she challenged him. "We do talk sometimes. Usually when your dad isn't around, I gather. I kind of wondered why, until you told me more about your parents' relationship."

"Has Mama said anything to you about him?" Alec looked curious.

"Mostly she worries about the kids and me. Lately about him, too. She thinks he's tiring too easily and is being stubborn about seeing a doctor."

"She said that to me, too." Alec gave a grunt that wasn't quite a laugh. "I offered to reinforce the message to him. When I did, he was annoyed she'd gone behind his back."

"Do you think it's his heart?"

"It's possible. Stress is one of the classic risk factors, right? Dad's always been angry. You know him. After he retired, instead of enjoying puttering around, maybe growing some vegetables the way he used to talk about doing, he turned the whole thing into a competition. His yard had to look better than any of the neighbors'. His zucchini had to be bigger. The lawn has a razor edge. God forbid the Finkels' grandkids should kick a ball into *his* yard." Alec's expression became distant. "My grandfather died when I was in college. It might have been his heart."

"You need to think about your own health, then," she said fiercely.

Alec rocked back on his heels, a slow smile spreading. "Hey, my diet is in your hands."

"Maybe we should cut back on the desserts."

"Don't you dare." He crossed the room swiftly enough to make her pulse pound. He sat, as he had before, on the coffee table, close enough they could have touched if they hadn't both been conscious of the kids only a room away. "Julia, I eat well, and I stay in good physical shape. Compared to my father, I'm downright easygoing."

Was he laughing at her? Julia eyed him suspiciously. "Sure you are."

"You ever seen me lose my temper?"

"Losing your temper is probably healthier than suppressing everything."

He was smiling again. "I don't do that, either. I

acknowledge what I feel. I just don't make a show of it. And, unlike my father, I'm capable of relaxing and having a good time."

She couldn't deny that. The day at Elk Lake, she'd seen a happy man. If it weren't for her darling son's behavior, she'd see Alec happy a lot more often. The thought brought renewed frustration.

"You're right." She *ached* to touch him, to be held in his arms. "I wish…"

"I wish, too."

They looked at each other, the naked wanting and a different kind of frustration on his face undoubtedly echoed on hers.

The stomp of footsteps and slam of a door gave warning that the kids were done in the kitchen. Alec tore his gaze from Julia's and looked past her.

"What are you talking about?" Liana asked.

Julia wanted to cry. Instead, she held out an arm for her daughter, who sank onto the sofa beside her and cuddled close. "Oh, all kinds of things."

"Cabbages and kings," Alec agreed, his tone light despite the near desperation in his eyes.

"No, really," Liana wanted to know.

"Oh, you know Grandma Raynor called today, and I was telling Alec about it."

Her daughter frowned at him. "Don't you talk to her? She's your mom."

"Yes, I do." The set of his shoulders relaxed as he smiled at Liana. "But she tells your mother different things than she tells me. Because they're both women."

She pondered that. "Oh."

"*Your* mother was threatening to cut off my desserts," he said, straight-faced. "She thinks I'm getting fat."

"I do not!" Julia exclaimed, laughing. "If anybody's getting fat, it's me. I'll bet I've put on five pounds since we moved."

His gaze raked her. "Bet you haven't."

"Uncle Alec's not fat. Neither are you, Mommy."

Julia loved being called Mommy. Liana had stayed childish longer than Matt, but lately even she was transitioning to the more socially acceptable Mom.

"I can't believe you're going into sixth grade," she said with a sudden pang.

"Are we really going back-to-school shopping soon?" her daughter asked eagerly.

Alec laughed and pushed himself to his feet. "That's girl talk. I'm going home."

Julia didn't argue. She hated to see him go—but it was getting harder not to give herself away, to him and to the kids. Over Liana's head, he and she said their good-nights, and, as happened so often now, their eyes said something else altogether.

Come with me.

You know I can't. But, oh, I wish...

MATT WAS SULKINESS personified when he trailed behind Julia into the swimming-pool complex the next couple of mornings, but she thought Alec was right. The most dangerous thing she could do was leave him alone too much.

Friday was the last day of the swim session, and close to the end of July, too. Partway through Liana's lesson, Julia glanced at her son and saw an unfamiliar expression on his face.

He was eying one of the instructors, a fresh-faced girl named Erica who might be sixteen or seventeen. Erica very likely wore a C-cup bra, which of course she didn't have on right now. Instead, a skintight, racing-style swimsuit outlined her body. Matt was not looking at her face.

Almost gulping, Julia convinced herself that any boy Matt's age would be noticing girls as sexual beings. The fact that he was suggested he was actually heading into puberty, which—well, she didn't know that it was good or bad, except increased hormone production might prompt his body into starting to grow, which would be a positive.

She was so not equipped to handle any of this. A little boy, sure; a testosterone-ridden teenager, no. If Josh were here instead of her, she reflected, he would probably have clapped his son's back, laughed and agreed that Erica was hot.

The very thought made her wonder— But no. She had never let herself do that. She couldn't have borne knowing he wasn't faithful to her.

Thank God for Alec.

Julia felt a funny, warm glow of pleasure nestling in her chest. Alec would never betray his wife, sexually or in any other way. She didn't know why she was so sure, but she was.

I trust him, she thought, and it felt like free fall. Like Josh had once described skydiving—exhilarating, life-affirming, not terrifying the way it would be for her. That was what this felt like.

A whistle blew sharply, recalling her from her reverie. She surfaced to find Matt staring suspiciously at her. She waited for him to ask what she'd been thinking about, but of course he didn't. He couldn't admit to any curiosity about her at all. It was like, she imagined, American soldiers in World War II thinking about the Japanese. Dehumanizing the enemy was essential.

What a cheerful thought.

"Matt," she said impulsively, but she was looking at the back of his head now. After a moment, she said, "Never mind," and went back to pretending to watch Sophie's swim lesson.

Liana emerged from the locker room and climbed the bleachers to join them, her hair wet and stringy, her swim bag bumping her leg.

"Did you see me? Joannie said my dive was fantastic! She passed me to advanced. Look, here's my certificate."

"I saw." Julia admired the certificate and then patted the bleacher seat beside her. "Look, Sophie's class is going off the diving board."

The ten-year-old gazed enviously. "I wish we could have."

Not ten for long, it occurred to Julia. Usually the birthday party would have been dreamed about and planned way longer in advance than this.

"We'll come back to a free swim," she promised. "Hey, kiddo. What are we going to do for your birthday party this year?"

Her small face lit. "Do you think we could go horseback riding? And then out for pizza or something?"

"Who is we?"

Besides Sophie, Liana wanted to ask Jenna from her swim class, and maybe Lauren from the swim class, too, 'cuz Liana liked her better than she had thought she did. And Sophie had had a friend over a couple of times and Liana liked her, too, so…

Laughing, Julia agreed to all. So much for her social butterfly of a daughter's fear that she wouldn't make new friends after the move.

If only Matt… He was hunched to show her not only the back of his head, but his entire back, as if he had to physically reject his sister and her cheerful adaptability, too. Matt apparently *had* made friends, Julia was reminded, if you could call them that; he'd gotten the marijuana somewhere. Alec had assumed the condoms were intended as bribes/payment. But after seeing the way her son studied the swim instructor, Julia wasn't so sure. Matt might be starting to dream about using them.

If so, she supposed she ought to be glad condoms were part of the dream.

"I've got to get Lauren's phone number," Liana exclaimed, jumping off the bench to go clattering back down the bleachers in order to catch up with a copper-headed girl walking out with a woman whose hair was the same color.

When, a minute later, the mother turned to look toward Julia, she smiled and waved, and got a smile in return. Then Julia had to applaud after Sophie leaped off the high dive and came up looking anxiously toward the bleachers. Her grin was as big as Liana's had been a minute ago at the idea of a horseback-riding birthday party.

I could be truly happy here in Angel Butte, Julia realized, *if only Matt weren't so miserable.*

Of course, she'd probably have considered herself happy back in L.A. if it hadn't been for Matt. Sort of happy, because Alec had never kissed her.

Would he ever have, if they hadn't moved in next door to each other?

SOPHIE HAD DINNER with them that evening, and Alec listened patiently to the two girls' excited descriptions of the final swim lesson in this session, their voices leapfrogging over each other.

"...this huge splash!"

"You should have seen me..."

From there, they progressed to telling him their

plans for the great birthday party. Liana would be eleven on August 3.

"I think we should just skip it," he decided. "You can stay ten. Eleven, hey, I'm not so sure about that."

His niece planted her hands on her hips despite being seated and gave him a reproachful look that reminded him of one from her mother's repertoire. "Uncle Alec! That's silly!"

"I guess it is." He smiled at her. "Okay, I guess we'll do it."

"And my birthday's on Saturday this year, so I can have the party *on* my birthday instead of after."

Man, he'd have hated to miss it. If her birthday had been the next weekend, he wouldn't have been able to be here. That would have sucked. Between work and distance, he'd only been able to make it to a few of their birthday parties over the years. The first for each—he remembered Matt's most vividly, his astonished gaze focusing on the lit candle atop the cupcake as his mom moved it in front of him and whispered, "Let's blow it out together, Mattie." She'd puffed up her cheeks and waited until he did the same. "Ready? Blow!" With a huge grin, Josh had been snapping pictures as fast as he could.

With a spasm of grief, Alec wished his brother was here to see his little girl growing into a young lady, even if that meant Alec would never have what he wanted.

Julia couldn't know what he was thinking, but

she watched him with an expression that suggested she knew something was wrong. He smiled ruefully at her and gave her hand lying on the tabletop a squeeze. Matt's eyes narrowed to slits. Alec summoned a grin for the boy that seemed to ease the suspicion.

Reluctant as he was to think about it, he asked himself how Matt would react to his mother and uncle hooking up. There was a time Alec would have assumed all would be good, but that was before Matt had turned on him and said with such ferocity, "You're not my father."

Uneasiness stirred in Alec, but also grim determination. Whether Matt liked it or not, they *were* a family. It wasn't as if Alec was asking them to forget their father or to call him Dad in Josh's place.

After dinner the two giggling girls went off to Liana's room, and Alec said tonight he'd let Matt off the hook and clean the kitchen. Julia, of course, leaped up and started trying to clear the table.

Alec removed the pile of plates from her hands. "Sit. You did your share. Now it's my turn."

With one last disbelieving look, Matt fled. They both heard his bedroom door close, but at least he didn't slam it.

Twice more, Alec had to dissuade Julia from helping. Finally she followed him to the kitchen and perched on a step stool to watch him rinse dishes and put them in the dishwasher.

"See? I'm capable. Haven't broken anything yet."

"But you're the only one of us who worked all day." She seemed to ponder that for a moment. "Did anything new or different happen today? You seemed in a funny mood at dinner."

"We had a really ugly domestic-violence situation." He grimaced. "Standoff for a good part of the day." He described the neighborhood and background as he started washing pans, ignoring the yellow plastic gloves Julia usually donned. The skin on his hands would never be lily-soft, no matter what.

"I stopped by a couple of times," he went on. "I didn't hover, but I also hadn't had a chance to see how my people handled something like this. As it turned out, our negotiator did a first-rate job, considering she can't have had that much experience. I was afraid the husband would react negatively to the negotiator being a woman, but her gender didn't seem to make any difference to him. She eventually persuaded him to put down the gun and come out. The wife…" He hesitated, remembering the battered face. "She's not in such good shape. Apparently he'd decided she was cheating on him."

"Do they have children?"

"Yeah, that's what made it especially ugly. The two-year-old was home and crying for what seemed all day. Getting the guy increasingly stressed. Not to mention all the officers listening in." He shook his head, ready to think about something else. "I also heard from a couple of city council members who'd read my proposal. Both claimed to be persuaded."

"Were they in your yes column already?"

He turned off the water and dried his hands. "Unfortunately. Not a peep from Greig or Miller."

She smiled. "You feel confident anyway."

He realized she was right. "I guess I do. They have to be idiots to vote no. If they don't go for this, one way or another we'll take the campaign to the voters, and several of the council members happen to be running for reelection in November."

"Do you dare go to the voters yourself?"

"No, I can't directly politick, but I can damn sure find a way to put a bug in the ear of any opponent to one of the wrongheaded council members. And that's assuming potential opponents won't already be attending Tuesday night's council meeting, where they'll hear my brilliant speech and see the vote tally for themselves."

Julia had an odd expression. "You sound energized. As though you're enjoying this part of your job."

He hadn't thought of it in those terms, but… "I guess I am. Good thing, too. I don't belong in this role if I can't represent the department effectively."

Her smile was soft. "You amaze me every day."

She'd give him a swelled head if he didn't watch it. "What brought that on?"

"I don't know. I just—" She broke off, lines appearing on her forehead. "Today I kept thinking how lucky we are to have you."

To keep his hands off her, he made a production of hanging up the towel. "Any particular context?"

"Oh..." She stole a look down the hall. "Matt was, um, all but drooling over one of the swim instructors. Who is *very* buxom, poor girl."

"Poor girl?" Alec asked with a grin.

Julia made a face then continued her thought. "It's the first time I've seen him look at a girl that way."

"That's not unexpected," he said, although this little story wasn't what he'd expected her to say.

"No, but how am *I* supposed to deal with it?"

"If you had a good relationship, I doubt you'd have any trouble. You probably would have teased him, he'd have blushed, and later he might ask you some questions."

"Would you have teased him?"

Something troubled her about what seemed to him to be a fairly innocent moment of awakened sexuality on her son's part. Instead of confronting that directly, he said, "No, I probably wouldn't have commented at all unless he said something."

"What if he'd asked if you thought the girl was hot?"

"What does it matter what I might have said? You can't react the way I might."

"No-o." Julia drew the word out. "I just had this picture of Josh—" She didn't want to finish.

Alec felt an uncomfortable mix: jealousy, because she was again summoning his brother, and curiosity. Whatever Julia was looking for, it mattered to her.

"I'd have tried to be tactful without getting too enthusiastic," he said. "When I was Matt's age, it would have grossed me out if my father was checking out the same girl I was. I might have said something like, 'Yeah, she's pretty. If I were your age, I'd definitely be looking, too.'"

"Oh." Julia's relaxation was subtle but noticeable, making him even more curious.

"What did you think, I was a dirty old man?" he asked, caught between amused and annoyed.

"No." She sighed. "I suppose I thought any guy would be going, 'Oh, hey, yeah.' I'm sorry."

Alec ignored the apology. "How old is this girl?"

"Um…sixteen? Seventeen?"

He shook his head. "I think I'm offended."

"Really?"

"A little bit."

"I didn't think…"

"No, you didn't. I want *you,*" he said flatly. "You and no one else. It has been one hell of a long time since I've so much as glanced at another woman, far less a…a kid, for God's sake."

Her eyes were wide, that swirl of color. "You mean, you haven't, um, been…?"

"No," he said irritably. He'd been seeing a woman right before Josh died. *Seeing.* What a euphemism, for a relationship that had been, for him, all about sex. After Julia called him that night, her voice both blank and stunned, he didn't think he'd so much as returned Elise's calls, which probably made him a shit. He was surprised he even remembered her name. "Once you needed me—"

Her mouth trembled. "Oh, Alec."

He groaned, "Come here, sweetheart."

She stepped into his arms naturally, as if that was where she belonged. Her expression was still remorseful. "Alec, I'm having trouble believing…"

"You are beautiful." He gave her a little shake. "You're also kind, gentle, graceful and loving. I like when you stand up to me or one of the kids, but I also like the soft way you touch one of them sometimes, as if you don't even have to consciously know they need reassurance. You do the same to me, too, lately." His voice had grown hoarse. "I like the way you come to me when you're troubled, and listen to me when I am. I can't imagine not wanting all that. Do you understand?"

She nodded, teardrops shimmering on her eyelashes. "Yes."

"Quit doubting." He bent his head, not thinking, only wanting. As if she felt the same, she rose on tiptoe and pressed her lips to his. He could no more have kept himself from kissing her than he could from going to her that night she had called and told him about Josh before, for the first time ever, saying that she needed him. He nipped at her mouth, small, biting kisses, stroked her lips with his tongue, gripped her ass with one hand to help lift her—and let himself be oblivious to his surroundings.

A scrape of sound was his first warning. Alec lifted his head. Too late.

Matt stood not ten feet away, his face contorted with rage and hurt. "I guess you had to pretend you wanted to be my father so you could sleep with *her!*" he yelled. Whirling, he ran for the front door.

CHAPTER TWELVE

ALEC MOVED FAST.

Shocked, momentarily disoriented, Julia couldn't have reached Matt in time. Alec had his hand flat on the door while Matt fought to turn the knob, screaming incoherent words.

Heart pounding, she followed them into the living room. "Matt…"

He tried to run again, this time toward the bedrooms, but Alec grabbed him and held on while he struggled like a wildcat, yelling, "I hate you both! I hate you! I hate you!"

"Mattie." Eyes blurred with tears, she reached for her son.

Arms held immobile by Alec, Matt kicked out, his foot connecting hard with her shin. She staggered back.

"Knock it off," Alec said grimly. "I'm not letting you hurt your mother. Do you hear me?"

"Let me go! Let me go! I hate you!"

A part of Julia knew the girls had emerged from Liana's bedroom and stood staring, white-faced. Matt's face was so twisted, he was unrecognizable. She had never felt so helpless and frightened, watching Alec fight to subdue this boy she didn't even know. There were grunts and the sound of Matt's wild kicks and blows connecting, an occasional muffled curse from Alec, screamed obscenities from Matt.

About the time Alec managed to plant a yelling Matt in a chair and hold him down, Julia pulled herself together enough to usher Sophie and Liana back to the bedroom. They crept backward like a pair of baby mice. For all Liana's exposure to Matt, even she looked shocked. The bedroom door shut behind the girls, but Julia had no doubt they would huddle inside, still able to hear too much.

She hurried back to fall to her knees beside the chair. "Matt. Oh, Mattie—"

"Don't call me that!" He renewed the battle. "I told you not to call me that! *I hate you.*"

She fell backward from the vitriol in his voice.

Alec swore again. "That's enough. What is *wrong* with you?"

"With me? It's *her,*" Matt cried. "You don't know her."

"I do."

The confidence in his voice, despite everything, gave Julia courage she'd been lacking. She looked into her son's eyes, dilated black. "Tell us both why I'm so awful."

Matt tried to curl away from her, head hunching as if he could pull it in like a turtle's.

All her shock and fear and distress became anger. "Oh, no, you don't!" she snapped. "I've had enough of this. What did I do that's so bad?"

He all but exploded. "You know!" he screamed.

"I don't know!" she yelled back.

Alec, crouched beside her, kept his hands on Matt.

"You killed Daddy!"

Her chest cramped in agony. Her mouth moved, but nothing came out.

"It's your fault he's dead!" Matt accused her. "You know it is!"

Julia hunched, as if to protect her vulnerable midsection, although there was no physical way to protect herself from his hate. "You heard," she whispered.

Tears streamed down his face now. He was a blur through her own tears. "You told him if he went away he shouldn't bother coming home. I heard you!"

She shook her head dully, then had trouble stopping. "You have to know I didn't want your father to die."

"You did!" He was trying for the same fury, but his voice had become smaller, more croak than scream.

"No. Never. I wanted...I wanted him to put us first. Don't you understand?"

"No! If you hadn't made him go away—"

A dry sob erupted from her. Julia barely controlled it, painfully conscious of Alec, crouching beside the chair and watching them both, his dark face inscrutable.

"I would never have wanted anything bad to happen to him. It was partly because I was always so afraid when he was away that I asked him to give it up. Not necessarily the navy or even the SEAL team—he could have done training or..."

Her son stared at her with hate. "*I* think you wanted him to die so you could be with *him*." He transferred his scathing look to Alec.

"No." Her protest emerged as a bare whisper.

Matt went back to staring at her. A sick hopelessness swept over her. Somehow she had lost him. Maybe he'd always loved his father in a way he hadn't loved her. Maybe...maybe she had some failing of character she hadn't known about. Or was he right? *Had* she, in some secret part of herself, hoped for Josh to die, freeing her?

Shaking her head again, she lurched to her feet. "I don't know what we're going to do," she said, voice thin.

Something changed on Matt's face.

"Julia." Alec's voice was rough-textured, worried, but she couldn't look at him at all.

"I can't..." She backed away. "Maybe tomorrow— I'm sorry. I'm going to bed." She all but ran then, desperate for the sanctuary of her bedroom. Alec called after her, but she ignored him.

Once inside her room, she looked around frantically. If only there was a lock on the door—but it would have been one of those flimsy, push-button ones anyway, that wouldn't keep anyone out. She could pull a piece of furniture in front of the door…but that reminded her unpleasantly of Matt's behavior. And it wasn't as if she could hide in here forever, she realized, the crushing weight of her responsibilities and failures crumpling her.

Back to the door, she slid to the floor. Oh, God. Liana and Sophie, scared. Poor Alec, left with the demon spawn. *And I am the demon who spawned him,* she thought, with wretchedness worse than anything she'd ever felt, even after learning about Josh's death.

Her face was already wet, she discovered when she lifted her hands. She pulled her knees up to her chest, wrapped her arms around them and buried her face. Curled in a ball as tight as she could make it, she cried, silently, hopelessly.

There were voices in the hall, doors opening and closing, and finally a knock on her door, but the best she could manage was a choked, "Go away."

Whoever it was—Alec—did finally.

Only thoughts of Liana finally got Julia to her feet. She was still a mother, even though she'd lost her son.

ALEC DIDN'T LEAVE until Julia came out. He wouldn't have gone then if she'd given any indication she wanted to talk, or even be held, but when she saw him sitting in the living room, lit only by a single lamp beside the chair, she only shook her head and mouthed, *Tomorrow.*

Weary and hurt, he nodded and let himself out.

The night air felt clean and cool. He stood outside for a while, but eventually let himself into his side of the duplex, where he realized he had no idea what to do. Go to bed? However exhausted, he wouldn't be able to sleep.

Not much of a drinker, he poured himself a shot of whiskey and sat down in the living room, contemplating it for a minute before he downed it in one long swallow. The burn slid down his throat and into his belly. He waited for it to bring numbness.

He didn't understand any part of that scene. It was tragic that Matt had overheard his parents' final argument, but how could he possibly believe his mother had wanted his father *dead?* Alec would stake his life on Julia's essential character—everything he'd outlined to her tonight, starting with goodness. The change in Matt had been almost overnight; it hadn't begun in some twisted relationship with Julia, a secret ugliness hidden from Alec. No, it had only to do with Josh's death, with the timing, with the overheard fight—but it still didn't make sense.

And the vicious way Matt had turned on Alec, who had loved the boy since the day he was born. Did he really think all the time spent with him had been a lie created so Alec could get into his mother's bed?

Alec had known that sooner or later Matt would blow, but he'd been convinced it would be healthy for all of them when it happened.

Now? He made a raw sound, letting his head rest against the chair. Now he wondered if there was any going back from the damage done tonight.

He had let Matt go to his room, only stopping him before he closed the bedroom door. "The bathroom's as far as you go." The harshness in his voice had shocked Matt, Alec could tell, but at that point he didn't give a damn.

Then he walked Sophie home, taking time to talk to her and then to her mother, and went back and sat on the edge of Liana's bed talking to her for a long time. How much good he'd done, he didn't know. He'd have sworn she had shrunk—lost weight, even her bones becoming more frail.

"I'm scared," she kept whispering, and he'd held her, his cheek pressed to the top of her head and thought, *I'm scared, too.*

What he said was, "It will get better, sweet pea. Your brother heard things he didn't understand and he's let them fester instead of talking them out with me or your mom. Now we finally *can* talk. I know it was frightening, but I really doubt he meant most of what he said."

She shivered, and he suspected she didn't believe him any more than he believed himself.

Alec had never wanted to see an expression on Julia's face like when she stared at Matt there at the end, right before she shut herself in her bedroom. She was bone-white, her eyes huge and dark; she looked like someone whose house was burning down in front of her with her family inside it.

Alec wanted even less to remember the expression on Matt's face when he saw Uncle Alec kissing his mother, or when he screamed that he hated them both.

As a cop, Alec had seen the worst of human devastation and degradation. Pain and bottomless hate, despair and hopelessness. But that hadn't been the people he loved.

Julia, he knew, wouldn't turn to him for comfort or for love. She *couldn't*. However they moved forward, she would never be willing to hurt Matt to that extent.

God, he thought, desperately wanting another shot of whiskey but unable to stand and get one. *I should have left well enough alone. Josh, I thought I was doing the right thing. I swear I did!*

Maybe he'd already loved Julia, but he'd loved the kids, too. He had only wanted to help, and he was beginning to think that, in trying to do so, he was partly responsible for the mess all their lives had become.

He hadn't thought he would sleep and only knew he had when he abruptly awakened. He blinked into the darkness a couple of times, groping for the dream that was slipping away even though it had been an uneasy one. Maybe he should be glad something had wrenched him out of the nightmare, he thought, glancing at the bedside clock. It was 3:14 a.m.

His brain finally cleared enough for him to realize what he was hearing. He frowned, focusing. An engine. Idling right outside the duplex. And damned if that didn't sound like his Tahoe—

"Shit!" He rocketed out of bed, grabbed the trousers he'd thrown over the back of a chair and hopped into them. Shoes—he fumbled his feet into athletic shoes and bothered tying them only so he knew he could run if he had to. Weapon.

He'd reached his front door when he heard the distinct sound of the vehicle moving, hesitating, shifting gears. Flinging open the door, Alec raced out just in time to see that his driveway was empty—and the SUV was accelerating away down the street, he could see clearly beneath the streetlamp.

Swearing, he went back in, grabbed his phone and called dispatch, reporting the theft.

"Whoever the son of a bitch is," he started to say, then thought again, *Shit.*

"Keep me in the loop," he snapped and ended the call.

Seconds later, he leaned on Julia's doorbell. When the response wasn't immediate, he hammered on the door.

It seemed like ages but probably wasn't even two minutes when the porch light came on and he heard the dead bolt being released. Julia appeared in the opening, wearing boxer shorts and a tank top, her hair tangled and her cheek creased. And, God, her eyes so puffy from tears they weren't much better than slits.

"Alec?"

"Somebody just stole my Tahoe," he said. "You need to check to be sure Matt's still in his room."

"Oh, dear God," she breathed and vanished. He opened the door and followed her inside, snapping on a table lamp. She was back in seconds.

"No. His window is open and he's gone."

"Look for your keys," Alec said grimly.

For safety's sake, they both carried spare keys to each other's vehicle and to the other side of the duplex. In case one of the kids got home and couldn't get in. In case either of them locked themselves out of a car. Standard precaution—and dumb as hell, it now seemed to him.

Without a word, she headed for the kitchen. Light blazed on. Almost immediately she returned, looking as if somebody had hit her. "The whole set of keys is gone."

He swore.

"Why didn't he take my car?" she asked. Begged.

"You know why. Mine's newer and cooler, with the bonus that he can hit out at me."

"He doesn't know how to drive." She sounded almost numb, and her expression was stricken.

He stepped forward and gathered her into his

arms, even if holding her was what had begun this whole mess. "I've already called nine-one-one," he murmured. "They'll pull him over."

Despite the distraction of her slim body leaning against his, he couldn't help speculating on how the kid *was* driving. Even with the seat completely forward, how was he reaching the pedals? And, since he obviously was, how the hell was he seeing over the dashboard? Or—damn it—had he somehow gotten in touch with an older boy to be a co-conspirator?

Alec wasn't a praying man, but he found himself doing it anyway. The Tahoe was insured; any vehicle could be replaced. But imagining Matt's too-slight body after an accident... He swallowed hard. The seat belt wouldn't fit right. And, man, what an exploding air bag would do to someone Matt's size— Alec didn't even what to think about it.

Julia mumbled something into his chest.

He eased back. "What?"

"We can't help him anymore." The grief in her voice tore at his heart.

"What do you mean?"

"Do you think he'd be better off living with someone else?"

"Like who?" His anger was inexplicable. He knew where she was coming from. If Matt wouldn't cooperate with counseling, maybe he'd be happier... but where? "Not with my parents," he said with finality.

"No. Or mine." She seemed to sag. "I could talk to my brother."

"The one you hardly know."

She gave him a wild look. "He's getting worse, not better. I'm not giving him whatever he needs."

Alec didn't want to agree, but she was right. Things with Matt were escalating. If he survived tonight… "Maybe a group home would be a good option for him," he said gently. "Trained counselors to work with him, us nearby."

She didn't say anything. His arms tightened again. She went back to leaning on him, or maybe they were leaning on each other. Neither spoke for a long time.

"Won't they call you?" she finally asked.

"Yeah." He cleared his throat. "There must not have been a patrol unit nearby."

"Maybe you should have chased him."

"I don't know. Your car doesn't have the horsepower the Tahoe does." He bent his head back. "My first thought was to find out whether Matt was behind the wheel or not."

Probably too late, he had considered going after Matt, but the thought of what he'd do if he glanced in the rearview mirror—could he *see* in the rearview mirror?—and realized his uncle was on his tail had scared the hell out of Alec.

Oh, damn. He should have ordered no lights or siren until the last second. Better yet, boxing the

Tahoe in and forcing it to ease to a stop. Surely Matt
wasn't foolhardy enough to make a real run for it—

Alec would have groaned if he hadn't known
he'd increase Julia's fear. Matt was self-destructing.
Foolhardy didn't begin to describe his recent behavior. Reason and self-preservation were no longer in his vocabulary.

Alec had set his phone and weapon on the end
table. Now he stared at the phone over Julia's head,
willing it to ring, scripting a reassuring voice.

*Pulled him over, no problem, Chief. Do you want
to come get him?*

But the more time that dragged by, the more unlikely became the easy end to Matt's ugliest and
most dangerous instance of acting out.

If they sent him to live with someone else, he'd
see that as rejection. But keeping him at home was
ripping Julia apart and harming Liana, too. Two
days ago, Alec would have offered to take him, giving Matt and Julia some separation. But now that
Matt hated him, too—

The phone rang and bounced on the wood surface. Alec let go of Julia and snatched it up.

"Raynor."

"Chief, this is Caroline." He had already recognized the dispatcher's voice and now nodded mean-
inglessly.

"Your nephew got out onto the highway. The
pursuing officer estimates he reached eighty miles
an hour." She hesitated. "I'm afraid he went off

the road and rolled your vehicle. I'm told he's unconscious." Her voice was kind, almost motherly. "Paramedics are responding. I suggest you go directly to the hospital. Um…I assume you can reach the boy's mother?"

"Yes." Somehow he'd shut down and succeeded in sounding emotionless. "She's with me. Thank you, Caroline." Very carefully, he touched the screen to end the call, then made himself look at Julia. "He's been in an accident. All the dispatcher knows is that Matt's unconscious. Paramedics are on their way or already at the scene. We need to go to the hospital."

She nodded, closed her eyes and swayed. But when he reached for her, she shook her head hard. "No, don't touch me. I…I have to pull myself together."

Alec didn't like the idea that his touch would weaken her, but he could only nod. Whatever she needed.

"You go get dressed. I'll wake Liana…."

"Mommy?" her daughter said. In shorty pink pajamas, she came into the living room. "Why are you up?" she asked in obvious bewilderment. "Why is Uncle Alec here?"

"Oh, sweetheart." Julia went to her and drew her into a hug. "It's Matt. He's done something *really* dumb this time." She explained without drama. "I think it would be best if you go spend the rest of the night with Sophie."

"I want to come with you!"

"Honey…" Julia's voice wavered.

Liana's face crumpled. "Mommy, please!"

Alec could see the escalation and knew Julia was in no shape to deal with it. He stepped forward.

"No. Sweet pea, your mom has to be free to spend time at Matt's bedside if that's necessary. Kids under twelve wouldn't be allowed in. We can't take you." He made sure she would hear that there was no give. "Now, go put on a robe and slippers. If you need a pillow or blanket or anything, get it."

She raced for her bedroom with a wail. Alec gave Julia a nudge, feeling the tremble in her fine-boned body. "Go," he said gruffly. "Get dressed. I'll be back in a minute."

She cast him a despairing look and went.

He returned to his side of the duplex and took the time to strip and get dressed again, including the extras like underwear and socks. He hooked his badge and a holster on his belt, sliding the SIG into it.

Liana was ready and still waiting for her mother, so he took her next door, once again waking an unsuspecting woman. Andrea responded quickly, hugged Liana and said, "Of course you can spend the night, pumpkin! Go climb into bed with Sophie. She's awake."

Liana's lower lip trembled. "But…I won't *know*."

If her brother was alive or dead, she meant.

For her benefit, Alec smiled. "I imagine he's

going to have a heck of a headache. He's also going to be in deep doo-doo. You sleep tight, sweet pea. We'll be back by morning."

She sniffed and went reluctantly. Only when she was out of hearing did Andrea ask for more information and reach out to squeeze his arm when he said Matt was unconscious.

"I'll pray for him."

He scrubbed a hand over his face. "Thanks, Andrea." He sounded hoarse. "I want to wring his neck for putting us all through this."

"But you want him to be okay so you can. I know the feeling."

He walked back across the dry lawn to Julia's car, parked in front of her tiny garage. They'd talked about installing a remote-control opener, but in the meantime she confessed putting the car inside was more trouble than it was worth.

She handed him the keys, as if it was a given he'd drive. Feeling the tremor in her hand, he was glad she had the sense to know she shouldn't be behind the wheel.

When they reached the hospital, an ambulance with flashing lights was parked in front of the emergency entrance. Two people in blue uniforms were lifting out a gurney, hospital personnel waiting to receive it.

Julia reached for her door handle even though the car hadn't come to a stop. "Matt!"

"Probably," Alec said, "but you don't want to

get in the way. Let's give them a minute to get him inside." Instead of letting her out, he kept her with him as he parked, then held her to a walk on the way in.

They went straight to the receptionist.

"Julia Raynor," Julia said, voice taut with anxiety. "My son was being brought in."

The woman glanced at her computer monitor. "He's already here, Mrs. Raynor. Let me check to see if the doctor can speak to you yet." She picked up her phone and spoke in an unintelligible murmur.

Neither Julia nor Alec made a move toward the chairs in the waiting area. Alec wanted to bust through those damn swinging doors and to hell with hospital protocol. He could only imagine how Julia felt.

The receptionist hung up. "It's going to take a few minutes. Do you have Matt's insurance information with you?"

Julia did. Once she'd filled out what appeared to be a sheaf of forms, the receptionist suggested they take a seat. "Someone will be out shortly."

Alec let out a ragged breath. After a moment, he steered Julia a few feet away. "Let's walk," he said. "I can't sit or just stand here."

Bemused, she looked at him. "Like Josh."

"Sometimes," he admitted. He could be still for long stretches, but not when he was tense. Then, he needed to be moving.

A long corridor opened off the E.R. waiting room, leading to the rest of the hospital. He and Julia walked it, back and forth, remaining within sight of the receptionist. They paced for what had to be the longest five minutes of his life. Neither of them said a word. Occasionally he laid a hand on her back, needing the small contact.

They had turned and were walking back toward the waiting room when Alec saw that a nurse was speaking to the receptionist and looking toward them. Julia groped for his hand and he probably crushed hers in his grip, but he didn't let go.

Please, God, he thought, let this woman smile, not meet their eyes with the compassion in hers that would tell them the unbearable had happened.

CHAPTER THIRTEEN

JULIA CLUNG TO Alec's hand as if it were a life buoy, all that kept her from drowning. She had never in her life been so terrified. Josh's death had been presented to her as a fact, something done and over with, likely days before she was notified, although officials were never willing to give her details. This, though, fearing the worst, was horrific.

The nurse waiting for them was small and well rounded with a bouncy blond ponytail. She wore blue scrub pants and a scrub top with a splash of blue flowers on white. Julia drank in every detail, knowing it was a self-defense mechanism.

They were within speaking distance when she began to smile. "Hi, my name's Carrie. We're ready for you in back. Matt got banged up some, but he regained consciousness before he arrived here in the E.R. The doctor will want to talk to you, but it appears none of his injuries are significant beyond a broken arm and a concussion."

A sob escaped Julia. Alec let go of her hand so he could wrap his arm around her and support her as they were led through those doors and down an even wider corridor lined with small, glass-fronted rooms. Carrie led them into the third room on the right, where Matt lay in a bed with the head halfway raised. A white bandage covered his forehead, and one arm was held awkwardly in some kind of temporary splint. He was going to have two black eyes, too, Julia saw, with what detachment she could summon.

"Thank God," she heard herself whisper, hurrying forward. "We've been so scared." She started to reach out to him, then stopped. When was the last time he'd let her hold his hand?

Her son gazed at her with incredulity. "You don't—" his voice cracked "—hate me?"

Beside her, Alec gave a strange laugh. "We're mad as hell at you, but of course we don't hate you. No matter how big an idiot you are, your mom and I both love you."

The boy's brown eyes filled with tears. "I'm sorry! I didn't mean..." He choked, his face spasming.

"To kill yourself?" Alec asked drily.

How did he seem to know what to say and how to say it? He could be sardonic and tender at the same time. Julia knew, *knew* Matt would respond better to that than he would if she threw herself on him weeping, which was what she wanted to do.

Her son's uninjured fingers gripped the white cotton blanket. "I thought I could drive," he said in a very small voice.

Julia stayed silent. Matt avoided meeting her eyes.

Alec studied him. "I'm told you reached eighty miles an hour."

Dark color flooded Matt's bruised face. "I was scared. I thought if I got away I could come home and you'd never know I took your car."

Alec only shook his head. "The cop would've had your plates run by that time, kid. Anyway, unfortunately for you, I'd already called in the theft of my vehicle."

His eyes tried to widen. "You heard me."

"I heard you."

"Oh." For a moment, it seemed that his face would crumple with emotion, but then he controlled it. He stole a glance at Julia.

"Were you trying to kill yourself?" she heard herself ask. *She* heard her own note of semihysteria, but prayed he didn't.

"No!" he flared. "Why would you think that?"

"Maybe because you came damn close," Alec suggested.

Matt's gaze fell, and his Adam's apple bobbed a couple of times in his skinny neck. "I was just...I was...I was..."

"Mad," Julia supplied, for lack of any other word.

He shook his head and cast her a desperate look.

"Mr. and Mrs. Raynor?" a man said from behind her.

Startled, she turned and felt Alec do the same. Clearly the doctor, the newcomer was tall, thin and had brown hair that glinted with strands of gray. He wore a white coat and had a stethoscope draped around his neck. He studied them carefully even as he held out a hand.

"I'm Dr. Beaumont. You're Matt's mother and father?"

"Mother and uncle," Alec said, shaking his hand. "Matt's father was killed overseas."

He nodded. "I gather this young man stole the vehicle he wrecked tonight."

Alec grimaced. "It was mine."

"I see." Dr. Beaumont's eyebrows twitched a few times. Who knew how much he guessed about their family dynamics. "Well, Matt was very fortunate, although he's going to hurt for some time. According to the paramedics, the air bag did expand, but it slammed him against the door, breaking his arm and giving him a heck of a bump on the head. It also protected him to a degree, of course."

He went on talking, explaining that Matt had apparently been unconscious for only a few minutes. His pupils looked good now, and he wasn't complaining of any dizziness or vision problems. To err on the side of caution, they would still like to do a CT scan. The break was his humerus, which was the bone in the upper arm. "Safely above the elbow," he said, "but he's going to need to wear a cast for a month to six weeks, which means he'll likely be starting school wearing a sling." He grinned at Matt.

"Matt tells me he's right-handed, though, so the cast won't get him out of doing his homework."

Alec asked a few questions; Julia had trouble focusing on the answers. Saying that he was going to arrange the CT scan, after which they would set and cast the arm, the doctor left. Watching Matt, Julia realized he must really hurt; they wouldn't have given him anything like morphine without her permission, would they? Or maybe they'd delayed because of the head injury.

"You know how lucky you were," Alec said, stepping closer to the bed.

"What's a CT scan?" Matt asked, low. "I mean, do they think, like, there's something wrong with my brain?"

That conversation wafted over Julia, too. She could tell that Matt was keeping an anxious eye on her. Maybe her silence was worrying him. Well, good.

"They said you rolled Uncle Alec's almost brand-new SUV," she said, then flushed when she realized she'd interrupted Alec midsentence.

He only smiled.

Matt hung his head. "Um…yeah."

"I imagine it will be totaled," Alec agreed. "I've never seen a vehicle yet that was in a rollover accident not sent to the wrecking yard."

"Are you… What are you going to do to me?" Matt's voice was high and scared, although it had begun, recently, to change.

Alec glanced at her; she nodded tacit permission. Her son's eyes widened apprehensively.

"That's going to depend on you, Matt." Alec leaned against the bed railing. "You have to talk to us about what's going on with you. Things have to change."

Matt didn't say anything.

"Let's start with why you were so angry to see me kiss your mother."

Once more the boy lowered his gaze to the bed-covers and plucked at them with his fingers. "I was, um, I mean, I thought you were hanging around for *me*. Well, for Liana and me. But then I figured you weren't. You know?"

To her astonishment, Alec smiled at him. "Your feelings were hurt."

"I guess," Matt mumbled.

"I *was* hanging around for your sake and Liana's. I was also trying to support your mom." He rubbed a hand over the back of his neck, as if giving himself a moment to frame what he wanted to say. "Matt, you can love more than one person at a time. Your mother didn't love you any less once Liana was born. You know that, right?"

Her son's dark eyes flicked her way. His "I guess" was just audible.

"No matter what happens between your mother and me, I will *always* be there for you and your sister. I've loved you since the day you were born. You know that, too, don't you?"

After a moment, Matt nodded.

"That has nothing to do with my feelings for your mother. You need to know I thought of her as my brother's wife and nothing else until after your dad died. But feelings can change. All of us together…" He shrugged. "I wanted us to be a family for real. Tonight, you made it pretty plain that's not what you want."

That brought Matt's gaze up. "No! I mean, I don't know. I just…I freaked out."

"We noticed," Alec said drily.

Julia looked over her shoulder to be sure no one was coming for Matt yet. She didn't see anyone at all. The E.R. was remarkably quiet—or maybe not so remarkably, since a glance at the wall clock told her it was now after five in the morning. As small as the hospital was, perhaps they were having to wait for someone to come in to do the CT scan.

"Matt," she said, past a lump in her throat, "we have to talk about what you heard between your dad and me."

Tears rushed into his eyes. Something awful was happening inside him. He started talking, but some of it was incoherent, squeezed out between gulps for air. "Dad…why didn't he want us? Really want us? Why did he *go?*"

"Oh, Mattie." The childhood nickname slid out, but he didn't seem to notice.

Seeing the way she pressed against it, Alec lowered the rail of the bed. Julia sat on the edge and reached for her son, the little boy she hadn't cuddled in so long. Mixed with her grief was astonishment and joy, because he burrowed into her, his good arm wrapping hard around her waist as he shook with sobs. Her own face wet, she murmured reassurances. "I love you. Oh, Mattie, I love you."

Once she lifted her head to see Alec watching them, his eyes near black with emotion. Seeing her face, he sat down, too, and wrapped his arms around both of them. They huddled together while she thought her heart might break from sadness and happiness both.

"It was me," Matt said finally, pulling back a little. "After…after I heard you, I asked Dad why he wouldn't stay with us. He talked about how important what he did was and how you didn't understand, maybe because you were a woman, but how *I'd* understand, because I was his son."

The horror on his face told her they had finally come to the heart of his misery.

"And you told him you didn't," she whispered.

"I yelled at him!" He vibrated with remembered anguish. "I said he was never there. That *we* were important, too. And how he missed most of my baseball games. And he kept on about how someday I'd understand and I said I never would. That I wished he'd go away so I could get a new father! And—" a huge, convulsive sob shook him "—and he did."

"Oh, Mattie," she said again, tightening her embrace until he was crying against her breast. "Your dad didn't die because of what you said, any more than he did because of what *I* said. He died because he had a dangerous job and every time he went away for real—" like her, Matt knew the difference between missions and training exercises "—there were people who wanted to kill him."

He was listening. What astonished her most was that, for the first time ever, *she* believed what she'd just said. She was no more responsible for Josh's death than Matt was.

Sniffling, Matt rubbed his face against her. "If I blamed you…"

"You could pretend you didn't blame yourself." She kissed his tousled head.

He didn't say anything.

The squeak of rubber-soled shoes on the shiny floor gave them all warning. A cheerful young man smiled at them.

"I'm here to take the young Mr. Raynor for a ride. I'm afraid the rest of you would weigh the bed down a little too much."

Alec only laughed as he stood. Embarrassed, wiping her cheeks, Julia gave Matt a last squeeze and stood, Alec's supporting arm helping her. Matt hastily swiped at his own wet cheeks and snotty nose with an edge of the sheet, making his mother wince.

The young man only chuckled. He suggested the two adults go get coffee, since this was going to

take a while. Matt lay back, and a moment later
Alec and Julia were left alone in a room that felt
strangely empty with the bed having been wheeled
out.

Alec reached for her hand, his eyes concerned.
"Okay?"

"Yes. I think I really am," she said in wonder.
"Oh, Alec. It wasn't just me!"

"No." He tugged her closer. "It wasn't you at all.
I'd begun to wonder. His reaction was too extreme
for it all to be rooted in anger at his mother."

"He really was trying to…maybe not die, but
punish himself."

"*Self* being the key."

She felt dizzy and nearly weightless as she rested
her forehead against Alec's strong shoulder. "Oh,
God. I was so scared. And now…"

"Now there's hope." His arms enclosed her se-
curely.

IT WAS A LONG NIGHT.

They didn't see Matt again for an hour and a half.
Coffee came from a machine; even in a hospital, the
cafeteria didn't open until six. Alec had his wallet
but no cash; he was glad when Julia turned out to
have plenty in her purse. He'd never needed a cup
of coffee more.

Matt was drowsy by the time he returned, his
arm and elbow encased in white plaster and sup-
ported by a sling. The doctor reappeared to tell Alec

and Julia that the scan had looked fine, but he'd like to keep Matt for twenty-four hours as a precaution. Concussions could be unpredictable, he said.

This time Matt was transferred to a wheelchair. Alec and Julia walked with him to the second floor of the hospital, where he was settled into a bed. Because another patient was trying to sleep on the other side of the curtain, they couldn't talk. Julia held Matt's hand until he fell asleep, and then she and Alec left the hospital.

The sunlight somehow surprised Alec even though he knew morning had come. Julia paused outside the doors, blinking bemusedly.

"Maybe we should have breakfast in the cafeteria before we go home," he said.

"I'd rather make us something," she said.

He smiled at her. "Fine by me." Even if she poured him a bowl of cornflakes, it would taste fantastic because she'd supplied it.

"Oh! It's late enough to call Andrea, isn't it?"

She already had her phone out and it was ringing by the time he had her car unlocked. He didn't ask if she wanted to drive; given his job, he'd become inured to interrupted sleep and even nights when he got no sleep at all. In the midst of a homicide investigation or when the chance for a big drug bust came, you didn't knock off at five for dinner and bed. Julia was always beautiful to him, but he also noted the bruised look beneath her eyes and the slowness of her usually quick, graceful movements.

She fumbled for the seat belt and he helped her fasten it as she talked to their neighbor, then to Liana.

"Yes, Matt's fine and really embarrassed," Julia told Liana. "He insists he thought he could drive." She actually laughed. "You may be jealous, because he has a cast. Think what an attention-getter that will be when you two start school." She listened and finally said, "Okay, let me talk to Andrea again."

They were almost home when she ended the call. He glanced at her. "I suppose Liana had a great night's sleep and is raring to go."

"Probably, but Andrea has an outing planned. They're going to a late-morning movie, out to lunch and then shopping. You know I'd promised to buy Liana boots for riding. Andrea's going to take care of that for both girls. Bless her heart, she says not to expect Liana until dinnertime. She knows I need to take a nap and then go back to see Matt later."

"We struck gold when it came to neighbors," Alec agreed.

"So…breakfast first."

He hadn't really expected her to reach for the cereal boxes. They were no sooner in her side of the duplex than she began to bustle. An omelet, she decided. Tomorrow morning, they'd have waffles before they went to pick up Matt at the hospital. Waffles were Liana's favorite, even Alec knew.

He liked the way Julia said *we*. She was including him, wasn't she?

Cooking seemed to energize her, although he suspected she'd wind down fast once the food settled comfortably in her stomach. She chattered over breakfast, a little too brightly, repeating herself several times.

"Listen to me!" she said finally, laughing. "I feel like I just walked out of prison. Free at last!" Her gaze sought his. "Am I being too optimistic?"

"No." He captured her hand across the table. "We had to find out what was really eating at him. Now we know. I'm guessing he's feeling as relieved as you are."

She shook her head. "He actually thought we'd hate him," Julia marveled.

"He's a teenager," Alec said matter-of-factly. "Everything is blown bigger than it should be. And this…this was big to start with. You've felt guilty yourself, and you're adult enough to know better."

"That's true." She smiled at him. "I feel giddy. Did I ever tell you I took dance lessons when I was a girl? I'm sure I could go en pointe now. *Swan Lake,* here I come!"

"I can see you as a dancer," Alec said seriously. "You have the body."

"I don't think our dance school was very good. Mrs. Hopper, who owned it and taught the classes I took, was in her fifties and had gotten a little pudgy. But we had fun and dreamed a little."

"Did you play any sports?"

She shook her head. "In my town, Little League

was for boys, and the first soccer league started when I was a teenager. Of course, the high school had girls' sports, but the skill level was pretty awful. How were we supposed to compete on a basketball court when the only time we'd ever played was in PE?"

He chuckled at her indignation. "Sorry, sweetheart, but basketball wouldn't have been your sport no matter what." The chuckle became an outright laugh. "I can just picture you under the basket trying to block a shot."

"I think I'm insulted."

"No, you're just short."

Julia blew a raspberry. "What about you?"

"Believe it or not, I actually did play basketball. Despite my height, I was a guard on my high school team. Neither tall enough nor good enough to play at a college level, though. Not really interested enough, either, I guess."

He rambled a little about the sports he and Josh had both enjoyed: surfing, mountain biking, hiking. "He was always more into high-adrenaline stuff. He took up hang gliding at one point. He earned enough summers to be able to afford to take flying lessons and try skydiving. Me, I'm not actually that crazy about heights."

"Really?" Julia looked fascinated. "I never knew that."

"I don't advertise it."

She tried to suppress the smile, but he saw it in her eyes. "Big tough cop with a weakness?"

"Reputation is everything," he told her.

Now she had the chance to laugh at him, and he enjoyed it. Damn, she was beautiful when she was happy. In one way he'd known how unhappy she had become, but the effects had been gradual.

Her smile slowly faded. "Why are you looking at me like that?"

"I'm thinking how beautiful you are," he said quietly. He pushed his chair back and held out a hand to her. "Hey, come here."

Her teeth momentarily sank into her lower lip. Her eyes never left his as she stood and rounded the corner of the table. Instead of taking his hand, she plopped down on his lap and slid her arms around his neck. "Alec," she murmured and pressed her lips to his.

He kissed her, trying to keep it gentle, although a sort of static wiped out most of his rational thoughts almost immediately. Her lips were so soft, so giving. She smelled good and tasted good, although he couldn't have described either. It was just…Julia.

He nibbled on her lower lip and shuddered when she did the same to his and then soothed it with her tongue. His hands dug into her. He'd never gotten hard so fast. Even so, Alec somehow kept the kiss slow, almost lazy, his tongue sliding against hers, stroking the roof of her mouth, swirling against the tantalizing flesh of her cheeks.

She made little sounds and kneaded his shoulders and neck while her tongue danced with his.

Pulling back took everything he had. It didn't help when he got a good look at her face, her eyes dreamy and shimmering with gold, her mouth swollen and damp.

"Julia…" Voice scratchy, he stopped. Lifting his hand, he cupped her delicate jaw and cheek, loving the way she tilted her face as if to nestle into his touch. "I know you must be exhausted. We don't have to do this."

She blinked, looking for a moment as if she had stepped out into the startlingly bright day. Then she seemed to focus. "*Have* to do this? What's that supposed to mean?"

"I don't want to—" God, had he been going to say *take advantage of you?* Really? "Push you."

It had to be pride stiffening her spine. Julia planted her hands on his chest and shoved herself away, wriggling to get off his lap. "If you don't want me…"

"You know damn well I do!"

"Then what?" She looked mad. "I'm tired of throwing myself at you and getting nowhere! Let's just forget it."

He easily prevented her from standing. As pissed as he'd been a second ago, he didn't know where the amusement had come from. "Throwing yourself at me? Is that what you've been doing?"

Glaring did not suit a face as finely made as hers. "Yes!"

God help him, he was still painfully hard. "There

is nothing in life I want more than to make love with you."

"Then what's wrong?"

"Nothing." His voice had become husky. "Nothing at all. Hold on tight." He slid an arm under her thighs and stood. Julia squeaked. Striding from the kitchen, he momentarily paused. "Did we lock the door?"

He saw from her face that he'd awakened dismay in her, too. Probably Andrea would keep the girls safely away from home, but who knew? What if one of them didn't feel good and they came home early?

"I think so," Julia said uncertainly. "But Liana has a key, you know."

"Oh, hell." After a moment, he let her body slide down his, increasing his torment. "Then let's go over to my side."

"Yes!"

"Bring your phone."

She spotted it on the kitchen counter and darted over to grab it.

Like two teenagers sneaking out into the night, they locked the door behind them and hustled from the small concrete pad that was her porch to the matching one that was his. Inserting the key almost took more concentration than he could manage. Once he had the door open, she whisked past him. He slammed it, turned the dead bolt and reached for her. He scooped her up again to bring her to his level, and when she wrapped her legs around his waist, he swung around and braced her back against the door. Two soft thuds told him her sandals had fallen to the floor.

They kissed deeply, hungrily. Alec quit holding back; he couldn't. She squirmed against him, driving him insane. His hips rocked, his head fogged. By instinct one hand found her breast, cupping it and squeezing, rubbing the peak of her nipple with his palm. He wanted to tear off her shirt, find smooth, bare skin, but he'd have had to back off to do that and he couldn't. He rocked his erection into the cradle her parted legs offered until he was painfully, excruciatingly close to coming without ever getting inside her.

He finally tore his mouth away from hers. "God, Julia," he said desperately.

She looked at him without comprehension.

This was their first time. They couldn't do it against the door. He turned his head and saw the sofa. Gripping her more firmly, he started that way. His legs didn't feel as steady as they had and his path across the small living room wavered. It didn't help that she was kissing and licking his neck. The feel of her damp tongue lapping at the base of his throat had him groaning his need.

About to lay her down, Alec clenched his teeth

instead. "Julia," he ground out, "are you on birth control?"

She bit the thick muscle that ran from his neck to his shoulder.

"Julia!" Even more desperate, he shook her. "Are you on the pill?"

Comprehension came slowly, but made it in the end. Her eyes widened. "No! After Josh, I decided to take a break."

"Bed, then." He stumbled around the back of the leather sofa and started toward the short hall.

"Do you have something?" She sounded stricken.

"Yeah." He'd thrown away the box of condoms he'd kept in the bathroom at his Los Feliz place before he moved, disconcerted to see the expiration date. He hadn't gone that long without sex since his first experience at sixteen. But within a couple of weeks of Julia's arrival in Angel Butte, he'd bought a new box. Hope in action.

"Oh, thank goodness," she breathed.

"I wouldn't be the police chief if I couldn't plan ahead."

She giggled at his feeble attempt at a joke, but then started nuzzling his throat again, and whatever limited blood was fueling his brain went south again.

He shouldered open the bedroom door, made it the last few steps and planted a knee on his bed, laying her down. He had to get her clothes off before he lowered himself onto her.

Funny thing, as he reached for the hem of her T-shirt, she was reaching for his. They struggled momentarily until he muttered, "Oh, the hell with it," and stripped off his own while she did the same. The color of a ripe peach, her bra was pretty. He didn't care. He had it off and tossed aside between one breath and the next.

"Julia" was all he could manage to say, and that was guttural. Now he did bear her back again, hungry to close his mouth over her taut, rose-brown nipple. He sucked it deep into his mouth, tugging rhythmically. She gave a strangled cry and her hips rose and fell, making him crazy. He wanted to savor her, but knew he couldn't hold out that long.

Lifting himself away from her, he worked on unfastening her chinos and pulled both them and her panties down. When he straightened, her small hands found the button on his trousers. It was ecstasy and agony watching her concentrate fiercely on getting him naked. He sucked in his belly as she tugged on the zipper, her fingers stroking him as she pulled it down. Then she gripped him through the cotton of his briefs, squeezed and slid her fingers beneath the elastic waistband to work the briefs down, too. Once she got them as far as his thighs, he took over, kicking off shoes and pants, wrenching off his socks and coming down on top of her for the hungriest, most frantic kiss of his life.

"Condom," she gasped at one point, and he managed to roll away to wrench open the bedside drawer, where he'd tossed a few loose ones. He used his teeth to rip open the packaging and rolled the condom on with careless haste.

Then Alec looked at her, the woman he'd wanted for so damn long, and felt a wave of euphoria. There she sprawled, arms and legs wide and waiting for him, her nipples dark and hard, her hair tousled against the bedcover, her slender body everything he could ever want.

With a ragged sound, he came down on her, stroking her silken dampness once and then driving inside her as if he wouldn't survive another minute if he didn't.

Her back arched. "Alec," she whispered and reached around to grab him.

It took them a minute to catch a rhythm, but it didn't matter. Every plunge was rapture, his senses so heightened that her fingernails digging into him, her high, helpless sounds, the whisper of her breath against his skin, all were more erotic than anything he could remember.

He couldn't have lasted long. He didn't have to. He knew the moment her heels drove into the bed and her body began to spasm. He let himself go.

The release rolled through him like thunder, long and powerful, deafening and blinding him.

In the end, he sagged down on her, his eyes closed. He said her name again, thankfully.

CHAPTER FOURTEEN

JULIA THOUGHT THAT DAY might have been the happiest of her life, even if, really, so much was unresolved.

She and Alec had finally made love. Twice, the second time coming after a lengthy nap. The experience had been so astonishing, she felt her cheeks warming every time she thought about the time in bed with him. She hadn't known she could lose her inhibitions so completely. She'd been sure she would feel self-conscious about the thin silver stretch marks low on her abdomen, but as he was stripping her, it had never even crossed her mind that he might be disappointed in what he found. She'd expected to feel self-conscious, period—she hadn't been naked with any man but Josh in a really long time. She hadn't known she could want so much, there was no room left for self-consciousness.

And then there was Matt. The way he'd flung himself into her arms that morning at the hospital and cried against her both warmed her and made her heart ache at the same time. She hated knowing he'd wrestled with the same pain and guilt as she had, but with much more devastating results.

When she and Alec had gone back to the hospital midafternoon, she'd worried that Matt would have retreated into the all-too-familiar sullenness, but he hadn't. He was shy and quiet, but no longer bristling. He seemed, if anything, to be in more pain than he was right after the accident, and kept shifting to try to get comfortable. Julia wasn't sure if he repeatedly adjusted the head and foot of the bed because he couldn't get comfortable or because he liked pushing buttons, but she didn't say anything about it.

He dozed in the late afternoon. Alec announced that he'd pick up Liana and bring her and dinner to the hospital. When Julia asked if they were allowed to eat in here, he just smiled, slow and sexy, and said, "To hell with 'em."

When Matt's dinner was delivered, the nurses pretended not to notice the odor of cheeseburgers and fries that permeated the room or the wadded-up wrappers filling the trash can. Both kids loved the idea that they were pulling a fast one on Authority, with a capital *A*. Amused, Julia wasn't so sure Alec wasn't enjoying it, too.

Finally, after Matt had taken some pain meds, they left him to sleep with a promise to be back to get him first thing tomorrow. Julia's biggest regret of the day was that Alec didn't come in with her and Liana. He waited while Julia unlocked and opened the door, hugged Liana, then bent his head to give Julia a swift, soft kiss on the mouth.

"Dream about me," he murmured and strode across the yard toward his own front door. When he reached it and noticed that she was still watching him, he gave a cocky grin. "Go on. Lock up."

Julia smiled sweetly, blew him a kiss and went inside.

It wasn't until she was alone in bed that doubts crept in.

Matt still felt embarrassed and chagrined because of the enormity of what he'd done. The effect might not last. He'd spent a year and a half rebelling with all the fervor he could summon. Could true confessions really restore them to the good old days, when he'd been an even-tempered boy? If nothing else, he'd become a teenager in the interval. Even if the worst was behind them, she didn't exactly know who the Matt who emerged would be.

And Alec. It hadn't really struck Julia until now that he'd never said the words *I love you.* Well, neither had she. But she was hampered by her upbringing in an old-fashioned town with old-fashioned parents. A lady would never say it first. And, oh, it was silly, because she knew Alec did love her, in one way at least. It just wasn't necessarily the way she wanted.

She kept thinking about what he'd said to Matt at the hospital. *I wanted us to be a family for real.* He'd also talked about how a person could love more than one person at a time. But…thinking back, it seemed to her that a lot of what he'd said had focused on thinking of them as *his* family. If he asked her to marry him, as she assumed he would, Julia didn't think, no matter what, she could bring herself to say no. He was too good to her and so good for the kids. She could not imagine living her life without him when she had the alternative of living it with him.

But that didn't keep her from wishing she could know for sure that he would have loved *her,* just her, whether Matt and Liana were part of the package or not.

And then there was the trial. She'd taken to eyeing the calendar daily, mentally checking off the days until he had to go. A week from tomorrow was August 4. He'd said they would probably want him that week, and it seemed likely he'd choose to fly out on the fourth, as it was a Sunday. So he'd be there for Liana's birthday party and then gone the following day. And even if the trial lagged and he didn't have to go quite that soon, he still had to go eventually. She was scared to death that Roberto Perez would find a way to keep Alec from testifying. Alec's very confidence in himself heightened her fear. Would he really let himself be kept in seclusion and guarded by federal agents, the way he should? Or would he take the threat too lightly?

The few hours of sleep she and Alec had gotten today hadn't been enough to make up for what they'd lost the night before, though, which meant she did sleep, and deeply. She awakened to the sound of voices. Straining to hear, she decided it was the television and relaxed. Liana was up.

Julia stuck her head in the living room and found her daughter curled on the sofa watching a favorite DVD rather than a television show. Julia bent over the back of the sofa, kissed the top of her head and said, "I'm going to take a quick shower."

"Uncle Alec said you promised waffles this morning."

"I did, and I'll deliver."

"Cool!"

"Let him in if he gets here, but look out the window to be sure it's him before you answer the door, okay?"

Liana rolled her eyes, looking disconcertingly adolescent.

By the time Julia emerged, feeling like a new woman, Alec had indeed arrived. His dark eyes surveyed her, and his approval of her shorts and skimpy T-shirt was obvious.

Over the breakfast table, he talked to Liana about her brother. "I think you're going to find he's different. He got some things out he needed to say to your mom and me, and that's going to make a difference."

Her high forehead crinkled. "What things?"

Alec shook his head. "I think right now it's better if Matt can keep that private. I don't blame you for being curious, but I'd suggest you don't push it with him. If he wants to tell you, he can, but let him do it in his own way, when he's ready."

Liana looked astonished and indignant. "But I want to know!"

Amusement crinkled the corners of Alec's dark eyes. "You always want to know everything, sweet pea. But this time—" He shook his head. "You want the old Matt back, don't you?"

She gaped, then looked at Julia. "Mom! Why can't I know what happened? He doesn't have to *know* I know."

Julia's laughter came more easily this morning than it had in a long time. "I hate to say it, daughter of mine, but you have a big mouth. You'd say something, and then he'd be mad that we told you."

"Humph." Liana crossed her arms and glared at them.

Alec laughed, too. "I like you better smiling than glowering."

He swept them out the door a few minutes after. Julia hadn't even finished cleaning the kitchen and didn't care. Matt was waiting for them to pick him up. He looked pathetic with the sling, the bandage on his head and, yes, a pair of black eyes.

He was also, if possible, even more subdued this morning and got grumpy when in the backseat his sister persisted in begging to be the first person to sign his cast.

"You'll do it in some girly colors and then I'd

have to tell everyone my *sister* wrote on it," he said disagreeably.

Julia sighed, but caught the grin twitching on Alec's mouth. Well, okay, the squabble probably was standard-issue brother-sister interaction. And besides, Liana *was* being kind of a pain, in revenge going on about her horse camp starting tomorrow and how especially with a broken arm Matt wouldn't be able to do anything.

"He can't swim," she said with satisfaction, "or ride his bike or—"

"Knock it off," Alec said mildly before she could continue. "One of these days you'll injure yourself and you don't want your brother gloating, do you?"

Fortunately, Sophie was sitting on her front steps, apparently waiting, because she bounced to her feet as soon as the car turned in. Given permission, Liana raced off to her house. Andrea's car was in the driveway, so presumably she was home. Julia couldn't help noticing that Alec had gotten out and looked around carefully before he let her go.

When Matt climbed out slowly, he gazed toward Alec's empty driveway. "Are you going to have to drive Mom's car from now on?" he asked in a small voice.

"No, I talked to my insurance agent yesterday," Alec said. "The rental company is supposed to deliver a comparable vehicle by midday." Of course, he had to explain that a comparable vehicle meant an SUV. And no, the agent hadn't seen the Tahoe yet, but would be looking tomorrow morning. Julia already knew that the officers who *had* seen it had told Alec it was a miracle Matt had escaped with relatively minor injuries and that the Tahoe would never drive again.

"Will they replace it?" Matt asked almost meekly.

"I'll lose some money," Alec said. "Because I've been driving it for four months, it's considered used. It'll cost me if I want to start with another new one."

Matt seemed to shrink. "Oh."

"I can afford it." Alec clapped him on the back, but lightly. "Although I may deduct what I lose from how much I'm willing to contribute to buying you a car when you get your driver's license."

"*If* you get your driver's license," Julia said sternly, glad Alec hadn't sugarcoated the reality of what Matt had done.

Alarm flared on her son's face. "They can't keep me from driving, can they? I mean, when I'm sixteen?"

She crossed her arms. "I don't know about the Department of Motor Vehicles, but *I* can."

He opened his mouth. Their gazes held. After a long moment, he slowly closed his mouth.

Alec laid a hand on Matt's shoulder. "Let's go in."

"Did you get fed at the hospital?" Julia asked.

"Yeah." Matt sounded dispirited. "But the eggs were gross. All I ate was this little box of Cheerios."

"I left the waffle iron out. Want one?"

"You mean, you'd make me one?"

She discovered she didn't like to see him quite so humbled. "Yes," she said gently. "I cooked for you even when you were being a snot, didn't I?"

He lifted his head. "I guess so."

"If you're heating up the waffle iron again," Alec said hopefully, "I wouldn't mind seconds."

He made coffee, poured Matt a glass of orange juice and got out the butter and syrup again while Julia produced two more waffles. Man and boy both devoured theirs with astonishing speed.

"I guess you won't buy kayaks now," Matt said when his plate was empty, eyeing his uncle side-long.

Alec raised his eyebrows. "That depends. You need to show us that things are going to be different."

There was no familiar flash of defiance or anger on her son's face. He only nodded with apparent docility. "I couldn't paddle anyway." He sounded depressed.

"Not for a few weeks," Alec agreed. "You know I'll be away for a little while anyway."

The reminder chilled Julia. Matt only nodded. Neither adult had made him aware of the danger Alec would be in during this trip to Los Angeles.

Matt's expression was desperate when he looked at Julia. "Were you really going to divorce Dad?"

She set down her coffee cup. "Are you sure you want to talk about this now?"

"It's all I can think about."

"All right."

Seeing her hesitate, Alec said, "Would you two rather talk without me here?"

"That's up to Matt," she said. "I don't have anything to say you can't hear."

Matt hung his head and mumbled, but they both heard him clearly enough. "I guess I don't mind."

Alec nodded and stood to replenish his coffee. Julia shook her head when he lifted the carafe.

She looked at her son. "Matt, it's taken me time to realize something."

He lifted his head, and the eyes that caught hers were almost as deep a brown as Alec's. She could see Josh in his face, but increasingly saw Alec there, too.

"I blamed your dad's job for all our troubles," she began. "I was resentful because I thought he was choosing it over us."

"He did!"

Julia shook her head. "In the end, he chose it over me." She emphasized the *me,* wanting to be sure he heard. "But he loved you and Liana, you know. I think he'd have kept being a good father within his limitations even once we were divorced. There was nothing that made him happier than teaching you to surf, kicking your butt at…I don't know, whatever video game you two used to play for hours."

"We played a bunch of different ones." Now he sounded sullen.

"There was a lot he enjoyed doing with you. I don't want you to forget that. He loved being with you."

His shoulders jerked. "When he was home."

"That part had to do with his job," she agreed. "But this is what I finally realized—if your dad and I had loved each other enough and had a good marriage otherwise, I could have lived with his job. What he did *is* important. Our country needs people like him. He could never tell me where he'd been or what he did when he was away, but a few times I had a pretty good idea. I think his team rescued those American aid workers in Mali, for example. Every one of them survived and came home. How could I not be proud of your dad for pulling something like that off?" She saw something ease on Matt's face and was glad. The fact that he was listening so closely gave her hope, too. "The job was hugely important to him. I think in a way it was his identity. He didn't know what would be left if he gave it up."

"So—you *didn't* love him?" her son asked.

"Of course I did. But I think now I was too young when I married him to be sure what I wanted. I compared him to the boys I knew back home and even the college boys I'd dated, and was dazzled. It turned out we didn't have an awful lot in common. For both of us, I think the stresses wore away at what we felt for each other. If he had gone back into the regular navy or asked for a transfer to training at Coronado when I asked, I suspect he'd have felt resentful and that would have done more damage. All of that doesn't mean I didn't still love your dad enough to mourn when he was killed. The part we have to remember is that he died doing a job he loved. He didn't die because he quarreled with us. He was killed by this country's enemies. Both of us need to be proud of him for risking so much every time he went. He wouldn't want us to feel guilty. Your dad didn't dwell on things like that. He'd have said, 'Forget about it,' and taken you fishing."

Matt gave a choked laugh, but tears were also streaming down his face. "I miss him!" he wailed.

Sitting closer to him, Alec wrapped an arm around him. "Yeah," he said, his face against Matt's head. "I do, too. We all do."

Julia was crying now, as well. Her vision blurred, as if she was seeing through a rain-washed window, but she couldn't look away from the man holding the boy, their hair the same tousled, shiny shade of dark brown. Seeing them so close together re-inforced her awareness of the blood they shared and increased her sense of gratitude. Having Alec would mean everything to a boy who'd lost his father.

Alec finally handed Matt a cloth napkin from the table. He used it to wipe his cheeks and give his nose a resounding blow. He looked both pathetic with those black eyes and absurdly young when he crumpled the napkin and gazed at her.

"What did you mean when you said 'within his limitations'?"

Julia had to cast her thoughts back. Maybe she shouldn't have said that. She didn't want to disillusion either of the kids. At the same time, maybe everything would have been different if she'd been honest since Josh died. She thought Matt was old enough to understand.

So she talked a little about her frustration and her feeling that Josh was too often more friend than parent, leaving her, always, to be the bad guy, and how unfair that was.

Matt listened, unblinking. When she finished, he sat for a moment without saying anything. When he finally did, he glanced between her and Alec.

"Are you two, like, getting married?"

Alec's dark gaze flicked to her, then back to her son. "You were pretty angry at the possibility."

Matt's shoulders moved uncomfortably. "I didn't really mean it. You know."

"Good." Alec wrapped him in a neck lock that apparently qualified as a hug, because it had Matt grinning sheepishly. "As for getting married, your mom and I haven't talked about it yet, but I think she knows my vote is yes."

Her heart gave one of those sharp, almost painful squeezes. "You," she said to her son, "are not to say a word to Liana, because we haven't talked to her yet about anything like this. Okay?"

"She doesn't know why I, um, flipped out like that?"

"No, she doesn't," Julia said. "Alec and I do need to talk between ourselves about the future, but probably not until he gets back from L.A. He's leaving—" She transferred her gaze to him. "When are you leaving? Do you know?"

He grimaced. "Looks like a week from today. They've started jury selection already. That's a long and involved process for a trial of this magnitude."

"I can imagine." She frowned. "Will they be sequestered?"

"Probably," Alec answered. "Both for their safety and to be sure they can't be pressured."

She shuddered. He saw and made a quick movement, but didn't follow through on it, not with Matt beside him.

He had to explain to Matt what sequestration meant, and she saw her son's face grow grave. He was old enough to grasp the implication. If the jurors faced possible threats, so might the witnesses.

"Oh," he said finally. "Are you... I mean, do you *have* to go?"

"Yes. It's part of my job. Investigating is the first stage, and making the arrest is the second, but that's all wasted if an officer doesn't testify at the trial to help ensure a conviction. In this case, the guy who is being tried is a real scumbag. I want to see him go to prison for a long, long time."

Matt gnawed on his lip. "You'll only be gone, like, a week, though, right?"

"That's my hope. But prosecutors can't be sure how fast things will move and exactly what day they'll need me. I have to be in town and available."

"Will you see Nana and Granddad while you're there?"

"Maybe." Alec smiled. "I plan to try."

Julia had been watching Matt, who, despite the questions, seemed to be flagging. "Do you need another pain pill?"

"Maybe," he said. "Can I watch TV?"

"Of course you can." She stood, smiling. "Let me grab your pillows and an afghan so you can get comfy on the sofa. Alec, you have the pills, don't you?"

He doled one out. By the time she returned to the living room, Matt had picked out a DVD, and Alec had put it on for him.

Then Alec stretched. "Damn it, I'd better go mow the lawn."

Feeling guilty, Julia said, "I could do that, you know."

He shook his head. "Walk me out."

They stepped out onto the small front porch, Alec pulling the door almost closed behind them.

"Hey," he said softly, "that went well."

"It did, didn't it?" She was still having trouble believing she might have her son back.

"Don't try to surprise me by mowing someday. I don't want you exposed outside for any length of time any more than I want either of the kids out here."

"No, but I could do the back," she offered. "Now that the fence is up."

He shook his head. "You do enough."

They had a brief skirmish over who worked harder, but he held firm. She wasn't sure whether this was a gender-role issue—only boys and men did the hard yard work—or whether it was all his need to protect. Either way, she decided not to argue too much. Mowing was boring, and it would be a great job for Matt once they could be sure nobody wanted to hurt him. When Liana was a little older, Julia would insist on her doing her share, too.

Alec's gaze rested on her. "You're worrying more about my trip to L.A. than you need to."

"I can't help it."

"Because of Josh."

"Maybe." *Yes.* "And because somebody already tried to kill you or Matt."

He tilted his head in acknowledgment. They stood for a moment, neither saying anything, a sudden awkwardness between them.

Are you two, like, getting married?
I think she knows my vote is yes.

He bent his head and nuzzled her hair. "I don't suppose you'd like to leave your bedroom window unlocked tonight," he murmured.

Julia felt a cramp of longing. "You know I can't."

"Yeah, but how are we going to get away from the kids at all?" He sounded…accepting, but also a little disgruntled.

"It would be easier if we weren't trying to keep them under lock and key."

"Damn it." He lifted her chin so he could kiss her. "You could offer me a glass of lemonade in an hour."

Julia laughed. "I can do that."

With reluctance, they separated, him loping across the grass to lift his garage door, her slipping inside.

THE WEEK THAT FOLLOWED was pretty damn idyllic in some ways, and yet for Alec undermined by constant tension.

Matt stayed quiet and thoughtful, but he also grew bored, for which no one could blame him, and whiny, for which they could. Alec wanted to avoid, if he possibly could, explaining why he thought those shots had been intended for Matt rather than him, which left Matt failing to understand why he couldn't leave the house without Julia or Alec.

"I could go for walks, at least!" Matt complained.

Alec settled for saying, "I need you to stick close

to home until this trial is over. My family could be used to pressure me into changing my testimony."

"But Liana gets to go places," Matt said mutinously.

"Only under supervision. If you think of something you want to do, I imagine your mom will take you."

A shadow crossed Matt's face. "I still have to go to court, don't I?" he asked. "I mean, for shoplifting."

"Yeah, you do. And," Alec added sternly, "if I didn't believe you'd learned something from it, you'd have been arrested for motor-vehicle theft, too."

"But it was yours—" Matt glimpsed the expression on Alec's face. "Oh, um, I guess."

"So count your blessings, kid. You'd have gotten time in juvenile detention for that for sure."

It appeared some actual thought was going on, which Alec saw as a good thing.

"Do you think that time someone shot at us had to do with this trial?"

"I don't know," he said truthfully, angrier than he wanted to admit at the lack of answers.

That was the other thing about the week. He was waiting for that second shoe to drop. Whatever the motive for taking those potshots at him and Matt, why hadn't there been a follow-up? Why no phone call saying, *You've had your warning. Next time's for real?* Matt had mostly been unavailable for a second attempt on his life, but Alec had half expected one on *his* life, although he hadn't said that to Julia. It didn't happen. He'd taken to worrying increasingly about Julia and Liana, but so far, nothing there, either.

Julia didn't seem to notice how often a patrol car swung by the duplex or hovered on Bond Road outside the ranch where the two girls had their riding camp. Somebody thinking of snatching one of them or threatening them would notice, though. Maybe the precautions were enough. Alec had checked out the ranch and been glad to see how open the surrounding countryside was. No cover for a sharpshooter.

He was dreading getting on that damn airplane and leaving them alone. The riding camp ran into the following week, and that was when the participants were to be taken on trail rides, leading into some partially wooded areas. Brian Cooper had found a horseman among the young patrol officers; he was to be inserted as a wrangler who'd stick close to Liana and Julia. Alec understood the owner of the ranch wasn't thrilled to learn about the possible danger, but had accepted the assurance that the precautions were really just designed to placate the police chief, who was overprotective of his niece.

Alec had had to shake his head and laugh at that.

He engaged in daily phone calls with the federal prosecutors in Southern California, who were getting jumpy. They'd have liked to have him down there now and didn't like his refusal to come any sooner than he had to. He'd explained his concerns about his family but had the sense he wasn't being taken seriously. The phone threats had been specific and unrelated to Perez, he was reminded.

Yeah—but he wasn't convinced.

And the sexual tension was killing him. The kids were always there. Matt especially. He not only never went anywhere, he was keeping a close eye on his mom and uncle, too. A couple of times he made excuses to follow them to Alec's side of the duplex. Maybe out of boredom, maybe because he was old enough to suspect what Alec had on his mind. Matt had, after all, stolen those condoms. Even if he was sort of okay with his mother and Alec getting married, the idea of them having sex was another story. Alec could only imagine the poor kid's horror.

The result was no sex. Alec and Julia managed to sneak kisses a few times, but those frustrated him as much as anything.

He'd have liked to propose and have an answer before he went, too. A ring on her finger. Alec discovered how much he hated uncertainty in his personal life. He kept thinking about how firm she'd sounded when she said, *Not until he gets back from L.A.* He had a bad feeling that being pushy would have the opposite effect of what he wanted.

Was she unwilling to commit herself until she

was convinced he no longer courted danger on the job? In one way, Alec couldn't blame her, given how she'd been widowed and how recently. But a part of him wanted to know she loved him enough to marry him whatever the risks. They'd moved to a small town for Matt's sake, but Matt would be going to college in a few years. What if, in the future, another opportunity arose that Alec wanted to take? Would Julia ask *him* to choose between her and his job?

He might know what his answer would be—but that wasn't the point.

Oh, hell—he was probably worrying about nothing. Maybe all she wanted was to be sure Matt *was* okay with the two of them, and he couldn't blame her for that.

But, damn, he wanted to make love with her.

SAYING GOODBYE TO ALEC at the airport was unspeakably awful. Julia knew she was overreacting—he hadn't had to tell her—but she couldn't shake a terror that felt too much like a premonition.

Something wicked this way comes.

Who knew she'd remember that much from *Macbeth*?

Stupid.

Now she wished she hadn't brought the kids along to the airport, but of course she didn't like leaving them alone, either, or insulting Matt by asking Andrea to sit with them. There was also no way she trusted him on his own yet, even if she couldn't blame him for chafing at the confinement.

The Angel Butte Regional Airport had only one gate for commercial flights and nothing that exactly qualified as security, except that everyone had to step through a scanner and she supposed bags were X-rayed. The whole family was able to walk Alec right to the doorway leading onto the runway where the prop plane waited for the ten passengers who had bought tickets on this particular flight.

The kids hugged him, and then she did. When she tried to straighten and regain her dignity before she did something like break into tears—just what he needed as a send-off—his arms locked around her.

In response, she melted against his hard body. "Please, please come home safely," she mumbled into his collarbone.

Cheek pressed to her head, he said, "I swear." He didn't seem to want to let go any more than she did.

Finally she wiped her damp cheeks on his formerly crisp white shirt, sniffed and tried again to pull away. His arms tightened briefly before releasing her, his hands lingered on her shoulders and his dark eyes were intense on her face.

She kissed his cheek and, while her mouth was close to his ear, whispered, "I love you." Then she backed off.

Hands falling to his sides, he looked stunned. "God, Julia."

She tried valiantly to smile. "Go."

He gave his head a dazed shake. "Yeah. Okay." One more intense look, and he said, "I'll call," and went.

Both kids stayed silent as they went to the wall of windows, watching as he walked across the tarmac and ducked to disappear inside an airplane that seemed awfully small. The propellers turned until they blurred, after which the plane taxied onto the runway, raced down it and rose into the air.

"Mom? Why are you crying?" Liana asked anxiously, reaching for her hand.

This time, Julia's smile felt more natural. "Because I'm being silly. I hate goodbyes."

"Oh." Her daughter's face relaxed, and she skipped along as they headed for their car.

But Matt, Julia noticed, kept watching her, and she wondered if he was as easily fooled.

CHAPTER FIFTEEN

ALEC CAME OUT of the bathroom rubbing his wet hair with a hotel towel, a second one wrapped around his waist. When a knock came at the door, he tensed, but it was followed by three more, lighter knocks in a prearranged pattern. He let in Michael Bishop, the middle-aged, sharp-eyed federal agent who was serving as his bodyguard and, at the moment, room-service waiter.

"Breakfast," Bishop announced, setting the tray on the table.

"Thanks. We getting anywhere?"

"Afraid not."

Opposing attorneys were still dueling over the selection of the last couple of jurors. He was pissed that they'd let him come down without telling him the whole damn circus had been delayed.

It was Wednesday now. Since his arrival Sunday, Alec had learned things about himself. He hated being cooped up with a passion. The feeling wasn't claustrophobia, but it was close. Maintaining an appearance of pleasant civility with his guards—or captors—was straining his composure.

Of course, he'd always known he preferred to be in charge. Handing over control like this was scraping him raw. He tried to imagine himself laughing about this later, preferably with Julia. Telling her, *I'm officially a control freak.*

"Later" felt like a mirage, a shimmer in the far distance that would fade when he got too close. And yeah, he'd been confined in this damn hotel room for barely—no, his gaze found the clock, *exactly*—sixty hours. A drop in the sea, when it was becoming clear his testimony wouldn't be called for until next week, at least.

He wanted Julia. He wanted the kids. They'd have all enjoyed the room service, the selection of new movies available at will. Together, they could have played board games, talked, laughed.

Made love.

He grimaced. No, not that, unfortunately. Even if the feds had been willing to spring for a suite, he doubted Julia would go for sharing his bed with the kids only a wall away.

Tossing the wet towel aside, he dressed in chinos and a T-shirt, then unenthusiastically sat down to eat.

By early afternoon, he'd skimmed all his notes—again—in preparation for his testimony and read half of a thriller Bishop had bought for him in the gift shop downstairs in the hotel. It might have been riveting under other circumstances. Under *these* circumstances, he found himself reading and rereading pages because he'd lost track of the fictional events.

Damned if he didn't owe Matt a huge apology. Recalling his impatience at his nephew's intolerance for sitting around, day after day after day, Alec smiled reluctantly. Unlike Matt, *he* would be thrilled to go grocery shopping with Julia.

Speaking of... He called once a day. Usually evening, but she ought to be home by now and he was eager to hear about the first lengthy trail ride. Yesterday's had lasted only half an hour, following a session in the corral. At this point, she couldn't call him—fear that he could be traced via his cell phone, or any call from her phone, meant he'd left his own phone behind and had been given a throwaway.

Anticipating the sound of her voice, he dialed and sat on the edge of the bed.

One ring.

If they'd ridden for the entire hour, Julia and Matt, at least, would probably be sore. Liana might have gotten over that last week—

The second ring was cut off. "Alec?" It was Julia, and she sounded semihysterical.

Shit, he thought, sitting up straighter. "What's wrong?" he asked.

"Matt's gone. Oh, God, I'm so scared."

His pulse had accelerated like an Indy car. "Tell me what happened." Somehow, he'd spoken calmly.

"He begged not to go with us this morning. Riding yesterday was really awkward for him and most of the camp participants are girls so I know he feels self-conscious. And then his arm hurt last night and he didn't sleep very well, and I thought— I'm such an idiot, Alec! I trusted him!"

"How long have you been home?"

"Forty-five minutes. Well, off and on. I made Liana go with me, and we drove around for probably twenty minutes, but there was no sign of him. Oh, I'm going to kill him!"

Not if Alec got to the kid first, he thought grimly.

"Call Colin," he said.

"I already did." The stress in her voice was almost more than he could stand. "He's coming over himself, and he said they'd go door to door and find out if any neighbors might have been home and seen Matt leave. To…find out if he was alone." Her voice was shaking at the end.

His jaw was clenched so hard it was a wonder he hadn't cracked a molar. He wanted, like he'd never wanted anything, to be *there,* not trapped in purgatory.

"You know he's probably done nothing more serious than go for a walk. I've let my paranoia infect you. I'm sorry, Julia."

That dialed her stress back a little and they spoke for another few minutes. Finally, he said, "I'll call back in half an hour," and let her go.

He paced, looking at his watch every minute or two. Time had never crept so slowly.

This time when he dialed, Alec wasn't surprised when the call was picked up midring.

It was Colin McAllister, though, who said, "Alec?"

"Yeah?"

"A neighbor three houses down across the street saw a police car in front of your house." Tension made his voice flat. "A uniformed officer went to the door. She isn't sure she'd recognize him if she saw him again, but she saw a boy come out and the officer put him in the back of the squad car."

Alec let out a blistering obscenity.

"The car wasn't blue. It was white with a navy blue band. She's sure of that."

County sheriff's department, not Angel Butte P.D. Jesus. What did that mean?

"Nobody I've talked to at the sheriff's department has a good goddamn idea what one of their officers would have been doing picking up a kid within our city limits." He paused. "We have to assume that Matt's been abducted."

"Nobody could reach me," Alec said numbly. "They won't know I don't have my phone. They may not even know I'm out of town, unless someone saw Julia take me to the airport."

"Is your phone here?"

"On the dresser in my bedroom."

"Do I have your permission to go in there and listen to your voice mail?"

Alec gave him his password and the number to

call him back, too. To hell with Bishop and the rest of the prison guards.

Then he paced some more, the phone in his hand. Although he expected it, he got a jolt of adrenaline when it rang ten minutes later.

"Colin?"

"Nothing. Not a single goddamn message. Not even a missed call."

Air huffed out of him as if he'd been smacked in the chest. "I'm coming home," he said. "They won't like it, but to hell with 'em."

"You can't do anything we aren't already doing."

"I have to be there."

"I don't blame you," Colin said. "You going to have this phone with you? I'll call if we learn anything."

A minute later, Alec was dialing the emergency contact number for the agent in charge.

IT WAS ALL Julia could do to hold it together. Grateful as she was for Colin McAllister's presence, she desperately wanted Alec.

She sat on the sofa for most of the afternoon, her arm around Liana, who was frightened into silence. Alec's iPhone lay on the coffee table in front of her, the gleaming black the center of her existence. Beside it was her mobile phone, as well as the home phone. Matt would probably call one of her numbers. Anyone else would call Alec's.

In the kitchen, Colin worked his own phone. She

heard the rumble of his voice, the occasional ring. Other officers came and went. Eventually, a plain-clothes female officer stayed. She was the only one to stop and introduce herself to Julia.

Her hazel eyes were kind. "Hi, I'm Lieutenant Jane Vahalik. I know you're scared, but we'll find your son."

"Thank you," Julia said stiffly. "This is Liana, my daughter."

Liana mumbled something, and Jane smiled at her.

Lieutenant Vahalik had to be about Julia's age. Alec had mentioned her and Julia knew Jane headed the detective division. He'd been concerned about her relative lack of experience, but also expressed his growing belief that she was smart and com-posed. Julia knew there were increasing numbers of female law-enforcement officers, but was amazed at one Jane Vahalik's age who'd risen to command a whole bunch of men. She wasn't exactly beauti-ful—pretty, maybe—but there wasn't any way she could have disguised her femininity even if she'd tried. Maybe an inch or two taller than Julia, she was fit but also curvaceous. Julia could too easily imagine the way men's gazes would stray to the lieutenant's generous breasts.

Well, more power to her, Julia thought, in one of the few moments she had been able to focus on anything but Matt and where he was, or her des-perate need for Alec.

The lieutenant disappeared to the kitchen, but took a minute to pop back out and say, "Chief Raynor has gotten on an airplane. It lands in Portland at 7:16. There are no evening commercial flights to Angel Butte or Bend, so we're arranging a charter. He'll make it here this evening."

"Thank you" was all Julia could manage to say.

Jane seemed to understand. She nodded and went away.

Eventually Nell McAllister arrived, hugged Julia and insisted on cooking dinner. Nothing fancy—only hamburgers and homemade macaroni and cheese and corn. Julia managed a few bites, if only to set an example for Liana.

Alec's phone rang, galvanizing all of them. The number was announced as restricted. Colin nodded at Julia to answer it.

"Hello?" she said breathlessly.

Not a word was said, but she knew somebody was there. After a pause, she could tell that whoever it was had ended the call.

Everyone in the living room stared at each other.

"It could have been a wrong number," she said tentatively.

Colin's expression was grim. "More likely, they want Alec, not you. I hope like hell they call back."

"Of course they will!" Nell exclaimed. "Nobody would go to all this effort and just…just…" She didn't finish, and didn't have to. They were all thinking the same thing.

And just kill a thirteen-year-old boy.

Kill Matt.

Julia's teeth chattered.

Jane was sent to the airport to pick up Alec. Julia wondered what was happening with the trial. Probably nothing—from what he'd said, he wouldn't be needed for days anyway.

Ten o'clock came and went. She decided not to send Liana to bed until Alec arrived.

When she heard the vehicle stop in front of the duplex, she shot to her feet and faced the front door, straining to hear a voice, so hungry for his presence she was shaking.

A key turned in the lock and he stepped in, his gaze going straight to hers. Finally, she could move. They collided halfway across the small room, coming together with desperate need that wasn't all on her side. It couldn't be.

"I'm so sorry," she cried. "So sorry. If I hadn't left him alone…"

If it was possible, he held her closer, his cheek scratchy against hers, his voice rough. "It's not your fault. If it's anyone's, it's mine. Somebody took him to get to me. Has to be."

"You trusted me to keep him safe, and I didn't."

"No. You couldn't watch him 24/7. We always knew that. If a cop's involved… God, I can't even get angry at Matt. He didn't take off on his own. This took real balls, abducting him so openly."

She blinked a few times and managed to let go of

some of the physical tension that had had her strung so tightly she'd felt as if she might snap.

Finally he eased her away, his eyes never leaving her face, sending her messages she couldn't decode but that comforted her nonetheless. Then he went to Liana, who had stood up but waited stiffly by the sofa. He held her tightly for a moment, too.

Julia saw him look at the array of telephones lying on the coffee table.

"No more calls?"

She shook her head. "You know about the one that was a hang-up?"

"Yeah." He turned to Colin. "Nothing new?"

The police captain grimly shook his head. "Sheriff Brock is dragging his feet about letting our witness look at photos of every deputy. He calls it a witch hunt."

Alec made a rumbling sound.

Colin continued, "He insists she could be mistaken about the color of the squad car. It would help if she could give a better description of the officer, but unfortunately, she was more scandalized that a neighborhood boy was being arrested than she was in paying attention to some policeman's face."

"That's the vibe she got? That he was being arrested?"

Colin grunted. "With good reason, from her description. The deputy kept a hand on Matt's back from the front porch to the car. Kind of stiff-armed." He demonstrated. "Opened the car door, blocked any escape with his body until Matt was in. The car was in the driveway, not parked on the street, so it partially blocked the woman's view the entire time."

"They were watching the ranch," Alec said flatly. "Saw that they had their chance to grab one of the kids."

With dread, Julia saw the look the two men exchanged and knew they agreed.

If only I hadn't left Matt alone.

NOBODY WOULD BE sleeping much tonight.

Alec went along when Julia tucked Liana into bed, taking his turn to kiss her on that high, curved forehead and murmur, "Sleep tight, sweet pea. Matt'll be back plaguing you before you know it."

Her laugh was half sob.

He stepped back into the hall and waited for Julia, who pulled the door almost closed, leaving about a six-inch gap. He tugged her down the hall toward her room.

Still holding her hand, he took in the near unbearable strain on her face. "Do you have any kind of sleeping pill? You need to get some rest."

Her stare held no comprehension.

"Julia, you should go to bed. Nothing's likely to happen now until morning."

The hitch of her breath was half sob, too. "I can't."

"You can." He hesitated, thinking of McAllister and Jane Vahalik, both out in the living room. He could hear them speaking quietly. To hell with what they thought. "I'll lie down with you."

"But what if there's a call?" she asked in panic.

"I'll set the phones next to the bed."

Those wide, green-gold eyes studied him for a long moment before she nodded. "Yes. Okay."

He smiled faintly and brushed her mouth with his. "Give me a minute."

When he stepped back into the living room and told Jane and Colin that Julia wouldn't lie down if he wasn't with her, they both nodded their understanding.

"Won't hurt if you get some sleep, too," Colin said. "I sent Nell home. Jane and I are going to stay, take turns on the couch." He shook his head when Alec offered to find some bedding; the throw pillows and afghan out there would do fine, he said.

Earlier, in a phone conversation, they'd debated going public. Someone might have seen the county sheriff's unit with a kid in the backseat and at least wondered. Or not. Trouble was, with the courthouse inside the city limits and the sheriff's department headquarters barely outside Angel Butte, the county's largest city, it wouldn't be unexpected to see deputies in town.

Still, all it would take was one witness. One person who'd caught a glimpse of the deputy's face.

The downside was that Matt's danger increased the more public his predicament became. The Butte County deputy sheriff who had been suborned into kidnapping a thirteen-year-old boy would feel a lot more secure once that boy was dead and couldn't say a word. The fact that Matt had been allowed to see his kidnapper's face told Alec that no one had any intention of releasing him alive at the end of the ordeal.

The debate about whether to call in the FBI was something of an echo. Trade off the feds' undeniable expertise in kidnapping for losing control over the decisions. What if *they* chose to go public, say, plastering Matt's picture everywhere? In Alec's heart, Matt was his kid, and by God, he wanted to be the one making the decisions. Simple as that.

Now he and Colin threw around the same arguments, with Jane making an occasional contribution. They all agreed not much could happen tonight. In fact, not much would happen at all until the call came in. The only other possibility of a break would come from the sheriff's department. The undersheriff, a guy named Josh Sherfield, was being a lot more cooperative than his boss was. Sherfield was quietly engaged in making sure all county cars were accounted for and determining whether there'd been any oddities—say, one not responding to a call in a timely fashion. Alec suspected Sherfield wouldn't learn anything useful, not without alerting the entire department to the fact that one of their own had committed an ugly crime—and thereby panicking him into the very action they were trying to prevent.

Finally, Alec checked to be sure all three phones still had some battery life and carried them along with his suitcase back to Julia's bedroom, where he laid them out in a row on the bedside table. *Like corpses laid out for burial,* he couldn't help thinking, hoping Julia hadn't had the same thought as she stared all afternoon and evening at them, praying for a ring.

She returned a minute later from the bathroom and he took his turn. He found her in bed when he got back, lying with her eyes fixed on those damn phones. Alec stripped to his shorts, laying his clothes over the upholstered chair squeezed into a corner of the bedroom. Not caring if that was her usual side of the bed, Alec nudged her over and got in closest to the nightstand. Then he rolled to face her. Their knees touched and he wrapped his hand around her nape, gently massaging.

"Hey," he said softly. "They won't have hurt him. No matter what they want from me, they have to know I'll insist on talking to Matt."

"But then what's to stop them—" A shudder traveled through her.

Nothing. But there was no damn way he was admitting that.

"I think we can rule out the election as a motive. It's too far out. Even if I were a more important player than I am—and the truth is I have no meaningful influence on voters in this county—nobody could expect to hold Matt until November to force me to take a public stance. The idea is ludicrous. I think those phoned-in threats were nothing but misdirection. At that point, maybe they intended to kill me. If that had happened, nobody would have been thinking about the Perez trial. They'd have been looking at Brock's campaign."

Julia's teeth sank into her lower lip, but she nodded.

"It has to be the trial."

He could see that scared her as much as it did him, but it also didn't surprise her.

"That limits the time frame. Even so, even if it proceeds as planned, I wouldn't be testifying until Monday at the soonest. Which means, were I to agree to their terms, I'd be demanding to talk to Matt daily."

"*Were* you to agree?"

"You know I'd do anything for Matt."

She relaxed minutely.

"My point is, we have time," he said. "We can't trust them to release him in the end, though." It had to be said. "We have to find him."

"Oh, God," Julia whispered.

"Come here, honey." He pulled her closer, shifting so that her head lay on his shoulder and he could wrap her in both arms. "He's probably asleep right now. He knows we'll be looking for him. Matt's a smart kid. He'll help in any way he can."

Her head bobbed slightly. Her breath was a warm caress on his chest. Alec felt his body stirring and cursed it. She'd have every right to be offended if she noticed him getting aroused.

Think about Matt. Picture him locked up alone, maybe tied up, bruised, scared out of his skull. No pain meds, so he hurts.

It worked like a douse of cold water.

"If you don't sleep," he murmured, pitching his voice to soothe, "it'll be hard to be strong tomorrow."

"I know, but…"

"But?" Of course he knew.

She didn't say anything.

"Yeah." Alec rubbed his cheek against the top of her head, his eyes closed. Behind the lids, his eyes prickled and burned. "Me, too."

Neither of them talked after that. As the hours passed, there were a few times he could tell she'd dropped off, although her sleep never lasted long. His didn't, either. He'd start awake and grope for his phone or the weapon that lay on the table, too, before realizing that if he'd heard anything at all it was Jane or Colin moving around the living room or kitchen.

Somewhere in the middle of the night, Alec heard a faint squeak of the door. His eyes had adjusted well enough to the darkness for him to make out the paler shape of Liana in her pink shorty pajamas.

"Mommy?" she whispered.

Julia bolted upright. "Liana?"

"I'm here, too," Alec said.

"Uncle Alec?" Her surprise didn't last long. "I can't sleep."

"You can get into bed with us," Julia said. "Go around to the other side. Uncle Alec needs to be able to reach the phone."

Alec was really glad she hadn't suggested Liana climb between them. Tonight he especially needed the contact with Julia. Though this wasn't how he'd hoped to spend a first night with her.

The small figure hurried around the bed. The mattress barely depressed beneath her slight weight, but the bedclothes rustled as Julia shifted to put an arm around her child.

Alec rolled to spoon her. Operating by feel rather than sight, he smoothed Liana's hair back from her face, then Julia's in turn. She and Liana whispered for a minute until Julia finally whispered, "Shh. Let's try to sleep."

Alec slid his hand along Julia's cheek and jaw in a final caress and felt the kiss she pressed against the pad below his thumb. She didn't say anything, but he heard the echo of her last words at the airport.

I love you. The most precious words in the English language.

He mouthed them himself, knowing she wouldn't hear him, but wishing he'd said them earlier. But how could he, when this was all his fault?

Still wide-awake, his arm lying loosely across

the woman and child he loved, he lay there wondering if Josh could have done any better than he had in the same place.

IN THE GRAY LIGHT of dawn, Julia felt Alec trying to slip out of bed without waking her or Liana, who slept heavily. She let him go, waiting through the rustle of him pulling on trousers, at least, and the tiny scrape of plastic against wood when he scooped up the phones and his holstered weapon, then left the bedroom. A minute later, she got up, too, leaving Liana to sleep. The light seeping through the cracks in the blinds was enough to allow her to pick out clothes and get dressed.

The bathroom door was closed when she passed and she heard the shower go on. She continued to the kitchen, where she found Jane Vahalik leaning against the counter, apparently waiting for coffee to brew.

"Colin asleep?" Julia asked quietly.

"No," he said behind her.

"I'm sorry." She turned. "Did I wake you?"

"No, I was just lying there." He shook his head at her expression. "I got a few hours. Don't worry." His gaze fastened hopefully on the coffeemaker.

He was as sexy a man—in a different way—as Alec was, Julia realized belatedly. The two men had that same self-contained air, but Colin was taller, with sun-streaked brown hair and perceptive gray eyes. No easier to read than Alec, and she might have found him intimidating if she hadn't seen the expression on his face when he looked at his wife.

Jane started pouring coffee. "That Alec in the shower?" At Julia's nod, she poured a fourth cup. "Your daughter still asleep?"

"Yes, thank goodness. She got in bed with us in the middle of the night and finally conked out completely."

"I was tempted to join you, too," Colin said. "Your couch is a little too short for me. When I saw your daughter sneak down the hall, I thought, where there's three, why not four?"

Julia surprised herself with a chuckle, if a weak one. She couldn't help picturing them all in bed together, having to roll over in concert.

"Sadly, my bed's full-size, not a queen."

"Ah. Maybe not, then." He turned his head. "Alec."

Even as Alec nodded at the others and laid the collection of phones on the kitchen table, his gaze was on Julia. She could see him running the same checklist she was on him: *Did he get any sleep? How is he holding up? Does he need anything I can give him?*

Finally, he stepped forward, kissed her cheek and accepted the coffee Jane had just poured for him. After a long swallow, he transferred his gaze to Colin.

"Anything?"

"It's early."

Julia hadn't even looked at the time. Now she did. It was 6:39 a.m. "I'll make breakfast," she offered.

Nobody demurred, although Jane offered to help. *A woman's role,* Julia thought ruefully, exchanging a glance with Jane, whose eyebrows had lifted at the two oblivious men.

"You can do toast," Julia suggested.

She went for easy—bacon and scrambled eggs, with ricotta and pepper Jack adding some flavor. Jane located jam and honey, and they all sat down around the small table to eat. Julia felt a burst of rebellion—this was the wrong four people. She wanted these two near strangers gone, Matt and Liana in their place. The next moment, she was ashamed. Jane and Colin were here to help. They'd been incredibly kind. She didn't think she'd have survived yesterday until Alec arrived if they hadn't been here.

At first she didn't do much but stir her food around on her plate, but beneath Alec's stern eye, Julia finally took a few bites. He was right—she had to stay strong. He ate mechanically, without his usual enthusiasm. Jane said, "Whatever you did to these eggs is good."

Colin had risen to replenish their coffee cups when a phone rang, the sound shocking. Julia jolted and her eyes met Alec's. From her peripheral vision she saw Jane looking down to check her own phone.

A muscle flexed in Alec's jaw and he pushed back his chair. "It's mine."

Julia swiveled in her chair to stare at it. On the next ring, it gave a tiny jump. Of course it was set to vibrate, too. Colin had done that.

Alec picked it up, his eyes on Julia, then on the third ring touched the screen. "Raynor here."

CHAPTER SIXTEEN

"GUESS YOU KNOW we have your nephew, *Chief* Raynor." The voice was muffled, just as the earlier phone threats had been. Maybe some cloth between mouth and receiver, Alec thought coldly. Same speaker. Male.

"I'm aware," he said.

"Simple deal. You refuse to testify in the Perez trial. Do a memory wipe. Claim not to remember a thing. Or you've got a lot of doubt about what you thought you saw or heard back then. Tell them anything you want, except that we're holding the kid. If the trial gets put on hold, the kid is dead. If we see cops sneaking around too close to where we're holding him, he's dead. When the trial is done, we let him go. Got it?"

"Got it." How the hell he was sounding so unemotional with Julia watching him, he didn't know. "I need to talk to Matt. Confirm he's okay."

"We'll call you back." Dead air.

Alec slowly set down his phone.

"Number?" Colin asked.

"Restricted."

The other man nodded and walked out of the room, already dialing. They had to try—but Alec was willing to bet the caller had used a throwaway or someone else's phone, as he'd done in the first call from the tavern.

"What did he say?" Julia asked in a stricken voice.

"What we expected. If I refuse to testify against Perez and the trial goes on without me, at the end of it Matt will be released."

Her eyes asked the question.

He shook his head and saw no surprise, only anguish.

"Matt?"

"They're supposed to give me a call back so I can talk to him."

"Either the caller isn't where they're holding Matt," Jane said, "or he wants you to think he isn't." She frowned. "Which do you think?"

"Don't know. I couldn't hear any background noise."

He touched Julia's shoulder, then started to pace. He was incapable of sitting and waiting.

Eventually, when the phone didn't ring, Jane stood and began to clear the table. Julia seemed oblivious. All she did was watch Alec, her complexion as pale as marble, her face as frozen. One hand was balled into a fist on her lap. The other clutched the rung of the chair.

Alec tried to make himself think calmly. What

could he ask Matt that would give them a clue? Was it realistic to hope Matt had any way of knowing where he was being held? Chances were good he'd been blindfolded or transported part of the way in the trunk of a car so that he couldn't help even if Alec knew the right question to ask.

Alec had dealt with hostage situations a few times. He'd empathized with the terrified parents, spouses, friends, waiting for this same kind of call. But he hadn't really *known* until now.

I'm not sure I can *make the best decisions,* he realized in agony. Only a couple months ago, he'd called Colin McAllister on the carpet for not stepping back when his sister was threatened. He'd been right—a cop *needed* to operate with a certain detachment—but he wasn't going to do the right thing any more than Colin had been willing to then.

His phone rang.

Julia jumped. Or had she shuddered?

Aware of Colin stepping back into the kitchen, Alec automatically checked the caller ID. This time a number showed. The number wasn't local, and the fact that they hadn't blocked it shouted throwaway.

He closed his eyes for a moment, centered himself and answered, "Raynor."

"Uncle Alec?" Matt's shaky voice said.

"Matt." Alec couldn't look away from Julia. "Are you all right? Have they hurt you?"

"Not really." A gulp. "I mean, I guess I'm okay."

Somebody said something curt in the background.

Alec hardened himself. "Tell me something that proves this really is Matt. Something no one else would know."

He prayed he hadn't shocked the boy, who must know his uncle had no doubt about who he was talking to.

"Um…you remember what I said about Sister Regina? How she can see, you know?"

Out of the back of her head.

"I remember."

"This place is okay," he said hastily. "Liana would like it. Mom always says— Hey!"

His last word was muffled. A different voice came on. Not muffled, not familiar. "We got a deal?"

"We have a deal," Alec made himself say. "But I need to talk to Matt every day, or it's off. Understand?"

"Yes." The caller was gone.

Alec verified that the call really had been dropped, then set his phone down. "He's being held out somewhere on the back side of Angel Butte."

"How do you know that?" Colin asked.

"I took Matt to see the angel up on the butte. The day we went hiking," he added as an aside to Julia. "He said she reminded him of a Sister Regina he had as a teacher at the Catholic school he used to attend. The students were all sure she could see out of the back of her head, even wearing the wimple." Alec repeated what Matt had told him, then looked

again at Julia. "Another thing. Just before they took
the phone from him, he got out something about
how Liana would like where he's being held, that
Mom always says…?" He let the words hang out
there.

She barely whispered, "That Liana would rather
live in a barn. That's what I always say."

A harsh burst of air escaped Alec. Behind him,
Colin said, "Ms. Raynor, you've got a smart boy."

A dry sob tore through her. She clamped a hand
over her mouth.

"Our jurisdiction doesn't extend far that direction," Alec said, trying to sound more composed
than he felt.

"Nobody will stop us from looking," Colin said.
"But we could use some help. Jane, do you know
any deputies with the county you'd swear are honest?"

"Three or four," she said after only a brief hesitation.

"I'd say the same."

They sat around the table again, discussing ter-
rain, how to avoid being noticed, who knew that
area best. Colin was able to go out to his 4Runner
and return with a detailed map they all pored over.
Jane had patrolled that edge of the city limits, al-
beit five or six years ago. None of the new growth
in the county was taking place there. There were
a couple dozen small ranches and more properties

that had a pasture and small barn of some sort, Colin and Jane agreed. In one way, Alec was intensely focused, but, as if his mind had developed a split screen, he was also painfully aware of Julia's every fleeting expression as she listened in silence.

Eventually, the three of them began working their phones, handpicking their team and passing on instructions. Every officer they spoke to would drive a personal vehicle, not a marked one. No one would report on the police band—mobile phones only. Two deputies, one of whom had been the wrangler at the horse camp, would ride cross-country on horseback.

The doorbell rang, surprising Alec, but Colin stood as if expecting someone. Nell, Alec saw a minute later.

"I thought Julia could use some company," Colin murmured as his wife went straight to Julia and hugged her.

With the lump in his throat, it was a minute before Alec could speak. "Thank you," he managed at last.

Alec would ride along with Jane, they decided, in case Matt's captors recognized his rental SUV or Julia's VW. Best if both stayed visible here. Colin left; Jane waited while Alec went next door, changed clothes and added his backup weapon in an ankle holster.

When he stepped back in, Nell was nowhere in

sight and Vahalik hovered right by the front door, as if trying to allow him a private moment with Julia. She stood stiffly, waiting, arms crossed tightly. He went to her, gripped her upper arms and bent to rub his cheek against her head. "I'll stay in touch," he said softly. "Don't panic. As long as they believe I'm cooperating, nothing will happen to Matt."

She tilted her head back. "Do they think you're still in L.A.?"

"I don't know." He'd wondered that himself. "They probably know there were no commercial flights I could have taken last night or yet this morning, and I arrived in the dark. It's possible."

"Please—" she said, and her voice broke.

The band squeezing his chest tightened, making it hard to breathe. What if he couldn't bring Matt home to her alive and well?

"I'd do anything for him," he told her again, wishing he could make the promise she wanted but knowing there was too good a chance he wouldn't be able to keep it.

Her cheeks were wet. "You have to come home safe, too."

Blown away, he stared at her.

"I love you," he said hoarsely. "I'm so sorry. I never thought—"

She only shook her head. "Forget blame. Just—" He could tell her throat had closed.

"Yeah." He kissed her more roughly than he

should have, taking something from her that he needed if he was to get through the next hours.

Then he left her, knowing her part was the hardest. He'd go crazy if he couldn't do anything at all.

WHEN LIANA FINALLY made an appearance, rubbing her eyes, Julia had a minute of wondering if she could function at all as a mother. How could she pretend she believed everything would be fine? She wanted to go back to bed, pull her knees up to her chest and suck her thumb, become a floating, unconscious being who didn't know love and pain.

But she was a mother no matter what, so she held out a welcoming arm and hugged her daughter. "Hungry?"

Liana searched her face anxiously. "I can get my own cereal."

"If you want something else, that's okay. It gives me something to do."

"Can I have a waffle, then?"

"Sure."

Nell had gone to the bathroom and now came into the kitchen. "Can I do anything?"

"Have you had breakfast?" Julia asked. "I'm going to make waffles. Oh, Liana, did you meet Mrs. McAllister last night?"

"Yes. Kind of."

"Nell," the other woman said kindly. "I've only been a McAllister for, um, not even quite six months yet. It's taking a little getting used to."

She poured Liana some orange juice and answered questions about why she was here and was her mister really that policeman. That made Nell chuckle.

"Yes. He scared me the first time we met. I had secrets, and I thought he was seeing right through me."

Liana's brow crinkled. "What kind of secrets?"

Normally Julia would have intervened, but she guessed Nell had thrown that out there because she was willing to talk about her life to distract Liana.

And me, too, probably.

She'd have sworn she couldn't *be* distracted, but Nell's story was astonishing. Julia had never before met anyone who had suffered amnesia, even the fleeting variety, never mind the kind that had allowed a fifteen-year-old girl to create a new life out of whole cloth and live it until she was twenty-eight.

"You really didn't remember *anything?*" asked Liana, obviously fascinated.

Nell looked pensive. "I did have memories, but they had no context. There were faces, voices, brief scenes, but I didn't know for sure that the man I remembered was my father, or the woman my mother. What I finally realized was that I didn't *want* to know. I hadn't had a very good relationship with them, and when I desperately needed help, they didn't listen, so I knew I couldn't trust them. So I think I partly had real amnesia—when I was attacked, my skull was actually fractured—but partly

I was afraid I'd be forced to go home if I remembered my name or who my parents were. The worst part was, I knew someone had tried to kill me, but I had no memory at all of who. I wasn't even sure it *wasn't* one of my parents."

Now Liana was aghast. "Was it?"

Nell shook her head. "No, thank goodness. I'm still not close to my mother or father, but we do talk. And I'm really glad to have reunited with my brother. He's one of my best friends now."

Julia had heard about Felix, but hadn't met him yet.

Nell had agreed that she might be able to eat a waffle, so she and Liana ate while Julia cleaned up and then poured herself yet another cup of coffee.

She knew there were things Alec hadn't said in her hearing. There had to have been threats. And how could Matt possibly know where he was? Would they really have driven him directly there, letting him see where he was being taken? If so, he must know they didn't intend to let him go. Almost as terrifying was to wonder if he could be wrong and everyone was out looking for him in the wrong area altogether.

And if he was right, hadn't whoever was with him wondered about him talking about a Catholic sister and what she could see? But they couldn't possibly relate that to the angel, could they? Please, God, no, she thought, because if they did, they would move him at the very least.

"Mom?"

Liana's puzzled voice penetrated Julia's agonized speculations. Clearly, this wasn't the first time she'd tried to get her mother's attention.

"I'm sorry, honey." Julia even managed a smile. "My mind was wandering."

"Do you think Uncle Alec will find Matt?"

She leaned over to hug her daughter fiercely. "Yes. I know he will."

And as scared as she was, she discovered something she hadn't known: she believed Alec could and would move mountains to save her son.

KNOWING THERE WAS even one dirty cop involved meant taking even greater precautions than they would otherwise have done.

Every member of Alec's team out prowling these country roads ran the risk of being recognized. The kidnappers, and especially any cops among them, were unlikely to believe a fellow officer just happened to be out for a midweek drive, taking the air today of all days. The last thing the searchers wanted to do was panic them.

Alec felt at a particular disadvantage, because his high profile meant he'd be identified easily, while he doubted he'd recognize more than ten or fifteen sheriff's deputies at a glance.

He gave Jane an appraising glance. Before they drove away from the curb, she'd pulled her thick mass of curly hair into a jaunty ponytail that made

her look ten years younger. She'd dug in her hand-
bag and produced some makeup, too, that changed
her look considerably. For him, she'd found a royal-
blue Seattle Mariners baseball cap. With dark
glasses, he doubted anyone would immediately
know him.

She'd asked him if he wanted to drive, but he
had shaken his head. "You know the roads better
than I do."

She didn't slow as they passed driveways. Without turning his head any more than he could help,
Alec scanned each homestead. They ruled out
any house without an accompanying barn or with
a crude lean-to instead of a closed structure. He
got especially tense when he saw several vehicles
parked around the home and barn. Only twice did
they pass oncoming vehicles—once a woman was
driving and he saw a baby in a car seat in the back,
but the other time the driver was male and alone,
and his head turned as he went by.

Colin called Alec a couple of times. Then Jane's
phone rang. She answered and her expression tightened. "Just a minute," she said and handed the
phone to Alec. "Clay Renner. He wants to talk to
you."

A sergeant with the sheriff's department, Renner
was one of the people Jane had suggested. He was
directing his handful of people and wanted to report on the whereabouts of the two who'd started
cross-country on a pair of quarter horses.

"They won't be able to get close to the barns," Alec said, his frustration rising.

"No, but they have binoculars. And a different perspective. The roads will be watched more closely than the open land behind the ranches."

"Stay in touch," Alec said finally. He handed the phone back to Jane, scrutinizing her as he did so. "If you don't like Renner, why did you recommend him?"

She shot him a look. "Did I say I don't like him?"

He was too good an interrogator to comment.

Color splashed across her cheeks. It was the first time he'd ever seen her discomposed. "We dated a few times last fall," she said tautly. "And you're right, I don't like him. But he's a good cop."

Alec weighed her tone.

"He's ex-military. Army ranger."

Didn't mean he couldn't be corrupted, but maybe lessened the chances. Alec nodded.

The road they were driving ended at a T. Jane turned right and found a bumpy, half-overgrown dirt track to pull into. "We need to get a closer look at some of those places."

"It's not going to be easy." He'd thought about nothing else, including the advantages of waiting until nightfall.

There were some he knew they couldn't get near in broad daylight, but they agreed there'd been places she could drop him where there was enough cover for him to get a better look-see at some of the barns.

"Or we can take turns," she suggested.

He shook his head. "If anybody notices the car coming and going, it better have the same driver. They're more likely to dismiss you, too."

She grimaced. "Happens all the time."

She found a place to turn around and, wincing a couple of times as the brambles scraped the sides of her shiny GMC Yukon, inched back to the main road. The truck was black and loaded, he'd been mildly amused to note a few months ago when he was first assessing his personnel and was still capable of being amused. It was a hefty vehicle for a woman who didn't top five feet five inches. Alec guessed the Yukon was a little bit of an equalizer, in her eyes.

On the first pass, she'd spotted a house with a carport rather than a garage that they agreed looked deserted. They took a chance now and turned in. While Jane trotted up to the house to knock, her excuse prepared, Alec slipped out and headed into a stand of woods separating the property from the pasture that lay beyond it. The sparse undergrowth didn't give as much cover as he'd like, but he had dressed much as he had the day he and Matt went hiking, in khaki trousers and a sage-green T-shirt. He took the too-colorful baseball cap off and stuffed it in a back pocket. When the pasture opened ahead of him, he crouched and lifted his binoculars.

The barn was ramshackle enough that he could see straight through it in places. It appeared to hold a rusting tractor and not much else. The roof sagged and the whole structure leaned, making him suspect a good load of snow this winter would bring it down. No way was there a room inside it secure enough to hold a hostage, nor any sign horses had grazed this overgrown pasture in the recent past. Would Matt have said what he did if he hadn't seen horses or smelled them, or at least a stack of hay or straw bales?

Out of the corner of his eye, Alec caught furtive movement near the barn. He brought the binoculars back up and watched a skinny coyote trot through the long, golden grass.

When he got back to the Yukon, he shook his head.

JULIA HADN'T KNOWN time could move so slowly. She pictured the icy rim of a glacier melting, drip, drip, drip, receding in what might, in geological terms, be worrisome haste, but in human years was scarcely discernible. Matt's previous escapades were nothing, her worry about them shallow. The worst had been when he'd stolen Alec's SUV, but at least that time the climax had come quickly.

The doorbell rang at 9:00 a.m. *Oh, damn,* Julia

thought numbly, jarred back to the fact that the world went on, whether she wanted to be part of it or not. Sophie was expecting to go to the horse camp.

"Come on in," she said, closing the door behind her. Liana hovered right behind her. "Honey, I'm sorry, I should have called your mother. I can't take you today. And Liana can't go, either."

"Oh." Sophie's face fell. "How come? Is she sick?"

"Matt's been kidnapped," Liana explained in a burst. "We have to stay here in case—" she stole a look at her mother "—in case...I don't know, we hear something."

"Do you want to call your mother?" Julia asked. "She might be able to find someone else to drive you."

"I could do it," Nell offered. "Unless she wants to stay to keep Liana company?"

"Could I go, too?" Liana asked, sudden hope on her face.

"No!" Seeing the way her daughter shriveled at her sharpness, Julia closed her eyes. "No," she said more quietly. "I'm sorry, but whoever took Matt might...might..."

She was dimly aware that Nell was steering the two girls toward Liana's bedroom and talking to them on the way. *I'm shaking,* she realized. *And... oh, God, it's only been five minutes since the last time I looked at the clock.*

SWEAT DRIPPING FROM his face and plastering his shirt to his torso, Alec squirmed forward on his belly, a metal trough his goal. He'd almost reached it when he heard a whuff and the crunch of hooves on dry grass. *Oh, shit.* He turned his head and found himself looking at a pair of hooves not two feet away from him. Man, they were big, the edges horny and cracked.

He knew nothing about horses. Would this one step on him? But the enormous brown animal bent its head down and blew out heavily, inches from Alec's face. He—she?—seemed interested rather than enraged, but what did Alec know? And would someone keeping watch out a window of the house or from the barn wonder what had caught the horse's attention?

It chomped a mouthful of grass near him and began grinding it. Bits flew, as did slobber. Neither would make him any filthier than he already was. Hell, even if he did get stepped on, a few bruises would only join the scratches he'd already gotten today.

He took a chance and wriggled forward, using his elbows to propel him.

Evidently still intrigued, the horse wandered after him. Close to the metal trough, Alec rose to his knees. The horse nudged him with its big head, almost rocking him to his butt. He gritted his teeth and peered around the trough at the barn, built recently enough to still be the color of newly stained timber. The peak was crowned with a fancy little cupola. The place was plenty solid to hold a captive. A dusty green SUV sat parked by the closed double doors.

Keeping his head down, he dialed Vahalik's number. When she answered, he murmured, "Run a plate number for me."

"Go."

He focused the binoculars with one hand, then read the number off. He was tempted to ask if she knew whether horses were inclined to trample people, but gritted his teeth and kept the worry to himself. "I can't get any closer," he said. "I'll be back as quick as I can."

Halfway across the field, his phone vibrated. He groaned and pulled it out of his pocket. Clay Renner's number.

"Yeah?"

"Olvera thinks he might have something."

Pedro Olvera was one of the two men on horseback.

"What?" Alec asked.

"He was watching a barn on Grass Valley Road. A pickup just pulled in. He knows the driver."

Alec felt a jolt of adrenaline. "A deputy."

The sergeant grunted unhappy agreement.

"Could be his place," Alec suggested in fairness.

"Olvera says no. He also says Hansen knows shit about horses."

"Okay. Tell him to keep watching."

Alec resumed crawling, the horse wandering behind. Intensely grateful when he reached the fence—a couple of boards reinforced with a strand of barbed wire—Alec squeezed under it, rolled a few feet until he was among a stand of scrubby trees and rose to his feet. His joints protested. Ignoring them, he broke into a trot.

It could be coincidence that an off-duty Butte County deputy was visiting a friend out here today—but Alec had been a cop too long to believe in coincidences.

ONCE THE AFTERNOON shade stretched across the backyard, Julia had finally gone to sit outside, leaving the girls in the bedroom and Nell using her laptop in the kitchen. This was as alone as she could possibly get, and she needed that. Weirdly, she found herself fixated on the butte and the angel atop it. The duplex wasn't ten blocks from the foot of the butte, and Julia could see the angel's upper body and an arch of one wing.

Julia remembered Sister Regina, too. She'd been her favorite of the kids' teachers at that school, a sweet-faced young woman who still had the gift of soft-voiced discipline. Sister Regina had used a glance, a touch on the shoulder, a smile, to quiet the kids when they got rowdy. That Matt had used her name seemed a sort of blessing to Julia.

Phone clutched in her hand, she sat in an Adirondack chair they'd brought from California. She'd pulled it off the hot concrete of the patio onto the lawn, which was turning brown despite Alec having moved sprinklers around a couple of evenings a week. She'd kicked off her flip-flops and rotated her ankles to feel the sharp prickle of dried grass blades against the sensitive undersides of her feet.

She used to shake her head over people who freaked at the idea of going anywhere without their phones. Who needed to be accessible to every distant acquaintance at every moment? Now it had become her teddy bear, her blankie, her string of rosary beads, never out of her hand.

Ring, she willed it, feeling the cool, smooth surface beneath her fingers.

Alec had called every couple hours today to let her know how the search was going.

"In other words, you haven't found anything," she had said once, more sharply than she had meant.

"We're narrowing the possibilities," he'd corrected her, his voice gentle.

Now she heard the sliding door and her head turned. It was Nell, carrying a glass. "Lemonade," she said.

Julia struggled to summon a smile as she took it. "Thanks."

Her new friend nodded, seeming to understand her desire to be alone, and went back inside, closing the door behind her.

Despite the shade, it was baking-hot in the yard. She'd have to go back in soon, Julia realized. She tried to make herself think about what trees and shrubs they ought to plant this fall to begin transforming the characterless rectangle, to believe Matt would be here to sulk because she was making him help dig holes, but her mind balked.

The phone rang. Her heart skipped a few beats as she stared down at the screen.

"Alec?" she answered breathlessly.

"We're pretty sure we've found where he's being held, Julia." His voice held a vibrant note. Hope. "We'll move on it after dark."

A wave of dizziness struck, and she bent forward to put her head between her knees.

"Julia?" he said urgently.

"I'm here." The dizziness was relief and fear in equal measure. "I wish—" she started, before thinking better of it.

"What do you wish?"

She told him. "I wish I was there, with you, seeing for myself."

"I know, sweetheart." The mere sound of his voice strengthened her. "I know."

CHAPTER SEVENTEEN

ALEC POCKETED HIS PHONE, reeling at some of the things Julia had said. He didn't even know why; she'd said them all before. Apparently he hadn't believed her. He sure hadn't expected her to worry about him so much, not consumed as she was by fear for Matt.

She wanted to be sure he would wear a vest and had asked anxiously whether he intended to go in first. He'd evaded answering. No, he probably shouldn't; two members of the search team, one county and one city, were SWAT. But Matt was *his* nephew, his responsibility, and hanging back wasn't in his nature.

It was the words *I love you* that really got to him.

"You don't blame me?" he'd asked, his throat feeling thick and his tongue unwieldy.

"No. How can I?" she'd said. "How could you not arrest Roberto Perez? How can you not follow through and make sure he doesn't get a chance to damage more lives?"

"Matt wouldn't be in this mess if it weren't for my job."

"Weren't you listening to what I told him the other day? If I'd loved Josh enough, if everything had been right between us, I wouldn't have resented his job. I can't resent yours, Alec." She was quiet for a minute, then said words he'd remember for the rest of his life. "No matter what."

She loved him. *No matter what.* She was telling him that even if Matt didn't survive…

A guttural sound tore from his throat. No, damn it! He couldn't think that way.

He laid his head back in Vahalik's SUV, grateful for the momentary privacy.

As the afternoon had waned, a couple of watchers remained stationed on the rise to the south of the property owned, as it turned out, by a prominent area defense attorney. Ed Gulden, mid-forties, known to be sharp and ruthless. Divorced, no kids. He hadn't made an appearance as yet today; he might or might not know what the place was being used for. A background check had made clear that he was the go-to guy for drug traffickers arrested within the tricounty area, though, and had a hell of a success rate in getting them off, or at least reducing the charges. What he did for a living wasn't a coincidence, any more than the appearance of that deputy sheriff had been. Alec had no doubt this guy was on retainer and as dirty as his clients, but unless he showed his face, proving that would be a matter for another day.

If Olvera hadn't gotten lucky and spotted his

ellow deputy arriving, they might have passed
on this barn. The men inside were being smart.
There hadn't been a lot of traffic. Pedro Olvera and
the second mounted deputy, a guy named Carson
Tucker, had continued watching, though, and had
seen another two men arrive, glance around with
deceptive casualness and then disappear inside the
barn. A few minutes later, two others left. The dis-
maying part was that one of the new arrivals was
a detective with the sheriff's department, working
property crimes.

Alec had now met Sergeant Clay Renner, who
was steaming.

"Those sons of bitches," he kept saying. "I
worked with Bart Witten." Alec understood why
that especially pissed him off. To do this job, you
had to be able to trust your fellow officers in general and a partner in particular.

Yeah, Colin was going to have a job of cleaning
house once he won the election. Having now done
his share of it with ABPD, Alec didn't envy him.

They'd have liked to get a listening device close
enough to the barn to give them a more accurate
idea of how many men were in there, but it wasn't
possible. The pastures and corrals were extensive.
A few trees sprinkled the pastures, but none were
close to the barn, which had small-paned windows
looking three directions out of four, and the fourth
faced the detached three-car garage. Olvera and

Tucker had spotted movement through the one window they could see.

Best guess was, a minimum of four people were in there besides Matt. More could be a problem. But all vehicles were tucked out of sight in the garage, which limited the transportation. And why waste manpower guarding a scrawny kid?

The upside was they had a warrant. The sole witness had finally been allowed to sit down with photos of every employee of the sheriff's department and had picked out a deputy. Along with what they'd seen here, it had been enough for the judge.

Alec stayed where he was for a while, running through their operational plan, looking for flaws. He kept finding them, too many of them. He told himself no plan was ever perfect, but knew this one was a disaster waiting to happen.

Not hard to list the problems. Number one: nonexistent cover. Anyone approaching would be vulnerable. Two: obvious motion-activated lights mounted front and back. Three: the damn barn was solid, which meant entry had to be through existing doors and windows. Double doors on the pasture side were bound to be locked, possibly barred. Ditto the double doors on the front, where men had come and gone. Tucker had had the best angle to see the arrival. He thought there'd been a prearranged knock, but couldn't quite make it out, which eliminated the possibility of fooling anyone inside.

The part that worried Alec the most: they were planning multiple entry points. That raised the risk of losing officers to friendly fire.

They all knew the risks. They could think this through, hold off until tomorrow or even longer. But in the end, he, Colin, Jane and Clay Renner had all agreed to go. Putting off the assault held another risk that trumped the others—that someone on the team would open his mouth to a buddy he trusted. They'd spotted two deputies so far, but that didn't mean they were the only two cops involved. Colin and Alec had never been sure they'd identified every crooked cop in their own department. Best way to prevent anyone on this operation from talking to friends was to keep them here, where they couldn't have a few beers with their buddies and develop a big mouth, and were given little opportunity to make private phone calls. It was far from perfect, but it was the best option they had.

He didn't know how he would have endured waiting another twenty-four hours or more, either, or what that would do to Julia.

They had to get close enough under cover of darkness to look in windows and try to figure out where Matt was being held and whether anyone was actually with him. The plan was to shatter windows and toss in flashbang grenades even as the largest group was breaking through one set of doors with a battering ram. Jane and a young officer with ABPD were both small enough to follow the flashbangs through the windows if the going looked good. Renner hadn't said much, but he'd looked especially unhappy about Vahalik's inclusion in the assault team.

A rap on the passenger window beside him made Alec start. While he brooded, dusk had deepened the sky. He rolled down the window to find McAllister standing there, a bundle in his arms. "Change of clothes," he said, passing them through. He wore black himself now, as well as a vest.

"Thanks," Alec said quietly. "You see Julia?"

"Yeah. She's strong."

Good thing one of them was. He hadn't been able to face her himself, instead asking Colin to stop by and pick up dark clothing for him to change into. One of Jane's detectives had already brought back enough Kevlar vests to go around when he picked up the other equipment they needed.

Alec glanced at his watch. "Two hours, ten minutes."

"We'll be ready." Colin nodded and faded away into the murky, purple-gray evening.

Alec had an eerie vision, just a flash, of a group of kids playing in the neighborhood on a hot summer evening. His turn to be it. Hearing running footsteps, whispers, a far-off giggle. An engine as some mom or dad came home from work, threading the parked cars that lined each curb. In his memory, Josh was out there somewhere, hiding.

His own voice. *Ninety-six, ninety-seven, ninety-eight, ninety-nine. Ready or not, here I come!*

He groaned, scraped a hand over his face and unzipped his chinos to begin changing.

TWO HOURS LATER, he stood with his back to the rough barn siding to the right of the doors, 9 mm SIG gripped to go. He and Colin McAllister, who was flattened on the other side of the doors, had been able to slide into position from each side without setting off the motion-detector lights.

Only Clay Renner hung back. He had the radio and was listening to reports from Vahalik and Dunlap, a young ABPD officer assigned to go in the other window. The hope was that one or the other would see enough to give them greater certainty. The final call was Renner's.

So far the quiet was absolute. Alec couldn't even hear Renner's murmur. Not far away, the battering-ram team stood by, waiting for the sound of shattering glass.

When it came, there were shouts inside the barn. The pair of lights above the doors sprang on as two of the biggest guys, Carson Tucker and an ABPD officer named Abe Cherney, drove the battering ram at the seam between the doors. The wood groaned and splintered. They backed off and made another attack. Flashbangs were going off inside. The *pop, pop, pop* of gunfire, too. The broken doors fell open and Alec and McAllister went in.

The chaos was near complete, although from long experience Alec was able to see it in snapshots. Horses were screaming and bucking in stalls to Alec's right. Hooves thudded against partitions. The shocking light of the flashbangs burned his retinas. Goddamn, there were too many people in here. They'd estimated low.

He returned fire. To his right someone went down. He ran forward, one objective in mind: find Matt. He saw Vahalik dive in through a window, roll and come up ready to fire. Air brushed past Alec's neck and he knew it was a bullet. Something slammed into him, robbing him of breath. He staggered and crashed into a wall but shoved himself away and kept going, leaping over a card table that lay kicked on its side, getting briefly tangled in a folding chair that came flying out of nowhere.

People were yelling on every side. Ahead he saw a man shoulder open an interior door and duck out of sight. Alec went after him. Just before he reached the doorway, he heard, "Kill the brat. Do it. That's the order."

And he heard a second voice, rising. "What are you talking about? Jesus, they've got us."

On a burst of adrenaline and fear, he flung himself through the opening as someone yelled, "Then I'll do it," and a gun barked twice.

Too late, slammed through his head. *Goddamn it, I'm too late.*

A weak overhead light let him see the man who

swung toward him already shooting. Alec pulled the trigger, once, twice, again, feeling only savage satisfaction as the man reeled back, then fell heavily.

Another man was sprawled half over a cot that had collapsed at one end. He was bleeding, groaning, his body covering the slight form of a boy.

Alec advanced ready to fire. The man turned his head and his eyes met Alec's.

"Don't shoot."

"Let me see your weapon."

"Dropped," he moaned.

Alec looked, saw it half beneath the cot and stepped close enough to kick it out of sight. "Get off the boy."

With a guttural sound, the guy rolled and thudded to the packed-earth floor. Matt lay curled on his side, duct tape over his mouth and wrapping his wrists and ankles. The sling was gone. Surrounded by fading bruises, his eyes were wide and panicked, aware.

Not dead.

Blood soaked his shirt, though, and streaked his cheek.

No more gunshots behind him, Alec noticed with the very small part of his attention not taken up by the wounded man on the ground and the boy, who hadn't moved.

Swearing viciously, Alec yanked the man's arms

behind him and cuffed them, then fell on his knees beside the cot.

"Matt. Damn it, Matt, where are you hit?"

The kid made a muffled sound. Alec holstered his SIG and, in a quick, ruthless movement, ripped the tape from Matt's face. The boy whimpered, then whispered, "You came. I knew you'd come. How did you find me?"

"Where are you hurt?" Alec repeated. He pulled up the bloody shirt, searching for wounds on Matt's skinny body.

"I'm okay. I'm okay."

The blood wasn't his. The knowledge sank in. Matt was alive. Unhurt. Alec sagged.

"I need a knife," he said hoarsely.

"I've got one," said a voice behind him.

It was Sergeant Renner. He pulled a knife with a six-inch blade from an ankle sheath and neatly sliced the duct tape binding Matt's ankles and wrists.

With a cry, the boy flung himself at Alec, who gathered him into his arms and tried to hide his tears.

It was a while before he could stumble to his feet to carry Matt out.

"WE'VE GOT TWO WOUNDED," McAllister reported. He stood by the open back door of Vahalik's SUV. "Carson Tucker and Dunlap. Tucker's hurt the worst. Gut shot. He's not looking good."

Alec, crouched on the floor in front of Matt, turned his upper body to look at Colin. "What about the other side?"

"Two dead, including the one you shot in the tack room. Jane and Renner are arguing about who took out the other one." There was a wryness in his tone. He'd also noticed the tension between those two. "Three wounded. One got tackled and cuffed but is okay except for a bump on his head. The worst is the guy you rolled off Matt." Colin paused. "He's one of the sheriff's deputies, the detective."

"He saved my life," Matt said. He sounded half excited, half scared shitless. "When that other guy burst in and yelled that about killing me, he threw himself over me. I think he was going to shoot the other guy, too, but then you came in."

"You get to know them?" Alec asked him.

"You mean, like names or anything?" Matt huddled in the space blanket Alec had found in the back of the Yukon. "Mostly they didn't talk to me. I heard them sometimes, but I didn't know who went with what name. Until, like, everything started, I hadn't seen the one who saved me."

He wasn't the one who picked Matt up in the first place, then.

"Okay. Damn. I've got to call your mom."

Alec started peeling off the vest and only then noticed that he hurt like hell. He swore a couple of times, and Colin, who had started to turn away, swung back.

"What?"

"Nothing serious," Alec growled. "I think I must have been clipped by a bullet. Help me with this damn thing."

Colin eased it off. "Huh. Maybe in your back."

"Uncle Alec?" Matt whispered.

"The vest stopped it," he said. "It's just a bruise."

"Hold still. I'll take a look," Colin said.

Alec let him pull up his shirt. He doubted Colin could see much with only the dome light, but unerring fingers found what experience told him would be an ugly bruise. Alec winced.

"Might be a broken rib, too."

"Could be worse." Kneeling, he was able to extract his phone from an inside pocket. The screen lit up as he scrolled to his last call.

Julia answered on the first ring. "Alec?" she said frantically.

"We've got him, Julia. It went fine. Matt's here and not hurt."

"Oh, my God," she said. "Oh, my God."

"You want to talk to him?"

"Wait!" she cried.

Alec stopped in the act of extending the phone and brought it back to his mouth. "Yeah?"

"You're all right, too?"

"I'm fine," he assured her. "I'm going to send Matt to the hospital to get checked out, though. Can you meet him there? I need to stick around."

He should also call Sheriff Eugene Brock, who,

whether he'd had a clue what was going on or not, wouldn't be a happy man. There wasn't any way he could sweep this under the rug. Alec guessed Sheriff Brock's chances of reelection had just gone south.

Weariness swept over him as he half listened to Matt excitedly talking to his mother. *God,* he thought, *I'm getting too old for this kind of thing.* Yeah, it was past time he'd taken a desk job. He almost laughed. Next time Julia worried about whether he'd get bored as chief of ABPD, he could definitely reassure her that his interest in any future action and adventure was nonexistent.

Matt thrust the phone at him. "Why do I have to go? I'm fine! Can't I stay with you?" he pleaded.

"Do you have any idea how scared your mother has been? I think she needs to see you for herself." Alec's mouth crooked. "And after you get medically cleared, I'll bet she'd like to feed you."

"Um…I *am* kind of hungry." He was always hungry. "They gave me a hamburger, but it was, I don't know, *hours* ago."

"I need to keep an eye on the cleanup here," Alec explained. "It's not going to be an easy scene to secure." Understatement. Eventually they'd figure out how many rounds each individual had fired and who had shot whom, but it was going to be a job. What he cared most about was Tucker and Dunlap—and the guy who had shielded a thirteen-year-old boy with his own body. In doing that, he'd redeemed all of his sins in Alec's eyes. He'd be glad to go to court and say so.

He left Matt briefly and persuaded one of his own officers, who was itching to follow Dunlap to the hospital, to take Matt, as well.

"His mother will be waiting for him in the E.R.," he promised.

Then he walked past the aid car and the gurney being loaded to go back into the barn and start doing his job.

MATT HAD BEEN SUBDUED while a doctor checked him out, but they'd barely left the E.R. when he started talking.

"Uncle Alec was shot, too."

Julia, walking beside him, stopped dead. "What?"

"Yeah. Captain McAllister said he probably has a broken rib."

Hardly aware of Nell and Liana, both of whom had come—in fact, Nell had driven them here—and were now listening almost as anxiously as she was, Julia could only say stupidly, "But he said he was fine." Oh, dear God, she was going to cry *now*, of all times.

"He had one of those police vests on. It stopped the bullet. But I could tell it must have hurt anyway."

Something like a laugh escaped Julia. In horror, she covered her mouth with her hand. She was going to fall apart. Thank heavens Alec wasn't here to see. But Nell suddenly had an arm around her, and she was saying, "Matt, the car's right there. You and your sister get in."

He went, Liana chattering with him, and Julia stood there in the middle of the parking lot, shaking. "What is *wrong* with me? They're all right. They're both all right."

"Nothing's wrong with you. They almost *weren't* all right, and you know that. Of course you're reacting."

Julia looked into the other woman's warm brown eyes. "Do you ever get used to this?"

Nell gave a funny laugh that held no more humor than Julia's had. "I don't know. I haven't even known Colin for a year! You've known Alec a lot longer. And wasn't your husband Special Forces?"

"Yes, but when he was gone I didn't know where he was or what he was doing. Some of the time he'd come back and tell me it had only been a training exercise, so I never knew when to really get scared."

Nell nodded. "I have a librarian friend whose son was a freshman in college last year. She said she'd quit worrying about him because she didn't know what he was doing or whether he was out late. It wasn't like before, when she lay in bed listening for him to come home."

"It's like that," Julia agreed, "except then Josh was killed, and, oh, I'm so glad Alec isn't still a street cop."

"You don't have to tell *me*." Nell made a face. "Our two men are *supposed* to be in charge, waiting safely behind the lines while sending their troops out to do the dangerous stuff."

"Right," Julia said.

And now they both did laugh, really laugh, until Julia began to cry again with relief.

A LIGHT SHONE through Julia's front window. The relief Alec felt was huge. If she and the kids had gone to bed, he'd have done the same—but he wanted to see Julia with an intensity he'd never felt before.

He thanked Colin, who had given him a lift from the hospital, where they had both gone to check on the condition of the two wounded officers and he himself had been X-rayed, and climbed stiffly out. As the SUV drove away, Alec walked up to Julia's door and knocked lightly, not wanting to wake the kids if they were asleep.

She opened it instantly and reached a hand out to draw him in. "Oh, Alec! Thank goodness. I thought you'd never get home."

Home. Her side of the duplex. No, wherever she was.

He looked past her, glad to see that the only light was here in the living room.

"I'm filthy," he said, "but I had to see you."

Her eyes were luminous. Were those tears? "You lied to me."

"I lied?"

"Matt says you got shot."

"Yeah, but I wore a vest. I'm just bruised."

No more talking, he decided. He ended the conversation by pulling her into his arms and kissing her. He gave her everything, and the kiss exploded. They spun in place, him lifting her, the two of them straining together in a desperate attempt to meld their bodies. She whispered his name when he let her breathe. He might have been saying hers, but wasn't positive the sounds coming out of his mouth were anything that coherent. He held on to enough consciousness to know he couldn't lay her on the floor here, bury himself in her, but, oh, God, he wanted to.

"Next door?" he managed to get out.

"Yes," she gasped as his mouth traveled down her throat. Then, "No."

"What?" He lifted his head, stunned by her refusal.

"I want you to stay here," she said.

His brain had to be working slowly. "You don't want to leave the kids."

She shook her head fiercely. "You slept with me last night. We don't have anything to be ashamed of."

"Last night was different," he said slowly.

"No, it wasn't. I want to wake up with you tomorrow, Alec." Color ran high on her face, but her chin had a determined tilt, too. "Will you marry me? Soon?"

He groaned. "You mean that?"

"Yes." She swallowed. "If *you* meant it when you said you loved me."

"You know I did," he said, low and ragged. "I do."

"Then?"

It would be easy to think she was asking out of gratitude. But Alec discovered he didn't believe that. She'd told him often enough, in different ways, that she loved him. *No matter what.*

"Of course I'll marry you," he said, shaken to the core.

She blinked hard, sniffed and said, "Then why don't you take a shower? I'll make you something to eat and, well, then we can go to bed."

His body was primed for her *now,* but enough blood had returned to his head for him to remember that he had to stink, and he probably had blood on him somewhere, and damned if he wasn't starved. And maybe most of all he loved the idea of them doing normal things—him taking a shower in *her* bathroom, the two of them talking quietly while he ate, then walking hand in hand into the bedroom, where they would not only make love, but sleep tangled together and wake together in the morning. He wanted all of that, not just the sex part.

"That'd be good," he said, "but I'd better go next door and get some clean clothes."

"Hurry." Julia pressed her mouth to his.

He sank into the kiss, only for a minute. Hurry? 'That's safe to say," he told her.

JULIA WATCHED ALEC devour a huge sandwich, thinking how unreal it felt having him here late at night like this, knowing they were going to bed together—and how right it felt, too.

She could see how exhausted he was, but guessed e was still wired, too. A bruise darkened one cheekbone. He'd shaved after his shower out of consideration for her, although she'd found she liked him with stubble, too. He had looked dangerous when he first came in the door, wearing black, hair unkempt, jaw heavily shadowed. Sexy.

"Matt's changed," she told him. "Growing up, I guess. He said two of the officers who came to rescue him were hurt. He's really worried about them. I hope…" Her voice lurched. "Neither of them are going to die, are they?"

Alec shook his head. "One had a bullet graze his head. Bled like a—" He apparently changed his mind about what he was going to say. "Looked worse than it was. The other guy took a round just below his vest. Those can be bad, but they cleaned him up in surgery and they're optimistic. I just came from the hospital."

"Oh, thank heavens. Matt feels like this is all his fault. He says he was stupid to go with that police officer, that you'd told him he wasn't going to be charged for stealing your Tahoe, but the deputy claimed there was a warrant and he had to take him in."

"That's what the guy said?"

She nodded.

"And I wasn't available for Matt to call."

"Which isn't your fault." She aimed a stern look at him. "Don't you start."

She loved his smile, and never more than now, when it started in his eyes long before his mouth curved.

"Yes, ma'am."

Julia nudged a plate holding a generous piece of coffee cake in front of him. He picked up the fork, but didn't take a bite. Instead he kept looking at her.

"You know I have to go back to L.A."

Nerves balled in her stomach. "Do they even know what happened?"

"Now they do. We arrested four men tonight. Two of them are talking. We'll trace this back to Perez and he'll be in even deeper shit. But that'll take time, and he's already on trial. Conspiracy to commit murder is good enough for me right now."

"Me, too," she agreed. She hadn't let herself think about it tonight, but of course she'd known he would have to go. She took a deep breath. "I don't suppose we can get married first."

He smiled at her again, the heat in his eyes enough to sear her. "Yeah. Things are still dragging on down there. Let's see what we have to do to pull it off before I go. If you're sure that's what you want."

She reached out for his free hand. "That's what I want."

Somehow his face was more serious than she'd expected, though. "We got lucky tonight, Julia. I don't know how much Matt told you."

She searched his face, wondering what he was really trying to tell her. "I know that one of the men guarding him took a couple of bullets meant for Matt."

"If not for him, I'd have been too late."

"And you're going to beat yourself up over it."

His look startled her with its savagery. "Wouldn't you?"

She had to be honest. "Thinking about how close he came terrifies me. It feels like I'm standing in the open door of an airplane, not wearing a parachute, looking down and knowing I'm half a step from plummeting toward my death. But I'll get over it, because he *is* home safe."

He stared at her from those dark, dark eyes and said nothing.

Julia finished. "Alec, I know you well enough to be sure you did everything you could. Maybe you couldn't save him without some luck, too, but you did. It's over."

He suddenly bent his head. "I don't know if I can live through anything like that again," he said, voice muffled.

She pushed her chair back and went to him, wrapping her arms around him from behind and laying her head down in the crook of his neck. "I love you."

He shuddered and turned so that he could grab hold of her and bury his face between her breasts. He mumbled something she didn't hear, then repeated it. "I'm luckier than I deserve."

That made her mad and wrenched her heart, all at the same time.

"No." She tried to shake him, but he was too solid for it to do much. She did it again anyway, for emphasis. "You're an amazing man, Alec Raynor, and don't you dare let guilt come between us!"

His shoulders shook. Appalled, she wondered if he could be crying, but then she knew: he was laughing. He straightened and met her eyes. "Nothing is coming between us. And I'm not hungry anymore."

Warmth pooled between her legs and her knees grew weak. "Bedtime," she said huskily.

"You don't know how much I want this."

A smile trembled on her lips. "I do."

He surged to his feet, lifting her. With a gasp she clamped her legs around his waist and her arms around his neck.

"Just say that one more time," he murmured and kissed her.

Somehow, with no practice at all, he managed to turn off the lights and carry her down the hall to her bedroom without once bumping a wall or making any noise whatsoever that would have awakened the kids.

EPILOGUE

ONCE AGAIN, the Raynors were at the airport, only this time they were there to meet Alec's return flight

"I see it!" Liana suddenly cried, nose all but pressed to the glass.

Matt tore off his earbuds. "Where?"

By this time, Julia heard the rumble of an approaching prop plane. She abandoned the hard plastic chair to join the kids in front of the windows. They all watched the descent and held their breaths as the airplane touched down, gave a small bounce and braked. Her heart was pounding. He was home. Their daily phone conversations these past two weeks were all that had kept her going, that and poring over every detail about the trial she could find on the internet.

The plane slowed and came to a stop near the end of the runway. As it turned and began to taxi toward the terminal, Julia could see activity below. Stairs were being rolled out, along with carts to collect the baggage.

There was the inevitable delay before the airplane door opened and the steps were fitted into place. At last the first passengers disembarked. Julia felt as if she was in a state of suspension, unable to so much as breathe until she saw him.

"There he is!" Matt crowed, and Liana whirled and hugged Julia, who was somewhere between laughter and tears. It was ridiculous. Her emotions had been so unstable lately. Something told her that with Alec home, she'd be fine.

He carried a suit jacket over his arm and a laptop case over one shoulder. But his head was lifted as he looked for them. And then he gave a huge grin, reminding her of that day at Elk Lake.

Happy.

Moments later he strode through the door and they all threw themselves at him. He did his best to encompass his entire family in his arms, dropping kisses on tops of heads and on Julia's lips.

"God, I'm glad to be here," he said finally.

"Is the trial over?" Liana asked. "Did you win?"

He laughed. "No, it isn't over. The defense just started presenting their side. But you know what?" He winked at Liana, then met Julia's eyes. "I think it is over. I think he's going down."

"Really?" she asked.

"Yeah." He got them all started walking toward the baggage-claim area. The first cart of suitcases had already been rolled in. "I've testified in a lot of trials. You get so you can read juries."

"It was you, wasn't it? They believed you." Matt had a serious case of hero worship. Julia knew Alec worried about it, but she didn't. Matt was a teenager, after all. Alec would develop feet of clay soon enough.

"I actually think it was the young woman who witnessed the murder that night. She was amazing. The defense couldn't shake her. She kept saying no, she knew the exact words she'd heard. 'Roberto says you have a big mouth and it's time to shut it.' The entire courtroom was riveted. The jury believed her."

"How long until there's a verdict?" Julia asked.

"Another week, I'd guess. Maybe two, if the jurors have a lot to talk about. But I think it's going to be quick." He seized a large black suitcase off the second cart and smiled at them. "My part is over. What say we go home?"

Liana bounced on her toes. "Yeah!"

Home was going to change in the not-too-distant future. One side of the duplex was too small for all of them. In those daily phone calls, Julia and Alec had made plans. As soon as he was home, they agreed, they would start house hunting. They'd finish the basic remodel and start renting out the duplex.

As they walked out into the hot August afternoon, Julia didn't say much, and neither did Alec. They didn't have to. The kids chattered away. School would be starting soon, and although Matt was pretending to be nonchalant, even he was excited. Apparently Alec had promised to buy those kayaks as soon as he got home, and Matt thought they should do it now.

"And I know what I'm going to wear the first day of school!" Liana told him.

Smiling, Alec listened to both talking at the same time. He stowed his suitcase in the trunk of Julia's Passat, slammed it shut and said, "Your mom says the insurance check came, so tomorrow morning we can go buy a replacement Tahoe. With a rack. And I don't see why we can't pick out a couple of kayaks, too. Then I vote for a picnic." He squeezed Matt's shoulder. "No chance of taking those kayaks out until you get the cast off, but with a little luck we'll be able to get them in the water before the weather turns. What do you say?"

"Yeah, cool."

"How about we pack a lunch and go for a short hike, too?" Alec suggested. "Matt can do that."

The kids both cheered. Julia felt tears prickle again but smiled through them as she handed Alec the keys.

"Let's go home."

He slid behind the wheel, moved the seat back—way back—and put the car in Drive. He held her hand all the way home.

* * * * *

Look for the next book in Janice Kay Johnson's
THE MYSTERIES OF ANGEL BUTTE *series!*
Coming in July 2014 from
Harlequin Superromance.